I0594487

Twisted
Obsession

(FRIENDS IN CRISIS SERIES BOOK 2)

Lucy Appadoo

This book is dedicated to victims of family and domestic violence. It is also dedicated to my husband and two daughters who always give me unwavering support and the space to write.

Contents

CHAPTER 1
A SOUNDING BOARD

Liz Randiza rested back on her beige suede sofa, her laptop sitting on her lap as she clicked on icons to access information for a client. She didn't normally work on the weekends, but she'd had a recent influx of cases at the centre where she worked as a social worker.

She peered at the blue sky through the glass doors, finding comfort in her first-floor Altona apartment with a five-minute walk to the beach, gym, shopping strips, and cafes. She occasionally enjoyed a refreshing walk along the pine-lined beach foreshore or relaxing on the balcony on those warm balmy nights.

Liz turned off her laptop and put it aside. She rose from the couch and reached into the fridge for a jug of water. Pouring it into a glass, she took a sip and stared at the date on her calendar. She flinched at the sudden reminder of what was happening today.

No, it couldn't be today, could it?

Her hands suddenly shook as she closed her eyes briefly, squeezing her hands tight. In spite of the warm, spring air, a trail of coldness raced down her spine. *He's back and he's coming for me. This will never end.* Staring at the letter stuck to the side of the fridge announcing his prison release, she struggled to breathe. She had to get out of there.

Liz grabbed her bag, stepped out of her apartment in a daze, and headed into the basement car park. Her sweaty hands gripped the steering wheel as she drove towards her friend's home in Williamstown, not too far from her place. Her friend, Bella, lived in a cottage-style house that was inviting and cosy, and Liz always felt comfortable there. Right now, she needed company, but she had to get a grip on this. Maybe it wasn't as dangerous as she first thought. But who was she kidding?

On the drive over there, images flashed across her mind, but she couldn't think about it now. She had to talk to someone, and Bella was always there to lend an ear. Clearing her mind, she remembered that her friend Jamie was working a late shift tonight, but Bella should be home. As a psychologist, Bella had ways to make people feel safe.

She took calming breaths to ease her tight chest, turned into Bella's street, and parked. She leapt out of the car and walked through the white picket gate. Her legs wobbled beneath her as she looked around at her surroundings. Making her way to the front door was physically exerting as her mind ran rampant about this particular day. She tried to control her shaky hands as she rang the doorbell and waited for Bella to answer the door. Within seconds, the door opened.

Bella stared up at Liz. "Liz, are you alright? Come in?"

Liz stepped inside and cleared her throat. "My ex-boyfriend was released from prison and I know he's going to find me."

Bella remained silent for a moment. "Oh Liz." She grabbed her hand and led her towards the living room. "Come and sit down."

"What am I going to do, Bella?" Tears swept freely down Liz's face as Bella wrapped her arms tightly around her.

Marco, Bella's boyfriend who worked as a detective, intervened. "Surely he'd have conditions on his release, but I'll try and get answers for you."

She pulled away from Bella. "Thanks, Marco. I'd appreciate that."

Marco watched her with concern. "If your ex has been a model prisoner and the court feels he's served his maximum sentence, he may have minimal conditions upon release. Although, there are bound to be conditions such as not coming near you, Liz. And he won't be able to apply for a lot of jobs out there."

Bella touched Liz gently on the shoulder. "Now you listen to me. He'll be a fool to come near you, and we'll be here supporting you all the way. He will never hurt you again, and we'll make sure of that. Okay?"

Liz nodded. "Thanks, Bella."

Marco leaned forward, watching Liz closely. "Bella's right. If he steps out of line, most likely he'll go straight back to prison." He moved closer to Liz and smiled reassuringly. "Now, I'll make us a cup of tea. As Bella taught me, you have to find comforting distractions when you're upset."

Bella beamed in his direction and Marco gazed lovingly into her eyes. He whispered in her ear and kissed her tenderly on the cheek. "I'll be back, honey."

Liz grinned, her mood slightly lifted. "I'm struggling to feel calm right now, but I'll process this in time."

Bella nodded. "Come on, Liz. Let's sit down."

She suddenly couldn't breathe, experiencing a sense of entrapment inside the house. "Do you mind if we go outside, Bella?"

"Of course not. Let's go."

They ambled over to the courtyard and sat down, the fresh air brushing Liz's flushed face. The air outside almost soothed her weary soul as she peered into the dark night.

"Have you had anything to eat?"

Liz shook her head. "I don't have an appetite."

"Not to worry. I know Marco will, at least, bring us some light snacks. He's great with guests and makes a good host."

Liz beamed. Bella had changed so much over the past year. She'd had her fair share of trauma from her abusive parents, unlike Liz who had loving parents but an abusive ex-boyfriend.

Bella took a quick breath, leaning forward with a frown. "So when did you find out about this? His release?"

Liz recounted the story with trepidation. "Two weeks ago." She ignored the shock on Bella's face. "I was flicking through bills, but this letter on the bottom came from the Victims Register. And I thought, '*What the hell!* It couldn't be that time already.'"

She remembered how her body had become rigid, her hands gripping the envelope tightly, the whites of her knuckles showing. She forgot how to breathe as she ripped open the envelope and stared hard at the typeface. *No, no, no. Domenic cannot be released from prison so soon? Had it already been ten years?*

Bella shook her head. "Oh Liz. Why didn't you tell me two weeks ago? I would've been there for you."

Liz shrugged. "I thought I'd be okay and didn't want to burden you. I was just reminded of his release today, and seeing that letter on the fridge triggered me again. Now it's so real. He's out, but two weeks ago he was still in prison."

"Are you getting back into counselling now that he's out?"

Liz wondered about the same thing. "I'm thinking about it. That psychologist I saw a few years ago was great, and got me through a lot of that stuff with Domenic. I might see if she's still around."

Bella clasped her hands. "Good."

Marco brought them a tray of savoury biscuits, cheese, dips, and small mugs of tea. He leaned in and kissed Bella on the lips. "I'll leave you girls to it. You take care, Liz. I'll be in touch. And Bella, I'll call you tomorrow."

Bella eyed Marco with endearing love in her eyes. "I'll talk to you soon, honey." Liz nodded wearily. "Thanks, Marco."

A part of Liz felt guilt at what she was doing to her friend. Bella had faced enough trauma; she'd been tortured by a crazy person. For months, Bella had been stalked and terrorised until she had almost died. No amount of support by Liz and Jamie could help Bella at the time. That ordeal had been one year ago.

Ten years before that, Domenic had gone to prison.

Liz wondered if Domenic would try to find her. Surely he wouldn't dare? But then again, Domenic always had a way of outsmarting her. He was very resourceful, and that's exactly what she was afraid of.

CHAPTER 2
THE CLIENT

Liz sat at her desk in a cubicle of several other staff within her community not-for-profit centre in Eaglemont, jotting down notes. The centre worked with the Northern Metropolitan regions of Victoria and focused on family intervention. Its aim was to connect children with foster carers while case managing broken families, mostly sole parents.

Her desk was cluttered with stacks of case files, in-trays of assigned tasks, scheduled assessments, and scattered stationery. Behind her was a shelf of books about social work policy and guidelines, family interventions, and case management for families.

She shifted her weight on the chair and stared at the woman across from her. "Okay, Camilla. I've placed your daughter with a foster carer until your brother gets down here from Queensland. So your job now is to attend the rehabilitation program in the city." She handed her a document, and Camilla grabbed it with a shaky hand, the skin on her hands flaky and peeling.

"Is your mother coming down from Queensland too?"

Camilla shrugged. Dark circles under her eyes and her skinny physique showed how malnourished she was from substance abuse. Her blood-shot eyes made it appear that she'd relapsed recently. "Nah, Matthew said she's having another procedure, so she'll be staying with a friend until she recovers. She'll probably come down for a visit. But probably not for six months, maybe less. Who knows?"

Liz took a breath. "I see." She frowned. "Have you relapsed?" Camilla averted her eyes, pressing her lips together. "Camilla, it's okay if you have. I mean, the point of rehabilitation is to work on those triggers to relapse. The important thing is that you learn from them and look at each relapse as a learning experience."

"Hmm, maybe." Camilla's words were muffled.

"So what triggered you this time?" Liz wondered if the incidences with Camilla's father had triggered her. She'd given a sketchy outline of the trauma he invoked.

"I'm not saying."

"And why not? I'm only here to help, nothing more." She sighed. "Do you want your daughter back?"

Camilla shot her a glare. "Of course, I do. She's my life."

Liz nodded. "Fair enough but know that you also have to do this for yourself. Remember how we mentioned that you need to be your top priority? That way you can best care for Mariana. Now what happened?"

"My ex dropped in and wanted to see Mariana, but I wouldn't let him. He threatened to take her when I was asleep. Said he'd break into my house, take her, then disappear overseas. But he wouldn't be able to get a passport because of his criminal record. The bastard." She scratched hard at her skin. "But he doesn't know she's in foster care, thank God. But once I get her back, he might make good on his damn promise."

Liz fought back the images of her own ex-boyfriend. The large fist, pounding into her. *No*, she refused to go there. She focused on the woman in front of her. "So you took the drugs because of your fear?"

"Yeah, but no way he's taking her. No damn way."

"Listen, she's safe where she is right now, and later we'll take measures to keep him away. If it comes to that."

"No damn intervention order will keep him away. He won't care about breaching it."

The Victorian legal system had its faults, but that wasn't something Liz could fix. *Focus on what you can control, Liz.* "I'm happy to come with you to the rehabilitation facility and get you settled in."

"Thanks, Liz. Appreciate it."

"Wait for me in reception and we'll leave for the facility. Just give me a few minutes."

Camilla nodded then left, holding her weathered oversized bag like it was a piece of treasure. Liz hoped that Camilla would stay clean this time, but considering her dark past, it would be the ultimate challenge.

Her manager and friend, Penny, approached her, holding a case file. Penny watched Camilla walk away. Liz was fortunate to have her as a supportive and easy-going manager. She threaded her hand through her strawberry-blonde hair, topping a face with smiling green eyes and dimples on her cheeks. "Let's hope she stays clean." Liz nodded. "This is Judy Jonesan who has alcohol and gambling addictions. She has a three-year old daughter, currently staying with an aunt. It's yours. She's scheduled to come in tomorrow, but don't spend too much on the bio-psychosocial history as I got most of it in my notes there."

After Penny left, Liz inserted the case file into a locked cabinet. A voice caught her attention and she turned to see Penny returning.

"Oh, remember how I mentioned the work placement student starting with us?"

Liz nodded. "Yeah, wasn't it organised a few months ago? The one you said was adamant she work here because she loves kids?"

Penny held her hands across her waist. "That's the one." She cleared her throat. "Well, she'll be starting next Monday, so be ready."

"No worries."

They said their goodbyes then Liz bent down to retrieve her bag from the large drawer at the bottom of her desk. She rose to leave with Camilla for the clinic and waved goodbye to one colleague who remained after a few others had left. Walking outside with Camilla, she savoured the spring air as the setting sun cast a light glow around her. But the worried expression on Camilla's face made her wonder whether she'd relapse again.

Storm clouds were brewing in spite of the mild weather.

CHAPTER 3
A WARNING

After work the next evening, Liz got into her sports car parked behind the building, and drove to her Altona residence a half-hour drive from work. Along the way, her thoughts turned to poor Camilla. Hopefully, her brother was supportive and could care for Camilla's daughter, at least temporarily. Otherwise, she would need longer-term foster care.

She parked her car in the basement, entered by the side of a grey building, punched in a security code, then pushed open the elevator and headed to her apartment.

Unlocking her door, she stepped into her beige-carpeted residence and sank into her three-seater beige couch, fluffing up the green and blue pillows after throwing down the letters. She put her bag down on the coffee table.

Her apartment was small, and featured timber chairs around a long table next to a small kitchen with wall to wall abstract paintings and photographs of her parents and friends. She ignored the pieces of clothing scattered around the living room, deciding to put them in the laundry later.

Heading into the kitchen, Liz opened the fridge and frowned at its near-empty contents. All she had was spoilt milk, a few eggs, a block of cheese, mouldy lettuce, and dried out mushrooms. She'd forgotten to do the grocery shopping. In spite of her love of cooking, Liz hadn't cooked a healthy meal in a long time. She enjoyed going out and was hardly home to do any cooking, but the last two weeks had become much worse with her self-care. That damn letter had arrived.

At least she had the chicken that she'd taken out of the freezer in the morning. She seasoned it, placed it into a non-stick pan, and cooked it. Tiny flecks of hot oil splashed out of the pan. She ignored the mess it created and the pain it caused as they hit her bare arms. Once it was ready, she ate it and washed it down with a glass of wine. Her heart hammered as she glared at the letter informing of Domenic's release stuck on the fridge. Maybe she should throw it out. What was the damn point of that letter now?

She was too alone with her thoughts, tired of thinking about Domenic, and decided to head to the nearby coffee shop. Rushing out the door, she grabbed her bag and made her way outside into the street below with its strips of stores, cafes, and restaurants. The sun was still bright as she stepped into the small cafe, sat at a corner table, and waited for the waitress.

Liz watched customers coming inside, and spotted a chubby woman with tattoos and piercing in her nose. The woman slapped a grey-haired man on the shoulder. She enjoyed people-watching and interaction with others, and was grateful for the distraction.

Liz stared into her hands, wondering where the damn waitress was. She wanted her fresh cup of coffee.

"Excuse me," a voice sounded near her.

Liz looked up and stared at a short buxom young woman, sporting a dark brown, bob haircut with blonde highlights. Her dark brown eyes penetrated Liz's.

Liz swallowed even though she was not at all threatened by this young girl with innocent eyes and a reserved smile. "Can I help you?"

The woman clasped her hands together and stared into Liz's eyes for a moment before talking. "Hi, I'm Gabriella. I believe we both know Domenic." She took a breath. "My mum was married to Domenic."

Liz flinched. "What?" Did she hear right?

"I'm sorry to say this, but I came here to warn you. About Domenic. He was released from prison a few days ago, and I think he plans to hurt you."

Liz's chest constricted. She wondered if she was being threatened by one of his minions, or if she had been abused by him too. "Who are you?"

A stout male waiter came by at that moment. "What can I get you?"

She swallowed, her focus blurry. "I'll have a short black, thanks," said Liz.

"A strong cappuccino thank you," said the woman. She took a seat opposite Liz.

Liz leaned forward, looking into her eyes with curiosity. "Who are you? And what's this about?"

The woman hesitated. "I'm Gabriella. Domenic's daughter."

Liz gasped loudly and winced at the attention it drew. She bowed her head, thinking the worst. That bastard had sent his daughter to do his dirty work, probably concocting a plan to kill her while she visited him in prison. "What do you want from me? And why are you threatening me?"

Gabriella's hand shook as she drew it through her hair and twirled the strands around her fingers. She bit her lower lip as if processing her words. "I'm not here to threaten you. I want to warn you that he's still dangerous."

Liz shook her head, pushing back tears. "No, you're here to conspire against me with Domenic. Besides, I don't believe you are who you say you are. He never told me he had a daughter when we were going out. You could be anyone, telling lies."

"You have to believe me. He hurt my mother, and then he broke up with her so you two could go out."

Oh no! "He told me he was single and never mentioned a daughter. I would've known if he had a daughter."

Gabriella shifted in her seat. "My Mum read the trial transcripts from beginning to end. She told me the whole story. I'm sorry." She turned away, looking up at the waiter who had brought their hot drinks. He set them on the table, and she took a sip, her hands gripping the mug for dear life. "No-one should have to go through what you went through."

"Give me one good reason why I should believe you are who you say you are?"

Gabriella fixed her gaze strongly on Liz, as if undeterred in her mission. "My mum and I visited him in prison. He said, and I quote, 'No bitch wins over me.' Then he laughed, and said he was joking and that he was a changed man."

Liz cleared her throat. "I have to go."

Gabriella held her hand up. "No, we haven't finished. Wait."

"I'm sorry. I can't deal with this now." She ignored her drink, headed to the cashier and paid.

On her walk back home, her body was shaking and the world around her seemed to spin. She couldn't deal with a daughter. For all she knew, Gabriella could be playing his sick games, being used like a puppet.

Maybe she was as psychopathic as her father was. No, she couldn't even fathom that Domenic had a daughter. Not only was Domenic back in her life, but his daughter was too. A whole damn family affair! This trauma was happening all over again.

CHAPTER 4
A DISTRACTION

Liz rushed inside her apartment straight from the cafe, her mind still on Domenic and his prison release. She wouldn't let him control her life and was not entirely sure that Gabriella was telling her the truth. How did she know without a doubt that Gabriella was not conspiring to hurt her, as ordered by Domenic? Trying to get her guard down and to trust Gabriella, then — BAM!—she would be vulnerable in his hands. No, she had to play it safe and stay away from this woman, whoever she was. Maybe Marco could do a background check on her.

She planned to focus on the life she'd built, and that included her rewarding job, network of friends, her love of cooking, and going to the gym. What more could she want?

Liz picked up an apple from the fruit bowl on the kitchen table and munched away. She headed outside on to her private balcony, her bare feet pressing against the cold tiles as she looked over the street view of Altona.

Liz's parents had helped her buy this apartment as she couldn't afford much on her social worker salary. Not that she didn't get by, but hopefully she'd one day be promoted to a supervisory role that paid somewhat more than she was getting now.

The sound of the phone distracted her. She stepped back inside the apartment and picked up her phone from the coffee table. The screen displayed Marco. "Hello there."

"Hi, Liz. How are you doing?"

She took a seat on the couch. "I'm better now, thanks to you guys. How's Bella?"

"She's great, but she wanted me to get onto this straight away to give you time to process things too."

"What did you find out?"

"Domenic's been instructed to stay away from you, or you can put out an intervention order. I was hoping they'd put him on a supervision order, but no such luck."

"You mean he's free to do whatever he likes without being supervised or monitored?"

"Hmmm. They believe he is a changed man and served his maximum penalty, so he's been released without having strict conditions to follow. I'm sorry, Liz, but he shouldn't come near you. He knows he can go straight back to prison if he does."

Liz gripped the phone so hard she thought her hand might break. "But I don't think he'll ever change. He's pure evil, Marco." She calmed her breathing. "And he had a drug and escort business before prison. I assume they've been shut down?"

"I checked known escort and drug businesses he ran, and they were shut down, Liz. And no known associations with that kind of business now. But we'll keep an eye on that." He paused. "Bella told me your story, and I want you to know that I'll be looking out for you. I'll make sure he never hurts you again."

"Thanks, Marco, but you can't monitor me twenty-four-seven, and I wouldn't expect that. I'll be fine. I can take care of myself."

He scoffed. "I've heard that before." Marco was obviously implying Bella. "What I would suggest is taking a few self-defence classes. It'll help you feel more confident and give you added strength."

"I'll think about it. Thanks, Marco."

"No problem, but if there's anything you need don't hesitate to call."

She remembered Gabriella. "Marco, wait. I need you to check out something."

"Sure. What is it?" Liz recounted her encounter with Gabriella, a part of her hoping she wasn't Domenic's daughter. "I'll look into it and get back to you. But surely you would've found out during the trial that he had a daughter?"

"I was too gutless to read the court transcripts, so I don't know who else testified or whether any family members spoke about him."

"Understandable, Liz. You were only seventeen, far too young to deal with that."

"Thanks, Marco."

Liz hung up with a heavy heart. *The bastard's going to be released without supervision and no strict rules to follow. He is not a changed man. He could never change.*

Liz walked over to her bedroom and contemplated changing her clothes. Her room was her sanctuary, with its bare walls, white timber bed, white dresser with four large drawers, and a matching bedside table. The gentle light coming in through the bay windows gave her comfort. She debated in her mind whether to go to the nightclub—one of her favourite things to do. What if Domenic was out there? She might be putting herself at risk. But if he came near her, he knew he could go back to prison.

Liz paced the floor and looked through her window, but nobody was down below. She was being paranoid. It would be too soon for Domenic to show his face as he'd only recently been released. He'd need time to settle into a place, and maybe he'd moved in with his parents. Not that she'd ever met them.

She shook her head, fighting against his control over her. For ten whole damn years she had dealt with Domenic's abuse, and damn if she'd let him continue to control her life. He had controlled her for far too long. No more. She would be in a public place with plenty of people around, and she'd keep a bottle of perfume in her bag. Socialising was good for her spirit and she needed this.

Liz sat on her white quilt cover and had made her decision. She put on a tight-fitting black satin dress with matching red stiletto shoes. Then she put on dangly earrings, added natural-looking make-up, and was out the door. She needed to get out of this place, so clubbing it was.

Being a Friday the queue to the nightclub was long, so she waited for at least half an hour before gaining entry. The lounge area had a soft-glowing look. She walked up to the bar and ordered a dry margarita from the burly bartender. The buzz of the crowd surrounded her, giving her that adrenaline high as she licked her lips, desperately needing a drink to forget her current problem. Acrid smells and strong perfumes permeated the air. Couches were on either side of the lounge close to the dance floor. Lights suspended from the ceiling spotlighted a small stage featuring an all-male band playing soft jazz.

"Here you go, love," said the bartender with a wink.

"Thanks," she said. She stood up from the bar and searched for a man to distract her from her pain. A man with a beard and a square jaw stared at Liz with hunger in his eyes until a woman grabbed him by the arm. *Oh damn! He's taken.*

Heading closer to the dance floor, Liz found a few more potentials she could enjoy the night with. Mostly brunettes and a couple of blonde men, although some were with their partners. Taking a few more steps, she spotted another good-looking man sporting a moustache, talking to another guy near the couches. But he didn't even look her way, so she turned back to the bar. She might have better luck, sitting alone at the bar. Taking a deep breath, she held on to her martini glass and set it opposite her on the counter. It was still early in the night and she had time to find someone to take her mind off things. She refused to let Domenic spoil her night. He was history and she'd moved on in some ways.

Liz wrapped her manicured nails around the glass and downed the margarita in two easy swallows. She needed more alcohol to wash away her dark thoughts and have fun tonight.

"Woh, take it easy there lady," said a strange man with a moustache and wavy shoulder-length hair. He had black eyes and stubble, and appeared harmless enough. This was the guy she'd just seen, the one who hadn't glanced her way. He was even better looking close up.

Her mind travelled to Domenic and how he always had to dominate her, but now, she'd taken back control. No longer would she let men rule her. She'd take control with this man. "I think you talk too much," said Liz.

The man's eyes widened. "And what did you have in mind?" His eyes were inviting something more.

She grabbed his hand and moved off the stool. She led him towards an empty couch and pushed him beside her, his body close to hers. "Get over here."

The man tilted his head, his eyes dilated and his mouth parting with desire. "My pleasure." He leaned in and pressed his lips over hers, their tongues flicking in and out as Liz forgot her troubles. She pressed her body hard against his, touching his manhood as he massaged her breasts. His fingers found her dress and trailed down her leg as he probed in between her thighs with rough fingers. She moaned with desire, but when he was pulling down her panties, she grabbed his hands and pulled them away.

Liz moved off him, her desire spent but his eyes still burned with desire for her. *Oh why did she keep doing this?* She had gone too far with the man when all she wanted was kissing for fun. Nothing more.

He hid his disappointment. "Can I get your number? I don't even know your name."

Liz smiled. "I don't think so. Gotta go." She rose from the couch, spotting a look of shock on his face and ignoring a couple staring wide-eyed at them.

The man caught up to her and tapped her on the shoulder. "Listen, let's take a seat back there and talk. Nothing more." Her feet remained frozen. Why had she even come? "Listen, I don't know about you, but I can tell something's bothering you. And I know I'm just a stranger but sometimes it helps to talk things out." He put out his hands. "This is a public place and we can have a quiet chat on the couch. I promise to keep my hands to myself. No expectations."

Liz nodded and followed him back to the couch. She sat beside him but kept a wider distance between them. "I'm sorry. I shouldn't have kissed you. I get like that sometimes. I try to distract myself when I know it's wrong. Whenever something triggers me, I tend to get wild." Not that she slept around with strangers, but she'd had a few superficial relationships with men she'd met in clubs.

"So what happened?"

"I really can't talk about it," said Liz. "Why don't we talk about something else, like movies or books."

He beamed. "Sounds like a plan. You can start."

Liz thought about that initial control over men, but why did she always feel empty afterwards? In spite of not wanting a man to traumatise her again, why did she give herself that illusion of control again and again?

CHAPTER 5
THE STUDENT

The following Monday, Liz yawned and stretched out in bed. Her mind flashed back to the nightclub, a sense of guilt and shame over her behaviour. Initially, she was able to get that sense of relief and control, but later on, she'd always come to the realisation that her using men that way was only a temporary measure. She'd never had sex with a stranger but enjoyed having foreplay in nightclubs, and always with people around. Even that could prove to be dangerous, but she couldn't help herself. The relief never lasted, and she'd ended up feeling dirty and ashamed of herself. But she couldn't help it. She loved controlling men, and maybe it was her way of dealing with Domenic over the years.

The last time she'd had sex was with her ex-boyfriend after Domenic, and they'd been together for three years. In the end, she realised that he was too controlling and broke it off. Luckily, he didn't dominate her to the point of violence, as Domenic had.

Liz had definitely enjoyed the touching and kissing on Friday, and the man had wanted to see her again, but why date someone she only wanted to have fun with? Bella would chastise her about her behaviour. Liz realised it was a destructive way of dealing with her pain, but she had no control over it. The man appeared nice enough, but she couldn't focus on a relationship when eventually they would all control her. It was just a man's way.

After a light breakfast of eggs and coffee, she grabbed her bag and keys and headed out to work. She found a parking space next to a black SUV that was taking up two spaces, and cursed. No-one was in the car. Damn! Given there was an event in the nearby area, some people must've decided to park here illegally.

Once she arrived at the building, she waved hello to Penny and others in the office and settled at her desk. She took out a case file and flicked through relevant points. She had a consent form to speak to Camilla's psychiatrist so that he could write a report about the prognosis of her substance abuse, and the likelihood of having her daughter returned to her care. It was always a long process, but normally the centre had a high success rate with the families in crisis.

She picked up her phone when Penny approached Liz with a young woman behind her. When the woman moved beside Penny, in her line of vision, her body sat up straight and her mouth opened. She hung up the phone. *What the hell! Gabriella*? The woman was already stalking her, and she still hadn't heard from Marco about her.

She stared at the short woman with her dark brown hair and blonde highlights tied up in a short pony-tail. Gabriella wore a tight-fitting black skirt and white shirt that showed off her buxom, slim figure. Her dark brown eyes penetrated Liz's with curiosity as if sizing her up.

Penny was oblivious to Liz's shock. "Hey, Liz. This here is Gabriella Jamitsan who we spoke about. She's the work experience student doing the Certificate IV in Community Services course at the nearby college. She's here to start the work placement."

Liz didn't want to make a scene and decided to question Gabriella later. She leaned forward and shook her hand. "Nice to meet you, Gabriella. Take a seat and we'll have a chat."

The woman had a piercing gaze but smiled, which made Liz uneasy. "Hi, Liz. I'm happy to be here. Thanks for taking me on. I realise how busy you must get, and I really appreciate it."

Liz smiled without it reaching her eyes. "Not a problem."

Penny rubbed her hands. "Okay, I'll leave you two to it." She turned back and returned to her desk.

Liz whispered. "Follow me." Gabriella nodded, gripping tightly onto her satchel. She followed Liz to an empty interview room.

Liz closed the door behind them and took a seat behind the table while Gabriella sat opposite with her head bowed. "What are you doing here? You do know that stalking is a crime in Victoria?"

Gabriella frowned. "I honestly didn't know that you worked here. It's a coincidence. Besides, I love kids and have a passion to do this kind of work. Give me that opportunity, Liz. If I don't do this placement, I'll struggle to complete my course because right now there's nothing else available for me."

"What is really going on here?"

Gabriella pressed her lips together, shaking her head. "I meant it when I said my father's still dangerous."

She scoffed. "Are you my bodyguard now?"

"No, of course not, but I'm here, so can't we at least try to work together? I really aspire to be like you, Liz, a social worker. Please give me that chance to work in welfare. Please!"

Liz got the feeling there was more to Gabriella's story, and hopefully, she'd hear from Marco soon. Right now, she had a job to do, and she was always the professional here. "Fine, but let's keep this strictly business. I don't want to hear that man's name in this office. Do you understand?"

Gabriella swallowed. "Of course."

"Fine. Now let's get to work."

Gabriella's eyes darkened. "I'm so sorry to make you uncomfortable."

Liz ignored her comment. She'd remain professional. If not, she'd probably break down. "So do you have a copy of your units of study in the course. It'll give me an idea of what you need to focus on."

Gabriella handed her a document. "Here it is." Liz pulled over a chair from an empty desk and moved it beside her own. They both sat down, and Liz scanned through the document. "Okay, well obviously this is general stuff so what's your main interest of work?"

"I'd like to focus on youth work as I can sort of relate."

Liz rubbed her hands together. "I'll give you a quick run-down of our services here." She handed her a few brochures of their service then resumed. "We run a foster and kinship care service for children and youth who struggle to live with their parents, more often a sole parent. And we also provide residential care for those young ones who can't live safely in their home."

Gabriella nodded, jotting down notes in a small pad. "And what's the main reason they're not safe at home?"

Liz sighed. "Well, it could be drug or alcohol abuse, family violence, child abuse by the parents or step-parent. In some cases, we've had child prostitution orchestrated by the parents."

Gabriella's eyes widened and she leaned forward with interest. "Really? Child prostitution. Oh that's awful. Tell me more about that."

"Well, parents might take their child out of school and work with illegal companies by placing their child's photo on their private site. They get interest from buyers then work out the logistics, and the child stays home to provide the service." Liz briefly closed her eyes. "It's despicable how many of these cases the police have."

"I take it you've worked with the police on this?"

"I have," Liz continued. "Anyway, we also support young people with new accommodation, building personal skills, and engaging them with other support services. We support the homeless, too."

"Amazing work that you do here," said Gabriella.

"Thanks." Liz showed Gabriella a copy of the office policies and procedures. "I'll give you this document to read, and then I'll get you to observe a bio-psychosocial assessment of my next case. She's due in about an hour. Then I have a visit to a drug rehabilitation facility in the city so you can come with me."

Gabriella squeezed her hands together. "Sounds exciting. I can't wait to work with you, Liz."

"Okay, I'm just about to ring a psychiatrist about a client, Camilla, who presents with substance abuse. She's been having therapy with him for a month, and she's started drug rehabilitation. Her brother's coming down from Queensland to care for her daughter temporarily, so we need to make sure she stays on the straight and narrow, or she'll lose her daughter forever.

She's relapsed a few times and has no family here. Her mother's in Queensland and will be having surgery soon. Once she's recovered, she plans to visit Melbourne for a while to help care for her daughter. Depending on Camilla's recovery, the mother may or may not apply for custody of her granddaughter, but there's the brother too. If all else fails, we look into the foster care system on a more permanent basis."

"And where's the daughter now?"

"She's with a temporary foster carer until Camilla's brother, Matthew, comes down. He's due here in the next few days and we'll be meeting him and discussing arrangements for the care of the young girl."

"Sounds complicated," Gabriella said.

"It sure is." She grabbed the phone. "Now, listen in on the types of questions I'll ask the psychiatrist as you'll be doing this sort of thing. Remember the bounds of confidentiality, which is in the guidelines that you'll need to read by tomorrow."

Liz dialled the number, a burst of energy sending waves through her body. She loved helping people and keeping busy, and Gabriella seemed keen and interested in the field. She only hoped they could have a professional working relationship with no personal interferences.

CHAPTER 6
THE GYM

Liz waved to Jamie in the hospital cafeteria of Western Health, where her friend worked as a doctor in the emergency ward. She had met Jamie through Bella and they became fast friends. Jamie was the sensible one while Bella was the wise one. As for Liz, well, she was the wild one who probably needed to be tamed. Maybe one day.

Liz rose from the table and hugged Jamie, who patted her on the back. She wanted to tell her about Gabriella, and no doubt Marco would update Bella about her.

Jamie flicked her red fringe and fixed her with a strong brown-eyed gaze. "Oh, Liz, how are you doing after the news? I am so sorry I haven't seen you. It has been extremely busy here in the ward."

They sat down across from each other, the chatter of others filling the room around them. Long lines made service slow, but Liz only ordered salads for both of them as Jamie had limited time.

"So what are you doing here anyway? Do you have a day off work?"

"I had a few things to do, like renewing my passport, signing up for self-defence classes, and fixing a bank account issue. I needed at least half a day, but I decided to take the rest of the time off."

"Don't you have a work experience student starting soon?"

Liz averted her eyes. "Yep, she started a couple of days ago, but I got a colleague to take care of her today.

She understood I had a prearranged day off." She looked back up at Jamie. "I've asked Marco to look into this student. She claims to be Domenic's daughter."

Jamie's expression shifted into surprise mode as she leaned closer to Liz. "What do you mean?"

Liz explained the issue with Gabriella while digging her fork into the salad. "I still haven't heard from Marco. He must be busy."

"I take it you believe she has an ulterior motive. Or could she be telling the truth?" Jamie crossed her legs as she chewed on a radish.

"I don't know what to believe. I'll just see what Marco says."

Jamie nodded. "And how are you doing after the news of Domenic?"

She shrugged. "What can I do? It's something I can't control, but if he comes near me, he could go back to jail. Marco said he's got my back."

Jamie nodded. She dug into her Caesar salad then looked up. "I am here for you, as we all are. So if you need anything, please do not hesitate to ask, Liz. So do I need to ask why you are taking self-defence classes?"

Liz's gaze turned serious. "I might need to protect myself, Jamie, and I don't like feeling unprotected." She paused. "Marco said he hasn't been given a supervision order, which means they're not monitoring him in the community."

"Oh, Liz, I am sorry. But I believe you might have the right to make a submission if you feel he should be on a supervision order. If you consider him to still be a threat."

"Oh, what's the point? Marco said they think he's a changed man, so I doubt they'd even consider an order.

I just plan to live my life and forget about him. But if that bastard, Domenic comes near me, there will be hell to pay."

Jamie leaned over and stroked Liz's hand. "That's my girl. I knew you had that fighting spirit in you."

Liz's stomach tightened, and she needed to change the focus of this conversation. "So how's your love life, Jamie?"

"Hmm, what love life? Who has the time? And what about you? Anyone new on the horizon?"

She shook her head. "Just me and my vibrator. Oh, and the occasional good time."

Jamie pressed her lips together, squinting. "Oh, Liz, forever the joker, aren't you?"

"That's good old me." She munched on the last of her garden salad and took a sip of her lemon-lime and bitters. It soothed her dry throat.

Jamie wiped her mouth with a napkin and drained the last of her water. "I have to go, darling, but we will catch up soon. You take care." She wrapped her arms around Liz.

"You too, Jamie."

Liz walked out, got into her car, and drove to the local gym near her apartment. She changed into her gym wear, consisting of a black cotton tracksuit and a white tank top then proceeded to step on to the exercise bike. Five men and two women were using the gym equipment, some of them competing for the same equipment.

After spending twenty minutes on the bike, she rubbed her face with a towel, stretched out her body and tensed her shoulder muscles. A whiff of musky cologne wafted through the air, although she couldn't see anyone in front of her. She was making her way to the treadmill when a man beat her to it. Was it his aftershave she smelled? He must've come up from behind her, which was why she hadn't seen him. He fixed his gaze on her, and for a moment, they were speechless. The man had thick eyebrows and dark-brown eyes. His wavy black hair was tied up and looked as though it would run down to his shoulders. A few scars on his chin and chest added to his good looks, and his well-toned body showed that he had worked out a fair bit.

"I'm sorry. You take it. I can go do the weights."

Liz shook her head. "No, it's fine. I'll do something else."

"No, please. I think I barged in on you as I was behind you. So sorry. Take it."

Liz angled her head. "Are you sure?"

The strange man's eyes lingered. "Of course."

She blushed, averting her eyes. "Okay, thanks."

He walked away and grabbed a large dumbbell, proceeding to lift it above his head. The veins in his neck stood out, and his arms glistened as he stretched and lunged. She could barely breathe, watching him, and she turned away when he noticed she was watching him. *Oh hell!*

Liz's phone rang so she stopped the treadmill. "Marco. Tell me."

"Gabriella is Domenic's daughter, and her mother testified against him in court after you did. It's in the archived newspapers if you want the details. I'll send the article to your phone."

31

Her body froze. "Thanks, Marco." She breathed a sigh of relief, realising that Gabriella was a victim just as she had been.

CHAPTER 7
THE MEETING

Liz steered towards the Richmond area about to meet with Camilla's brother, Matthew, at the foster carer's house. Gabriella sat in the passenger seat, and looked wistfully through the window, appearing to be in a world of her own. So far, she had proven to be hard-working and keen to work in the community sector field. She didn't appear to take after Domenic in any way. She was the complete opposite.

Liz had read through the article about Gabriella and her mother, who apparently had reported his abuse to the police multiple times, but nothing was ever done about it. On one occasion, her mother, Jean, had been admitted into hospital with a concussion and broken ribs, and that was about the time he'd left her for Liz. If he'd stayed with Jean, he might've killed her the next time around. Domenic gave Jean her freedom and entrapped Liz, but he had never told her he'd been married or had a child. Not that she expected him to say anything.

A sound reverberated in Gabriella's large bag. She rummaged into it, stared at the display screen, and grinned. "Hi honey. What's up?" Liz watched as she nodded, her face blushing. "Sure. Pick me up at seven. Love you. Bye." She turned to Liz. "Sorry, that was Nick, my boyfriend. It's our first-year anniversary. He remembered. So we're having a special dinner."

Liz chuckled. "That's sweet. It's great that he's romantic."

She nodded. "And I'm head over heels. But it's hard with his travel."

Liz turned to her, frowning. "Why does he travel? For work?" They were close to Camilla's place, having turned into her street.

She nodded. "He works for himself as a motivational speaker, particularly about people empowering themselves against crime and violence. He's a forensic psychologist." Her eyes glistened. She had it bad. "In fact, he has a seminar in town coming up soon. I'll see if Penny can give us the time to attend as it is relevant to the work we do."

"Sure. Sounds interesting."

The conversation ended once they arrived at the house that Liz had visited several times for the regular check-ins and support. She pulled over by the kerb and exited the car. Her eyes roamed the all too familiar weatherboard house featuring a cracked pathway, wilting plants, towering trees, and potted plants set on either side of the front door. Two teenage boys rushed out of the house, throwing a ball, and almost bumped into Gabriella who shot them a glare. Liz smiled and nodded at them as they passed the ball to each other in the front yard.

"Boys, come back inside. You haven't had your breakfast yet." They turned back and entered the house when the foster carer beamed at the sight of Liz. "Liz, great to see you. How's my favourite social worker?"

"Great, Joan. And how are the kids doing?"

"Pretty good. Little Mariana's doing well. Just having her breakfast."

"Great." She turned to her student. "This here is Gabriella. She's a community studies student, learning the ropes of my work."

Joan put out her hand and Gabriella took it with a nod. "Great to meet you, Gabriella. I'd say you're in great hands with this one." She winked at Liz.

"Nice to meet you, Joan, and yes, I agree with you." Gabriella avoided her eyes and blushed as if she didn't like the spotlight.

They moved into the kitchen, and Liz's heart warmed when she saw Camilla's daughter Mariana. She was eating cornflakes, the milk and cereal dripping down her chin. Very carefully she wiped her chin with a paper napkin then sipped her cup of water. Her rosy chubby cheeks and light-brown wavy hair made her look cute, despite the trauma this young girl had been through in her short life at five years of age.

Joan touched Mariana on the chin. "Hey, sweetie. You remember Liz, don't you?"

The young girl nodded. "Liz, yeah."

"Well, she is here to bring you home to your Uncle, Matthew. He'll be here any minute now to take you home. Is that okay?"

The young girl shrugged then continued to eat her cereal.

Gabriella stared at the girl, mesmerised but she said nothing. Turning towards Liz, she whispered, "Where's the Uncle?"

Liz said, "He's due here any minute now." Turning to Mariana, she said, "You're a big girl now, Mariana, and starting school next year."

She turned to her. "Where's Mama?"

Liz hesitated. "Mummy is sick at the moment and getting help. Hopefully, you will see her soon. But for now, she needs to rest and get help."

"Okay," Mariana said with a cheeky smile.

Liz wanted to reach out and wrap her arms around the little girl, to tell her that everything would be alright. She wanted to assure her of that security, but she couldn't. For all she knew, the Uncle could be a creep who couldn't be trusted. But for now, she had to give him the benefit of the doubt and trust that he would take care of her on a temporary basis. Worst case scenario would be that her grandmother or a permanent foster carer would take over.

Liz jolted at the ring of the doorbell and Joan headed to the front door. She turned at the sound of footsteps and winced at the figure before her. It was the man she'd seen at the local gym—the one who had offered her the treadmill. His expression showed a hint of recognition as his gaze turned serious, his dark-brown eyes piercing her own. He flicked his wavy hair to the side, but this time his hair wasn't tied up in a bun. It flowed smoothly down his shoulders and added further appeal than when it was tied up.

She never got the chance to meet him yesterday as a fellow social worker had visited him at his sister's house.

Joan broke the silence. "Matthew, this is Liz and Gabriella. I understand you met another social worker yesterday? Penny, wasn't it?"

He shifted his posture. "Yes, I met Penny." He turned. "Hi, Liz and Gabriella. Very nice to meet you." His gaze lingered on Liz but he didn't mention anything about the gym, and why would he? "Now, where's that little niece of mine?"

Joan led him further into the kitchen where two other children sat at the breakfast table, munching on fruit and toast in silence. The two teenage boys headed upstairs, and now Mariana glanced at Matthew briefly. He pulled up his shirt sleeves, showing tanned, muscle-toned skin. His pants hugged his body to show a rugged and strong physique. He obviously worked out often.

He sat in a chair near her and moved closer, but Mariana moved. He was a stranger after all, and it would take time. "Hi Mariana, I'm Matthew, your mother's brother. I am sorry we never got to meet, but I was living in another place far away. I plan to stay here now, and I can take care of you for a little while."

"I want my Mummy." She finished her cereal and crossed her arms, looking up at Liz.

Liz leaned down, saying, "Sweetie. This is your Uncle, and he will take you back to your place and look after you."

Tears started to fall. "Will you come too, Liz?"

Liz hesitated. If that was what it took, she'd give her the time to adapt. "Sure, I guess I can come for a little while." Matthew frowned then turned away as if wondering what he had got himself into.

CHAPTER 8
FAMILIAL STRANGERS

Liz drove over to Camilla's house while Matthew followed in his sister's car. Gabriella sat in the back with Mariana and they chatted about children's shows. Gabriella had a way with children, and Mariana seemed to shine around her.

Liz got out of the car, aware of Matthew's strong presence behind her. She was conscious of his commanding persona but put that thought out of her mind. She barely knew the guy and was already self-conscious.

Gabriella held on to Mariana's hand while they waited for Matthew to unlock the front door. He gave them a reassuring smile as he led them inside. Luckily, the house didn't smell like dust and cigarette smoke, so she guessed that Matthew must've cleaned it yesterday when he'd arrived. The small foyer led to a large living area with a basket of toys and books set in a corner, a television sitting on top of a glass stand, a torn brown sofa etched with cigarette and food stains, and a discoloured blue carpet. The place was in serious need of refurbishment and care, but what did she expect when Camilla had issues?

Matthew's eyes darkened as he faced Liz. "I know this place needs a make-over, and I plan on doing just that. Rip up the carpet, get a new couch, and add in some new furniture. All in good time."

Liz nodded. "That's great." She looked at Gabriella. "Listen, why don't you play with Mariana here in the living room while I have a quick word with Matthew."

"Sure, boss." She led Mariana to the toys, and together they sat on the carpet and rummaged in the basket, which made Mariana's eyes light up.

Liz walked into the kitchen, and she and Matthew sat on chairs at a round table featuring a scratched surface. The dishes had been washed, and he had obviously cleaned the entire room. "Thanks for doing this. I know Camilla's grateful, and hopefully she'll get the help she needs."

He nodded. "Thank you for helping. She's a gorgeous little girl, and I am happy to do whatever it takes. I just hope I can get her to trust me. Not that I blame the poor child. I would've been here for Camilla much earlier if I'd known how bad she was."

"I know, but give it time. As Joan said, she likes to have a snack in the afternoons and likes watching cartoons too." She handed him a documented list of Mariana's needs in a manila folder. "This sheet here is all about her needs night and day. Luckily, she's mostly independent. If you come across any issues, just give me a call. My card's in that manila folder." She swallowed. "Now, we do provide twenty-four-hour support if you run into any issues. Here's another document that outlines the financial support and our policies and procedures, particularly details about peer mentoring, and education and training for carers. There's also access to the Foster Care Association of Victoria for further resources you might need. I'll be Camilla's case manager for the next couple of months. It could be less time, depending on Camilla's progress. So my job is to do home visits and check in with you through regular phone calls." She pulled back at the light in his eyes. "You might not even need this information, but it's there should you need it."

He nodded. "Thanks for that. I'll have a read of all this stuff." He paused. "So you like the gym, hey?"

She nodded. "I do, and thanks for the treadmill. Much appreciated."

His eyes lingered. "No worries. Happy to help a damsel in distress."

Liz chuckled. "Funny, but seriously, I have to go. My workday is not done yet, but I'm sure you'll be fine. I'll let you know when Camilla finishes rehabilitation, but she's got a while yet. The centre will help her get work once she proves she can stay off the drugs." She cleared her throat. "We'll also help sort out Mariana's educational needs, like school, for next year." She rose. "I will be in touch, Matthew."

"Thanks again," he said.

Liz felt herself blushing as he leaned forward in his seat, getting another smell of his musky cologne. She headed into the living room, watching Mariana build something with Legos. "Mariana, we need to go, but your Uncle here is going to play a game with you. Would you like that?"

She shrugged. "I want you to stay."

Liz bent down on her knees and stroked her hair. "Oh, darling, I wish I could, but I have to help other little children like you and their families. I will come visit soon, I promise." She turned back but Matthew was missing. He returned with a thick photo album.

"Hey, Mariana. I thought you might like to see some photos of your mum from when she was little. Would you like that?"

Mariana nodded and got up, making her way over to the couch. "Okay."

Gabriella waved goodbye. "Take care, Mariana."

She waved back. "Bye bye Gabi."

Liz nodded to Matthew and waved goodbye to Mariana, then walked out the door with Gabriella back to her car.

CHAPTER 9
COPING STRATEGY

Gabriella appeared sullen and quiet all of a sudden, as if lost in her own world. Drawing a hand through her hair, Gabriella focused straight ahead and remained silent.

"You and Mariana were pretty close back there," Liz said.

Gabriella fixed her gaze on Liz then shrugged. "She reminds me of me at that age." Liz nodded and waited for more. "I can relate to her pain."

When she didn't go further, Liz said, "I found out that you're telling the truth, and I'm sorry I didn't believe you."

Gabriella gave her a reassuring smile. "I guess you can say my Dad treated me like dirt, always controlling, demanding, never satisfied. He never hit me, but he made damn sure I witnessed his abuse of my mum. I was helpless then."

Liz could hear the deep sadness in her voice. "I'm sorry, Gabriella. That must've been hard. You would've only been nine years old. Too young for that kind of trauma."

Liz had heard it all before: broken families, and fathers who didn't deserve to be parents. She often wondered why the ones who deserved to be parents were never able to have children while those who didn't deserve them gave birth to many babies, and sometimes from different fathers.

"Anyway, enough about me. Tell me about you." Gabriella's mood brightened, obviously needing the distraction. "Do you have a family? Are you married?"

"No, I'm single."

Gabriella lifted up her palms and tilted her head. "A gorgeous woman like you wouldn't be single for long. You must have your pick of men, or maybe there is someone special in your life."

Liz's hands sweated as she stared straight ahead, thankful that the office was up ahead. She turned to Gabriella and grinned. "We're here." She swallowed and gazed at Gabriella. "Maybe I'll tell you another time."

Gabriella's eyes darkened. "I'm sorry. I never meant to pry."

She turned into the parking area, turned off the motor and rubbed her sweaty hands. Once they exited the car, they headed into the building and returned to work for the remainder of the day.

**

Liz lifted up her glass that evening and skolled down the Tequila shot in front of the bartender, who topped her up with another shot. She was at her usual nightclub. "Hit me again."

Staying home was out of the question. She needed the distraction of the club; especially after hearing Gabriella's story. Why bother Bella and Jamie when they had their own problems? She didn't want to burden them with this.

The bartender, with bleached hair and bright blue eyes, squinted. "Take it easy, Liz. I might need to drive you home if you have more." He winked at her.

Liz leaned forward in the stool, her arms resting on the counter as she wiped liquid off her lips. "I so need this."

The bartender shook his head. "Care to share?"

Liz shook her head. "I don't think so. I'd rather drown my sorrows if you don't mind."

The bartender frowned. "I think you have your pick of men to talk to right here, and looks like that guy from last time is coming your way."

She turned and nodded in greeting to the strange man from her last visit at the nightclub. She didn't know his name, but she appreciated his moustache and blond crew-cut style. His eyes were black with a hint of stubble. "Hey there, stranger. We meet again."

He took the stool beside her. "Hey, woman with no name. Can I get you a drink?"

Liz nodded. "Sure, give me another Tequila shot."

The man turned to the bartender. "A Tequila shot and a Jagermeister for me, thanks." He fixed his gaze on Liz, and the scent of a woody cologne penetrated her nostrils. "So what is your name?"

"It's Liz. And you?"

"I'm Johnny. Great to meet you with a name." He put out his hand and she shook it. "So what brings you here tonight?"

Liz swallowed, wondering how much to tell this strange man who was good-looking and appeared to be sweet and grounded. "Just need to forget a certain problem and looks like you can offer me the distraction I need."

He leaned forward and touched her thigh. "Oh yeah!"

She drank her drink then wiped her mouth. "Maybe I just need some innocent fun."

He shook his head then drank down his drink. Together they got off their stools and she followed him towards the exit.

She stopped in her tracks. "I don't think so. Why not the couch like last time?"

He smiled sweetly. "I want something more private."

Liz rummaged in her bag and gripped her small scissors and perfume. She'd be ready if he tried to hurt her. No man would hurt her again. "Let's go there. The couch is empty and has little light." She wandered away from him and sat on the empty couch as he leaned in close and wrapped his arms around her. He kissed her hard and hungrily, and Liz melted into his tongue as she moaned and brushed her hands through his scalp. He pulled away and kissed her neck, his lips trailing down the middle of her chest. He played with her breasts and was about to squeeze his hands between her thighs, but she stopped him.

She quickly lifted herself away, a sense of emptiness in her stomach, and avoided his eyes. She cleared her throat. What the hell was she doing? This had to stop.

Johnny watched her with concern. "I'll try again. Can I get your number?"

Liz averted her eyes. "Let's just leave things the way they are."

His eyes darkened, but the expression was fleeting. "Sure thing."

CHAPTER 10
RESPITE

Liz played with the strands of her jet black hair and sat on a wooden stool at a solid square timber table with light casting a glow on her friends' faces. She gripped her tall glass of skinny iced coffee and shifted her posture. She was with her friends, Bella and Jamie, at their usual cafe in Altona. Suspended light bulbs lined the centre of the cafe, and it featured pictures of bird designs on white-washed walls.

A number of patrons created muffled tones as they ordered food where they sat, scattered around the few tables in the small café. It gave her the buzz she needed to forget her troubles. The autumn season was mild with its intermittent sunshine and rain.

"So you never mentioned the sex between you and Marco. How was it?" Liz leaned forward with a cheeky grin and rubbed her hands.

Jamie shook her head, her short red hair prominent under the glowing light. "Oh, cut it out, Liz. That's personal and between her and Marco."

Bella chuckled. Her face flushed and she became occupied with her breakfast. "It's okay, Jamie." She stared at Liz with an almost defiant look. "That is private." She shook her head. "All I'll say is that he's amazing, and I am so in love with that man."

Liz touched Bella's hand. "I'm glad, girl. You deserve it after that psychopath tried to kill you."

Jamie almost cried. "I second that, Bella. It's about time you move away from all that trauma you experienced and settle down with the man you love."

"Thank you, girls. I couldn't have got through it without both of you." She fixed her gaze on Liz. "Now, it's your turn to find love, Liz."

Liz's posture stiffened. "I think Jamie'll be next. I don't do relationships, girl, and you know that. I'm happy to be free and have fun with any guy I please. It's the life." A sense of tightness pervaded her chest and her throat dried up. Who was she kidding? Pushing the sensations away, she shifted her posture and squeezed her hands. "I am all for us going to a nightclub next weekend. Just let our hair hang down and forget all our problems. What do you say?"

Bella's green almond-shaped eyes stared back at Liz with curiosity. She had a gorgeous yet innocent look about her. Liz almost wished she had the bright eyes of Bella rather than her boring, hazel eyes and tall frame. Bella's brown shoulder-length hair and green almond-shaped eyes gave her an innocent beauty. "Stop distracting yourself, Liz. You can't keep partying to forget your past."

Liz laughed. "Oh, come on, Bella. That's just your excuse not to come out with me next weekend. Your way of saying no, isn't it?"

Bella shook her head. "I'm happy to come with you next weekend. Not a problem."

Jamie gave Bella a reassuring smile. "You have come a long way, Bella. I never thought I would hear the day that you would easily say you'd go to a nightclub."

Liz focused on Jamie, whose soft brown eyes complimented her short red hair that rippled with her body movements. She had a more regal beauty than

Bella. The dimples on both cheeks enhanced her smile. "You'll really come?"

Bella nodded. "I must say, I don't feel so anxious anymore."

Liz bit into a lettuce leaf, the tangy taste of balsamic vinegar soothing her. It dripped down her chin, and she wondered if Bella was right. Was going out almost every night a distraction? She'd go out most nights to cafes, parties or nightclubs, in spite of weariness and fatigue from her intense work as a social worker. "What about you, Jamie? Are you in for nightclubbing? And please ignore what darling Bella says about me?"

Jamie's dark brown eyes pierced her own as if she could see right through Liz. It was unnerving when her eyes said so much more than her words. "Sure. I am happy to keep you company if I can change my shift at the hospital. I will make a few calls and swap with a co-worker." Her eyes turned serious. "Maybe Bella can teach you meditation techniques. I'm happy to brainstorm with you on ways you can spend more time on a hobby rather than going out almost every night. You love to cook, so do more of that. And you need rest, Liz. We don't want you burning out."

Liz clenched her teeth. "I don't need a plan, Jamie, and I would never have the patience or inclination to meditate. How boring!" She smiled. "But I can cook more nutritious meals, I guess."

Bella intervened. "I don't see Liz meditating, but she should go back to that psychologist."

Liz nodded. "I haven't got around to calling yet, Bella, but I will. I mean, you guys have been through hell and back in the last year, so maybe you guys should do counselling with me.

"Great," Bella said. "But you need to make a date to ring and stick to it. No more waiting. It's time."

"I know, and you're right. I will ring."

Bella nodded. "And how are your parents? Maybe you can spend more time with them after they return from their cruise."

"I'd love to, but they're not back for a month so they're living it up."

Jamie sighed. "Have you told them about Domenic?"

Liz shook her head. "I am not going to ruin their cruise. After all, me seeing Domenic was all my fault. They warned me against him but I was too stupid to listen. I thought I was in love, and I just up and leave home to live with a psychopath mechanic. Thank God they took me back and paid for me to go to university."

Bella stroked her hand. "Oh Liz. You were only seventeen and they love you. And you were even more wild back then than you are now."

Liz watched new customers come in, the glass windows giving her a clear view. She wondered if Mr Right was out there. She was tired of hooking up with controlling men or crazy psychopaths. It was time she focused on getting past things and moving forward as Bella did. Could she learn to feel at peace with her past?

CHAPTER 11
A SURPRISE VISITOR

The following weekend, Liz got off the phone with Jamie and Bella. She appreciated their concern, but it was getting tiring to hear Domenic's name. She'd rather get on with her day than think about the monster who haunted her dreams. He could no longer hurt her.

Liz put in a load of washing then headed to the front door to pick up a few grocery items for lunch. As she left her building into the quiet street, she stopped dead in her tracks. Her body turned numb and she wrapped her arms around her stomach. She squeezed her eyes shut then opened them again. Surely, she was dreaming. It couldn't possibly be Domenic standing in front of her, only a few metres away, wearing dark glasses and a beanie. He hovered over a black station wagon as if he was exploring a motor problem. He wiped a cloth over his face with a shake of his head then spotted her. Throwing the dirty cloth, he took a step towards her, but Liz moved back a few steps, her body feeling like lead. She wanted to head straight back into her apartment, but she stopped herself. She could do this; she wouldn't let him intimidate her any longer.

He looked surprised. "Wow, I never expected to see you. How the hell are you, Liz?"

She clutched her throat, feeling the perspiration around the base of her neck. She took another step backward. "You're not supposed to be close to me. Why are you here? I...I can let the authorities know. Please go." She fought back the tremor in her voice and refused to succumb to weak legs and dizziness. She was much stronger than all those years ago. A fighter. She'd always been a fighter.

"I didn't know you were here. Haven't seen you in ten friggin years. Do you live here?" Liz looked him hard in the eyes for any sign of deception. She wondered how he knew where she lived. But instead, he pretended to be fixing his damn car. He'd always been manipulative. At least this way, he'd make it look like they simply bumped into each other, but it was his quiet way of controlling her. She wouldn't respond. She waited, but he looked at her smugly with his large hands resting against his waist.

He hadn't changed in ten years, still sporting tattoos around his neck and arms—a solid and muscular man, who wore earrings in both ears, with a short beard.

She asked him again, "And how...How did you find me?"

He chuckled. "Like I said, I didn't know you were here. But if I did, you know how resourceful I can be. But I wouldn't hurt you, Liz. I'm passed that. Anyway, seeing as I am here, I'd like to apologise. Make amends. I'm a changed man. You can trust me this time."

She cringed. "I doubt that." She was struggling to keep it together, but she refused to let him control her any longer.

His eyes turned upwards towards her building and the nearby shops, assessing his surroundings. "I must say, it is a quiet sort of place. Probably not much excitement. Is there?"

What the hell was he playing at? Was he trying to intimidate her after ten freedom-filled years? "Anyway, take care, Liz. I won't be bothering you anymore, but it was good to see ya. Still as beautiful as ever I see. And maybe one day you can learn to forgive me." He turned away and pushed down the bonnet of the car, unlocked it and stepped inside. Turning the motor on, he sped off.

Liz bowed her head, the images of his beatings at the forefront of her mind. Her blurred vision and gasp made Liz crumple to the ground, retreating into a foetal position. A female passerby approached but Liz ignored her as she covered her face, shaking. She pressed fists to the side of her head to stop the visions of the past.

Liz's body froze at the dark look in his eyes. "I'm leaving," she said. The look in his eyes told her that she shouldn't have said anything. Maybe she should've just left without telling him. That would've been safe. He clenched his hands into fists, his posture stiffened, and he squared his shoulders as he gave a lurching walk. "Fuckin' bullshit you are. I own you!" Liz shook her head. "Please don't hurt me."

He gave a mocking smile. "You're not the only person I've hurt, bitch! And I can kill you with my bare hands. I can hurt anyone who doesn't do what I ask. And you're going to stay put."

Liz cried. "No, I can't take this anymore." He lunged at her.

Liz broke out of her flashback, and must've lain on the ground for a while when the woman asked, "Who can I call for you, love?" She blinked a few times before answering. "My friends, Bella and Jamie." She handed the lady her phone from her back pocket in a daze. The woman scrolled through her contacts and made the calls.

Sometime later, Liz looked up to find the woman smiling and nodding to Jamie and Bella who pulled her up from her position on the street. They made it inside her apartment and closed the door.

Bella led Liz to the couch with Jamie following behind. She couldn't stand to see their stricken faces and hated being in a submissive position. Surely, she was stronger than this? How could he still affect her this way?

Bella sat beside her and grabbed Liz's hand while Jamie sat on her other side. "Liz, what happened? The woman said you'd seen some guy who rushed off. Was it Domenic?"

Liz turned to Bella, a tear sliding down her cheek. "It was Domenic." She explained their conversation as Bella's face turned pale while Jamie held a curious expression.

"Dear God, Liz. I'll let Marco know. He has restrictions, and if he comes that close to you again, he can be arrested for trespassing on your property."

Jamie shook her head. "Liz, honey. What can I get for you? A drink? A tea?"

She closed her eyes briefly. "No, I'll be fine. You guys don't need to babysit me. I'm a big girl."

Bella leaned in. "Don't be silly. We're here for you any time, any day, just like you'd be there for us. Us girls stick together. Now, let's make a plan."

Liz's shoulders slumped as she looked to Jamie then Bella. "What's the point? He's too smart for any of these authorities. I doubt he could ever change even if he said he did. He wanted to see me in pain. His sick way of getting his kicks."

Jamie drew a hand through her hair and frowned. "Bella is talking about a safety plan. A crisis response plan. How can we keep you safe, Liz?"

"My apartment should be safe. He can't get in here without me knowing it. And as for out there, I don't know. I guess I have Marco on speed-dial."

Bella added, "The Victims of Crime Register can help you with support. Don't they have support groups? Use them, Liz. And I'll give you some contacts for women's crisis services."

She shook her head. "I'm fine, Bella. I really don't need a group or services. They can't keep me safe. Only I can. Besides, what good will it do if that bastard's roaming free to do as he likes? He can say he was in the area and accidentally bumped into me, but I don't believe in coincidences."

"He has restrictions and will be busy with his post-release programs," said Jamie. "He'll be stupid to do anything as he is aware he can return to prison."

"I guess." Liz shifted her posture and wiped her cheeks. "You know what? How about lunch? I'm making a vegetable frittata with whatever's in the fridge. I was meant to go to the grocery store but that plan didn't work. How about it?"

Bella nodded. "I'd love lunch, but I can make it for you."

Liz shook her head. "No, let me do this. I could use the distraction."

Bella nodded. "How about you, Jamie?"

"Lunch is what Liz does best. And whatever helps you to cope, Liz."

Liz smiled at her friends. She rose and scoured her fridge for the vegetables and eggs. No, she wouldn't let that bastard drag her down anymore. She was her own woman, and she was safe now.

CHAPTER 12
YOUNG DEFIANCE

Matthew watched Mariana play with her Barbie doll by dressing it up in a dress and stiletto shoes. She brushed the doll's hair, almost pulling her head out of its neck socket. Mathew sat on the couch, warmed by her cute face and placid manner.

She suddenly sensed him. "I want to see Mummy."

He swallowed and braced himself. "Your Mummy is still sick. She'll be back soon, Mariana. Very soon."

"I want a cheese sandwich, just like Mummy makes."

He got up from the couch. "One cheese sandwich coming up." Heading to the kitchen, he swung open the fridge and sighed. Grabbing the cheese slices and butter out of the fridge, he set them down on the bench and pulled out two slices of bread from the pantry. When he was done, he put the sandwich on a plate and called Mariana over from the living room. "It's ready. Come and eat."

She shuffled along, carrying her Barbie doll under her arm and setting it down on the kitchen bench. She looked down at her sandwich and strongly shook her head. "That's not the way Mummy makes it. She cuts my bread in a circle. I want it in a circle."

He nodded. "Okay then." Matthew found a biscuit cutter in the pantry then placed it over the bread on the plate to cut out a circle. Once he was done, he turned to her.

She shook her head again. "Not like that. Mummy uses a glass to cut the circle. It has messy edges. Not like that." She pursed her lips and squeezed her hands tight, breaking out in a cry. "I want my Mummy. I want my Mummy."

Matthew stood close by and touched her on the shoulder. "I'm sorry, Mariana. I'll do it again with the glass. So sorry."

She bowed her head and banged her fists on the table. "I want my Mummy. You can't make cheese sandwiches. Go away. Go away!"

Matthew watched her. "Why don't I make you another sandwich?"

She ran out of the kitchen as fast as she could. The slamming of the door jolted him in his place. *What the hell*! Running towards the front door in a panic, he swung it open but couldn't see her. Boy, she was fast. As the strong wind cut into his cheeks, he searched the front yard, but still couldn't see her anywhere. She had disappeared, but how could she be that fast? He had only missed her by seconds. He wasn't prepared because he never expected her to rush out of the house like that. Where the hell was she? He was in so much trouble.

He pulled open the front gate further then dashed around the footpath, looking behind trees and around parked cars on the street. Then he considered the nearby park. Maybe she ran to the park. Wouldn't that be where young children would head to? Running off in that direction, he scurried towards the park and searched everywhere, certain she was lurking somewhere. *I can't even care for a five-year-old child when Camilla needs me.* This wasn't happening.

His heart beat fast and his mind ran rampant, thinking that maybe someone had taken her. Maybe she'd been kidnapped, but his mind had to be playing tricks on him. Passersby around him watched him with suspicion as he was breathing fast, and he picked up his pace around the river, towering trees and a small playground area in the park. He headed over there and found Mariana crouching near a seesaw, crying. "Mariana. Are you okay?"

She faced him and cried some more. He didn't know what to do, and an image of Liz flashed before him. He had to call her. Maybe she could calm Mariana down more than he could. He'd never had experience with children, and she dealt with foster kids in her line of work. He was a firefighter, so what did he know about the emotional needs of children? Give him the policies and procedures of fire and safety any day and he was your man.

He fished in his back pocket for his phone, dialling Liz while watching Mariana in a cowering position, still whimpering. Once he hung up, the sound of her voice remained in his mind. She had a soothing, gentle voice, and his chest tingled at the words she'd used to calm him down. She'd be coming down to the park in about twenty minutes as she wasn't too far away.

Matthew sat with her on the seesaw. "Liz will be here soon, Mariana. Would you like to tell me what's on your mind?"

Mariana shook her head and took off on the swing set. He watched her in silence.

Footsteps later sounded behind him. He turned and stared at her flushed cheeks and smiling eyes. Boy, was she beautiful and smart. As she drew closer, he was tongue-tied all of a sudden. His rapid breathing started to settle.

"Hi Matthew. Give me a minute." She scurried over to Mariana who was drawing a picture in the dirt of the playground. Looking up, she walked into Liz's arms and beamed. Why couldn't Mariana hug him like that?

"Hi, cutie. I heard that you wanted a cheese sandwich."

She pulled away from Liz. "He didn't make it like my Mummy does."

"I heard, but Mummy isn't here right now, and you still need to eat. What if I make you my very own special sandwich with sprinkles and butter? Fairy bread."

"That would be nice, Liz. Thanks."

Liz held on to her hand and ushered her back to the house with Matthew following behind. He watched the way her body moved and he found his body responding. He didn't know this woman and here he was reacting to someone this quickly. What was wrong with him?

He had this sense of loss, and the grief of having lost his sister to drugs was making him all mushy inside. He was more emotional than he'd normally be.

CHAPTER 13
FRIENDLY BANTER

Matthew stood, cross-armed in his sister's kitchen while he fixated on Liz's sandwich-making skills. She dabbed butter on the bread shaped in circles then added colourful sprinkles on to the bread. She squashed the two bread slices together, and with long, dainty fingers and bright red, manicured nails, handed it over to Mariana on a small plastic plate.

Mariana's eyes widened. "Oh wow! That's nice. Thank you, Liz."

Liz put her hands together and beamed. "Anytime, Mariana. Now eat!" She headed over to Matthew. She stood by his side; her eyes focused on his niece. The sweet scent of flowers and spices penetrated his senses. He became aware of the slender curve of her body in the fitted pantsuit she was wearing and the nurturing way she handled his niece.

Matthew and Liz steered Mariana towards bed after she'd finished eating and drinking a glass of milk. Mariana snuggled up in bed with a yawn. He waited until her eyes started closing.

Walking back into the kitchen, Matthew sat across from Liz, who was checking her phone. She put it into her bag then looked up at him with a piercing gaze. "Is she asleep?"

He nodded. "Almost out like a light. She's exhausted after working herself up."

She gave him a reassuring smile. "Any other issues?"

"No, mostly she's been okay, but occasionally she misses her Mum, which is only natural." He clasped his hands together, his eyes focused on her rosy, red lips and the strong outline of her neck. *Damn!* He couldn't even think straight.

"We do have training sessions if you're keen. Mainly about dealing with these kinds of challenges. Otherwise, we can look at peer mentoring if you like."

He shook his head. "No, I'll be fine. I think it's about adapting."

She grinned. "Sure. And I guess you'll be going to work soon too?"

He rose from the table. "I applied for a transfer close by so I could be close to Mariana and my sister. But I don't start for a couple of weeks yet. They understand my situation with short-term foster care."

Liz nodded. "So what do you do?"

He lifted his posture. "I'm a firefighter."

"I can certainly see you as a firefighter." She peered into the distance. "I'm reminded of the show, Chicago Fire too. I absolutely love that show."

He swallowed. "And how do you see me as a firefighter?" He tilted his head, waiting.

"You look fit and you're pretty muscular."

"And the show? What do you like about it?"

"The men on that show know how to protect and serve the people. They're not too bad to look at, too. You have a reputation to uphold, Matthew."

His face warmed. "So are you saying that I'm good-looking and a stereotypical fire- fighter then?"

Liz blushed and averted her eyes. "I'm sorry. I shouldn't have said anything."

He leaned forward, gazing into her eyes that were still averted. "It's fine. I'm honoured that you admire my work and Chicago Fire. It is a great show. I watch it, too. And I can say that some of the women on that show are great to look at too. And beautiful like you."

Liz got up from the table, clearing her throat. "I'd better go. I have another house call to make before going home. I'll visit you soon and see how you're going."

Matthew rose. He wanted to hit himself for adding that last sentence, but he couldn't help himself. "Sure, Liz. And thanks so much for your help today. I appreciate it."

Liz half-smiled. "Any time. Bye, Matthew."

"Bye, Liz." He walked her out to her car and watched her drive off without looking at him. She couldn't have left the house fast enough.

What was he thinking when he mentioned her beauty? She was so mesmerising to him that the words slipped out. A woman had never had this much of an effect on him and he was starting to dream about her at night. But his focus had to be his responsibility to Mariana. He had to respect his working relationship with Liz, seeing that she was Camilla and Mariana's caseworker. Thinking about a relationship with Liz would impact his family responsibilities. He had to put aside his feelings and treat her as the professional that she was. He could do that. He had to do that.

CHAPTER 14
REFLECTIONS

Liz drew a hand through her hair as she sipped on a cafe latte in her regular cafe in Altona, drawing back as she almost burnt her lip. Once she recovered herself, the steamy hot liquid was soothing as she pondered last night with Matthew. He had a way with his niece, a gentle and nurturing side that tugged at her heart. She hadn't known many men who showed his kind of demeanour. It created a reaction in her. Her heart fluttered, and her hands sweated as she savoured the image of the way his biceps tightened when picking up Mariana or the way his lips parted when he wanted to say something but held back. "Earth to Liz! Earth to Liz! Where are you?" Bella said as she gave her a light slap on her hand.

She turned her eyes. "Sorry, just thinking."

"And what were you thinking about?" asked Jamie.

Liz shrugged, not wanting to talk about Matthew as whatever her reaction was, it was a conflict of interest. He was Camilla's brother, and she knew that most men initially appeared charismatic and trustworthy until they showed their true colours and violated your very soul. No, she refused to be so trusting next time. "Not that I can mention names, but my client's daughter reunited with her uncle and they seem to be getting along well. Except for the part when the little girl refused to eat the sandwich he made. But apart from that, I'm hoping the mother will be ready soon to come back home to her daughter."

Bella leaned forward. "That must be the best part of your job, right? The foster children getting back with their biological mothers?"

"For sure, girl. No doubt about that. So how about you guys? What's happening with you and Marco? Are wedding bells on the horizon or what?"

Jamie shook her head. "There will be no pressure from you, Liz. When Bella is ready, she will let us know."

Bella blushed and averted their eyes. "Actually, we have been talking about marriage, and I was going to mention it today…"

Liz slammed her hand over her mouth for a brief moment. "He proposed." She wrapped her arms tightly around Bella, almost choking the life out of her.

Bella pulled away. "I love you, Liz, but a little more breathing space please."

Jamie chuckled then hugged her. "Congratulations." She pulled apart from Bella. "So how did the famous detective propose? Was it formal or casual?"

Bella stared into her cappuccino while Jamie's eyes fixed on her, waiting. "He took me to this fancy Italian restaurant out in the country that was very dark, but romantic, and got down on one knee. I could tell he was so nervous because his hands were shaking, and his face was all puffy and hot. He took my breath away. I said yes before he even got the last word out." Her eyes lit up and peered into the distance. "He is amazing, and I love him so much."

Jamie shed light tears. "Oh, that is so romantic, Bella. I want what you are having."

Liz chuckled. "I knew he'd be romantic about it, and I'm so happy for you guys. Can't wait." She turned to Jamie. "So no guy on the horizon for you, Jamie?"

"I wish, but like I've said a multitude of times before. I am far too busy for romance."

Bella grimaced. "That's exactly what anyone would say to hide their true feelings, Jamie. You need to make time out of your busy schedule. It's not healthy to be all work and no play. Balance, like I always say."

"Exactly right," said Liz.

Jamie scoffed and blew on her herbal tea. She remained silent by drinking the hot liquid, then changed the subject. "Anyway, I want to know how you're feeling after the Domenic incident."

Liz swallowed. "I wish someone had seen him near my place, but then again, I don't want to do anything to escalate the situation. I really don't think he's changed. No-one can change that much. Those intervention orders aren't of that much value and can tend to make things worse."

Bella softened in her gaze. "Marco mentioned that an officer questioned Domenic but, of course, he denied knowing that you live in the area. The woman that was there didn't really get a good look at him either." She paused. "Marco said that if he gets close to you again, to take a photo of him with the surroundings and keep notes on what happens if he's around. That way you'll have visual and written proof he's near you. But I personally don't think you should be doing anything to aggravate him. If you see him and don't feel safe, call the police straight away, or make sure you have a secret weapon with you. It could be anything to incapacitate him."

"Thanks, Bella," said Liz. "I could do with your advice right now. But I'm sure he'll forget about me and not give me a further second's thought. He was always a ladies' man, and I do hope he has changed for the sake of his next girlfriend." One of the baristas with the bluest eyes she'd ever seen, who had recently started in the cafe, approached. "Would you ladies like another drink or a sweet? We have freshly-made scones if you like?"

Liz looked to the others who shook their heads. "No, we're fine, thank you." He walked away with a nod and a smile.

As Liz downed her hot drink, she wondered if she believed that he'd let her go. Surely after ten years, he'd want to get on with his life and not return to prison.

CHAPTER 15
COUNSELLING SESSION

Liz clasped her hands in the softly padded chair, waiting for the psychologist, Celine, to be ready for the session. The woman pulled out a note pad and took a seat opposite with a reassuring smile on her face. She recalled how ten years ago, this same psychologist had saved her from self-harm and terrifying nightmares. She owed her everything during that scary time. "Thanks for seeing me again."

"So what's happened, Liz? How can I help you today?"

She took a breath. "I've been having flashbacks and nightmares again. Domenic's been released from prison and he kind of made contact." She explained the time she'd seen him near her apartment.

Celine flipped her auburn fringe out of her vivid blue eyes. She hadn't changed much after all these years and was still petite in build with shoulder-length hair and well-manicured nails. Her eyes showed concern, but with any expression, her face was striking. "And you informed the police of this?"

"I did, but there's nothing they can really do unless he hurts me, or there's evidence he's following me. He's done his time, but I know it's his way of manipulating me."

"We can certainly discuss a safety plan before the end of the session, and I'm happy to extend it to do just that. Now, tell me how your life's been without Domenic in it over these past ten years. Have you had any other bad relationships after him?"

"I had one boyfriend who wouldn't stop calling me when I broke it off, and I kept telling him to stop ringing me. But he kept ringing me for months, and that triggered me over and over. I had the support of my friends, so I got through it eventually. My friend, Bella, gave me strategies once I finally told her about it. I could've saved months of heartache if I'd told her sooner."

Celine nodded, jotting down notes. "So what was Bella's advice?"

"She told me to listen to my intuition and stop answering the phone when I knew it was him ringing. But I felt I had to tell him to stop. It didn't work. I was telling him to do something, but I was inviting him to keep doing it by talking to him. I told him that I didn't want to talk to him and that it was over, but of course, he didn't listen because I kept talking to him anyway. He wasn't aggressive, but simply a pest."

"Interesting you say that, Liz. It's a bit like telling your child not to hit other children, but then you hit or abuse them in the process of telling them that." She cleared her throat. "So I take it he stopped calling after you ignored his phone calls?"

"He did stop."

"That can sometimes work. In some cases, if the partner has a huge emotional investment in the relationship, the behaviour can escalate." She jotted down notes. "And how are your parents doing?"

She smiled with fondness at how much she loved her parents. They'd always been supportive, but she didn't realise it when she was young. "My parents told me that Domenic was bad news, but I wouldn't listen. I still feel bad for running away at seventeen, in my last year of high school, to live with a psychopath. He supported me financially as a mechanic, but I lost my identity and school friends at the time. I was a virgin and I trusted him enough to end that. But in those early days, he was such a gentleman, and my parents were only trying to deal with a wild teenager. I felt stifled by them at the time, but boy was I stupid. In reality, they were only trying to protect me. They're on a cruise now and have decided to extend their vacation for a couple more months. I encouraged it because I don't want them being here knowing about Domenic's release."

"I understand, but you'll have to tell them eventually. For now, you'll need your support systems more than ever. I want you to use your intuition about Domenic at this point in time. What do you think his motivation would be to see you again?"

Liz didn't need to process that. "Revenge." She explained the situation with Gabriella.

Celine's eyes darkened. "I want you to be extra cautious. The fact that her working with you might be a conflict of interest. It might set him off if he thinks you're turning Gabriella against him."

"But she'd visited him in prison, and told him that she didn't want anything to do with him. That decision came from her."

She nodded. "Okay, but we'll monitor that and see how you feel as things go. I wonder what her motivation was to work with you."

"It's something, but she won't tell me the truth. I think she's hiding something."

In the rest of the session, the psychologist unpacked her feelings around the flashbacks and nightmares, discussed a safety plan, and shared support service numbers for women in crisis situations.

Liz rose. "Thanks, Celine. I will see you next week."

She beamed. "Of course. You take care of yourself."

As Liz walked out, she was able to breathe easily with a slight burden lifted from her shoulders. She was reassured that she could manage the situation and would be prepared should Domenic hurt her.

CHAPTER 16
A SILENT CALL

*They turned to their companion, sitting in a tinted car.
"Find me that runaway and make her pay."*

The companion nodded. "Same method?"

*They nodded. "Of course, but I want you to teach
her a lesson beforehand. I want her to suffer."*

"That's my speciality."

***

A week later, Liz took in the clear blue sky and light
breeze that feathered her cheeks. She sat back in her
padded chair on the balcony's tiled flooring outside.
Bella and Liz sat on either side of her, each holding a
flute of champagne to toast to Bella's upcoming
engagement party to Marco. Jamie steered her eyes
towards Liz who feigned a smile for the sake of her
friends. She didn't want to give them any clue that ever
since seeing Domenic she'd been a chaotic mess in her
mind. Dreams and flashbacks taunted her daily.
Besides, today was about Bella and not her.

Liz clinked her glass with theirs, and savoured her
special time with Jamie and Bella who'd been there for
her no matter what. Not so long ago, they'd been there
for Bella who was fighting her own demon. Now she
was relishing her newfound status with her soon-to-be
fiancé who was an amazing man and detective. Marco
would do anything for Bella, including die for her. Now
if only Liz could find a man even a fraction like Marco

who would cherish her like a princess. But that was surely only in fairytales. At least it was for her.

"In two months, we're getting engaged." Bella's eyes lit up like fireworks in the night. "I cannot wait."

Jamie beamed and took a quick sip of her drink. "And how was it meeting his mother the other night?"

Bella took a deep breath. She looked at both Jamie and Liz. "She's very protective of Marco, but such a lovely lady. She's a bit controlling, and spent about twenty minutes telling me how important it is that we invite the right people, especially the ones who showed her respect after her husband died. Your typical Italian woman who's keen on nice appearances and would do anything for her son." Her eyes drifted. "I can understand now why Marco didn't introduce us straight away. He said she's a bit of an acquired taste. But she means well."

Liz nodded. "It'll take time to adapt to her traditional Italian culture. But you finally got to know her. Getting to know the family is half the battle. And what about his father? When did he die?"

Bella's eyes dimmed. "He died when Marco was a teenager. It's only been them two, plus a few other relatives in the family. I'm yet to meet the others, but Marco's planning a get-together with them before the engagement. I'm a bit nervous. You know how I am with huge crowds, guys."

Jamie squeezed Bella's hand. "Take it one step at a time, Bella. You've healed since you were kidnapped, and with what you went through with your father. And like you tell us incessantly. Focus on the present, not on the distant future."

Liz said, "Yes, listen to your own advice."

Once they exhausted that topic of conversation, all eyes were back on Liz. She loved the attention most times, but understandably, she'd been somewhat socially withdrawn, which was unlike her.

Bella clasped her hands together. "How was your session with the psychologist?"

Liz flashed back to the session. "Great. She really gets me, but there's nothing much she can do about the insecurity I feel with Domenic so close. We talked about a safety plan and anxiety strategies. She knows I'm taking self-defence classes, too."

"And how's your student, Gabriella, going?" Bella asked.

Liz smiled warmly. "She's been great. Really relates to the foster kids —probably because she suffered at the hands of Domenic as a father. When you know how some of these kids feel, you have a secret understanding and rapport."

"For sure," Bella said. Frowning, she leaned forward. "And you think she's genuine, and not doing Domenic's bidding?"

Liz shook her head. She had wondered the same thing in the beginning, but her intuition told her that Gabriella had suffered. Marco must've kept Gabriella's information private. "I think she suffered like her mother."

Bella nodded. "Marco gave me a bit of information about Gabriella as it is public news now. But I still worry." She changed the subject. "And you mentioned you were meeting a client's brother who came down from Queensland. Is he good with his niece?"

She nodded. "He's amazing with her. Kind, considerate, and finding his feet in Melbourne. He's a firefighter."

Bella fixed her gaze on Liz, and it unnerved her. "Why are you blushing, Liz?"

"No reason." Liz fidgeted and shifted in her seat.

Jamie stared at her curiously. "Your eyes lit up when you mentioned this man."

Liz shook her head. "That's silly. He's my client's brother and a nice guy, that's all. Nothing more to it."

"Hmmm," said Bella, her eyes appearing to be unconvinced.

Liz turned to another topic. "How about a movie on TV? There's a comic love story I'm dying to watch."

Jamie laughed. "Are you trying to change the subject, Liz?"

Liz rose and ignored the comment while her friends followed. She slid open the black-framed door that led to the living room and picked up the remote. The others reclined comfortably on the couch as Liz clicked buttons, typing in a search of the movie she had heard about from Penny. As she was typing in her search for the movie, her phone rang. She put down the remote and picked up her phone, not recognising the number.

"Hello." Silence. "Hello?" A light breathing sound came through. "Who is this? Hello?" She waited a few more seconds but nothing, so she hung up.

Turning to her friends whose expressions were those of concern, she said, "Just a wrong number, I guess." Liz ignored the tight sensation in her stomach and shaky fingers as she turned back to the television and pushed down her nerves. She refused to think that it wasn't a wrong number, but Domenic playing with her.

She was being silly and letting her imagination get away from her. Domenic would be busy with his post-release programs and settling back into life. Surely, he wouldn't want to hurt her again and go back to prison?

CHAPTER 17
THE FIRE STATION

Matthew exited from his car after parking near the firehouse. His hands shook slightly as he closed the door and picked up the black satchel. He made his way down a concrete path and spotted the big sign that said FIRE 000 on the front side of the tall beige building. Hedges on either side of the path closed him in as he headed to the red-framed door. The side of the building held the fire truck garage with its transparent door wound down. A few men were loading heavy-looking bags onto the truck.

He was starting his first shift today. He'd taken Mariana to Joan's house until his sister was ready to care for her again. His niece was adapting to their daily routine, but what would happen once his sister returned? Would she stay off the drugs and finally be a mother to her five-year-old daughter? Only time would tell.

Matthew leaned in closer to an intercom built into the side part of the building. "Yes, hi, I'm Matthew Abila, the transfer from Brisbane, ready to report for duty."

He was buzzed into the building. A young man with a moustache and wavy, shoulder-length hair, and in uniform, met him at the entrance. He played with his stubble and smiled with his eyes. "Welcome to the North West Fire Brigade." He stretched out his arm and shook Mathew's hand firmly. "Hi, Mathew. I'm Johnny, one of the lead firefighters on duty today. Come on through to the chief's office."

Matthew followed Johnny down a narrow walkway with a multitude of doors on either side, some open and some closed. He passed a tearoom and nodded at a few firefighters in offices as he was led towards a larger office, assuming it was where the chief worked. A few uniformed men passed by them as they nodded in greeting.

Johnny smiled and approached the chief. "Chief Bradley, this is Matthew Abila, the transfer from Brisbane, here to get started today."

The chief was a large, bulky man with a dark, crew-cut hairstyle and moustache. He rose from his ergonomic chair and shook Matthew's hand. "Welcome aboard, Matthew. I have a few extra forms for you to fill in." He handed him the forms then his pass. "And here is your door pass. You have been highly recommended by your chief back in Queensland, particularly for saving a few of your men in past bushfires. Commendable."

"Thank you, Chief. I truly honour this work and strive to work hard as a team member."

"Well, it's a credit to you. Now, if you wouldn't mind getting those papers back to me by the end of the day, I'd appreciate it. Johnny here will show you around the place, take you to your locker, and uniform, and then we can chat further later."

"Of course." He followed Johnny out of the office, back down the narrow hallway. Matthew drew a hand through his black hair and scratched at the scar on his chin. It was itching like crazy, but he put it to the back of his mind as he walked behind his fellow firefighter.

Johnny faced him and pointed to a room. "This room here's the duty officer's room. So he's the one responsible today for the roster and any issues that come up."

Johnny peeked inside and introduced him to another solidly built firefighter who shook Matthew's hand. They carried on down to the walkway and Johnny turned to face him. "If you like history, we have displays of the old staff of the fire brigade over the years."

Mathew nodded. "Impressive." They made their way into another room that smelled of cinnamon and coffee.

"And here's the tearoom." He walked in behind Johnny and spotted wide, glass doors that held a view of the street. A television set hung high above a whiteboard that displayed important notices, events, and training information. Cabinets featured a large white fridge, cook tops, and stainless-steel range hoods high above them, surrounded by back-supported grey stools and a long kitchen bench.

They walked upstairs. "So how many staff work here at one time normally?"

He turned to him as they headed inside a gym. "Usually about eight or so. We do get about eighteen hundred calls a year, so it gets pretty busy 'round here."

Matthew nodded, and his eyes roamed the large gym that housed treadmills, a range of weights, weight machines, physiotherapy balls, and cardio machines.

Johnny led him to another room. "This is the multipurpose room." Matthew's eyes widened at the many trophies contained in a glass cabinet. He focused on the time the fire brigade first started and a trophy for first place in running in 1879. A set of hooves on display, showcased the time when horses dragged fire appliances around. This room then led to the backyard, which contained the fire trucks, parked cars, a Hazmat truck, a Bushfire or Grassfire truck, and a workshop for hose-patching and mechanical repairs.

Johnny introduced him to a few firefighters in training and a couple of firefighters on duty, then followed him to his locker bay. "So this is where you can store your personal items and keep your uniform."

Matthew nodded. As he started to change, he took out his wallet from his back pocket and something fell to the floor close to Johnny's feet. "Sorry."

Johnny bent down to the floor and picked up what he'd dropped. His eyes scanned the name on the business card, which must've come out of his wallet. The way his eyes distended at the name was cause for concern.

"Is everything okay?" Matthew asked as he took the card from his hand.

"Yeah, it's just that I was reminded of someone."

He angled his head. "Liz?"

"Yeah, I know a Liz, but don't we all. It's a pretty common name, so I suppose all the other firefighters here probably know a Liz too."

Matthew hoped he didn't know the same Liz. "Is she your girlfriend?"

He shook his head. "Nah, don't have a girlfriend. She's just someone I hooked up with a couple of times."

If this was the same Liz, he would surely know her surname or even her job as a social worker. It had to be a different Liz.

CHAPTER 18
A SMALL PACKAGE

Liz spoke on the phone while Gabriella sat near her desk, waiting to discuss her current performance review and report. "Thank you so much for the great news." She hung up and turned to Gabriela. "Camilla's due to leave the centre in about two weeks. She's apparently doing well and engaging in the individual and group counselling."

A dark shadow crossed Gabriella's face. "That's good for Mariana, I guess."

"Are you okay?" Liz wondered if Gabriela was reminded of her own past of a lost childhood, similar to Mariana's situation.

She shrugged. "I just hope she doesn't relapse, you know? That poor girl's precious. All children are precious."

Liz nodded and leaned forward. "I know, and we'll be monitoring her closely to make sure she's okay. She'll get strong. Besides, she'll have Matthew for support."

"But he's a firefighter. Don't they work all these crazy shifts?"

Liz gave her a reassuring smile. "I guess it is shift work, but they get days off in between, so it's just a matter of creating a system that works. They'll start a routine that'll work for them." She handed Gabriella's assessment report to her, and she read it through quickly.

"Thank you so much, Liz. A glowing assessment, and I'll make sure to work on these areas so I can improve. You've been a great mentor too."

"No worries." She took a breath. "Now, before I get you to do the biopsychosocial assessment for the new client, would you mind going to reception and checking on the mail? Mandy usually brings over the mail, but she had to leave early today and we don't have a back-fill."

"Sure, no problem," said Gabriella.

Liz picked up a file and made a case note from the previous client session then inserted the file back into her locked cabinet. When Gabriella returned, she sat beside her and handed her a few envelopes and a small box. She frowned at the box as she wasn't expecting anything of this size to arrive at her work. Anything she ordered online was usually delivered to her home address. If she wasn't home, she'd pick up the package from the local post office in her spare time.

She took hold of the mail and plonked the box on her desk. Gabriella peered at her when she grabbed scissors and cut into the sides of the package. An uneasy sense settled into the pit of her stomach as she opened up the flaps and dug into the box with quivering hands. Her eyes widened when she picked up a baby's rattle in her favourite colour. Orange. *What the hell!* Was this coming from Domenic? Her vision blurred as she dropped the rattle back into the box. She jolted out of her reverie.

"Liz? Liz, are you okay?"

She turned to Gabriella who leaned in towards her with a worried expression on her face. "Yeah, I'm fine."

"Who would send you that? And why? You're not pregnant, are you?"

She swallowed, the image of a heavy hand pounding into her cheeks. "No, I'm not." She was losing breath, and a coldness settled over her body. Was the baby rattle meant to symbolise her miscarriage? "I'll be back in a minute." She rushed into the ladies' bathroom and vomited into the toilet. Wiping her mouth with toilet paper, she flushed it, and sat on the lid with her hands resting on her forehead. The images wouldn't leave her as her mind took her back to almost eleven years ago.

Liz braced herself when she sucked up the courage. She was standing by the kitchen sink. "I'm leaving. I'm sorry, but I can't do this anymore. This pain. It's too much."

The chill in her bones grew at the rage in his face and the squaring of his shoulders as his glare suddenly turned deadly. Liz momentarily returned to the present, steeling herself to return to fragments of her past.

Domenic charged at Liz with full force, pushing her hard against the wall and making her hit the back of her head. He grabbed hold of her head and smashed it into the wall. The sharp pain made the room spin around her as he pushed her towards the couch, holding her arms over her head. She fought back by kicking him in the groin, but he was too quick for her as he dodged her kick and punched her hard in the face. "No, please. Stop! I'm pre…" His hand covered her mouth as if trying to smother her. She was knocked to the side, her hands now locked down as she sank into the couch, his body hovering over her. He swung his fist high into the air and swung into her face again and

again. She lost count of the number of times he kept
hitting her in the face. She forced her eyes away,
knowing she had to stop him.

"I'm preg....nant," she said, but he was in such a
psychotic rage, it didn't seem to register in his brain.
His fist landed forcefully into her abdomen. She cried
out, her face a bloodied mess, her front tooth knocked
out, and her whole body bruised. He was about to
punch her in the gut again, but she said more forcefully,
"I'm pregnant. No, no, no......" Her hand scratched his
eye as she attempted to wake him out of his fugue,
psychotic rage.

"Please...stop," Liz said as she cried in immense,
stabbing pain, almost blacking out. The look on his face
softened for a moment then hardened. He gave her one
last punch in the face.

Liz focused on her breathing as she brought herself
back to the present. Putting a hand against her heart, she
grounded herself and squeezed her hands into tight
fists. She rose and dabbed water across her face.
Wiping around her eyes with toilet tissue, she fought
back the tears. No more tears. She'd cried enough tears
over the years, but why could that horrific time and
other times, not be put in the past where they belonged?
Why was it still affecting her to this day, all these years
later?

With a resigned sigh, she straightened her posture
and forced her legs in the direction of her desk, where
Gabriella would be waiting to be observed for her client
interview. She was stronger than this, and she would
put Domenic out of her mind with the help of her
psychologist. She was better able to fight back now as
she was no longer a scared seventeen-year-old teenager.

***

Later that night, Liz walked towards the basement car park and winced at the sound of footsteps in the near-darkness. She looked around but saw no-one. All was quiet as she quickened her steps to her car. Maybe she didn't need to go to the nightclub tonight. Maybe it was time to stop going out almost every night to her usual nightclub. Wasn't it safer that way?

She steadied herself in her stiletto shoes and drew her hair behind her ears as she looked over her shoulder. The footsteps sounded distant now. Besides, her car wasn't the only one in this basement, as other tenants lived here too. Once reaching her car, something didn't look right. Was it her imagination or had her car been scratched on the passenger side door? She leaned over the car and noticed not only one scratch on her car but a dent on the front bonnet too. Her tyres had also been slashed and the words, 'FUCKIN' BITCH!' had been written in paint across the front windscreen. *Hell!*

Liz called Marco and explained the situation.

"Get back into the apartment and call me back when you get there."

"Okay." Maybe the perpetrator was still around as she'd heard the footsteps earlier. She rushed back the way she had come and unlocked her door. She stepped inside, cowered on the couch and called him back. She waited for Marco and his partner, Tim, to arrive. First, the packaged gift and now her car had been damaged. Was this both the work of Domenic? It had to be, given that nothing had happened until after his release.

CHAPTER 19
INVESTIGATION

Liz's hands shook as she stood in the basement. Marco shouted instructions to a team of officers after checking for the perpetrator at all exits of the building. "I want you to check CCTV and canvass for any possible witnesses outside the building and inside. Look for any suspicious lurkers." He pointed to another officer. "Go door to door to the other residents in the building and see whether they heard or saw anything suspicious. I want this area cordoned off, and I want you to check Domenic's alibi for earlier today." He turned to an officer who was tall and stout.

"Liz mentioned that this had happened after she came home from work, so check between the hours of six to nine at night. I'll speak to the team working in the prison release programs too, see whether Domenic missed any sessions or appointments tonight. And call Crime Scene." He faced Liz. "Can you give me access to your building?" Liz nodded. "I'll make a sweep of your place, just to make sure there's no-one there. The officer here will wait with you until I come back."

"Okay, I'll be here," said Liz. She gave Marco the details and her key, then watched him pull out his gun. He slowly crept out of the basement towards the elevator, peering in every direction. After briefly closing her eyes, she watched the officers standing by, waiting for the crime scene unit to arrive.

The young officer made small talk with her until Marco returned. "Okay, Liz, it's all clear, but you'll be staying with Bella for tonight just to make sure he doesn't come back. Luckily your place is fairly secure so you should be okay tomorrow. I doubt he'll come back here, but I'll get an officer to patrol the area tomorrow just in case.

Once the crime scene unit arrived, Marco recounted his version of events and then ushered Liz to his car outside. She entered the passenger side, and he drove to Williamstown where Bella resided.

"Bella's at a meeting tonight, but she'll be back home soon. I'll be staying the night, so you guys aren't alone."

Liz nodded. "Thanks, Marco. I know you have other cases to work on, so maybe shift this to someone else. I don't need preferential treatment."

He pursed his lips as he steered the car out of the Altona area towards Williamstown. She squinted from the setting sun. "So tell me again about the first time you saw Domenic. Was he malicious or angry? Did you think he would do this to you?"

"He seemed almost pleasant, but he was always a charmer. No, he didn't seem bitter towards me. Maybe prison has changed him. I don't know."

He shifted his eyes towards her. "So do you doubt that it might be Domenic?"

"I can't be sure, Marco."

"Do you know of anyone else who would do this to you? Any former clients?"

"None at all. I help people with foster caring and make sure that parents learn how to parent their children. There are no threats in this area of work. I mean, unless you're dealing with angry ex-partners of clients or those drug-affected, but other than that, nothing."

He nodded. "And this looks like a well-planned attack. Well thought-out and definitely not disorganised. It would've taken time to plan this out and make sure that nobody else would enter the basement area at that time. The perpetrator might've known your pattern, or might've watched the traffic to and from the building at certain times. They might've scouted everyone's routines to know entry and exit times for tenants."

Liz remembered the gift she'd received. She'd left it at work but had placed it into a sealed bag to possibly check for fingerprints. "I got an unsettling gift in the mail today too. It had no return address. I meant to call you to check for fingerprints, but I got busy all day. I'm sorry, but it's secure in a sealed bag." She explained the context of the gift.

"No worries, Liz. I'll get an officer to pick it up tomorrow. That might be purely coincidence or not. I don't want to speculate at this stage without evidence."

Liz racked her brain to think about whether Domenic would do this. Another flashback passed through her mind.

Large hands covered her mouth as Domenic shouted, "Fuckin' bitch! Shut up and give me what I want, or I'll make this less enjoyable for you." He took his hands away from her face and ripped off her underwear, the pain of the elastic causing her to wince. He shoved his hands between her thighs as he forced himself inside her. She screamed out in pain, her body ripped to shreds as he pumped into her fast and hard.

When Marco called her name, Liz jolted. "I'm sorry. What?"

"I asked if you were okay. Your hands were gripping the seat hard, and your eyes closed like you were dreaming." They'd stopped at a traffic light.

"I'll be fine." She remained quiet until they arrived at Bella's place.

CHAPTER 20
A BEACH DAY OUT

They walked over to a young street girl who was obviously a runaway, lying down on a dirty blanket outside a dilapidated building that looked abandoned. The girl looked up at them, hugging her body as if fighting the cold in the warm weather. "Got a proposition for you. Interested?"

***

The sun glared and Liz squinted while putting on her sunglasses, the granules of sand warming the part of her calves not covered by the towel. Looking out over the water, swimmers splashed, screaming with laughter, and couples strolled hand in hand along the shore. Seagulls fluttered in the distance, and a large float was dragged further into the water by the rising tide.

Liz turned to her friends, Bella, Jamie, and Penny who were lying lazily on their towels to soak up the sun. She sat up on her towel, her mind ruminating about the incident from a few days ago. She didn't want to be a downer about her current problem, but at the same time, her psychologist had encouraged her to access her support systems. She could no longer be that wild child who defied everything and everyone.

Bella sat up and straightened her sunglasses over her eyes and smiled at Liz. She lay beside her while Penny lounged beside Bella, and Jamie lay on her other side. They all sat up, and Liz hugged her knees with her bare arms, wearing a bikini that left little to the imagination. Luckily, the weather was warm enough for a beach day out.

Liz yawned. "I love this time of year, the October spring season and the approaching summer ahead."

Bella nodded. "It is a gorgeous day today." She fixed her gaze on Liz. "Are you feeling better about yesterday?"

Penny and Jamie turned their heads, both saying, "What happened?"

Bella crossed her arms and shook her head. "Don't tell me you haven't mentioned anything to them? They're your friends too, Liz."

Liz shifted on her towel, her back tightening as she leaned forward in both directions to focus on Penny and Jamie. "I'm sorry. I didn't want to worry you, guys." She explained the incident with her car and the gift she'd received.

"Oh girl. You should have said something. If you need to take time off work, then let me know. I'd be happy to take your cases for a while," said Penny.

"Thanks, but I'll manage. If I don't distract myself with work, I'll go crazy. You know that. Besides, you've got a hundred million more cases than I do."

Penny ran a hand through her hair. " Liz, you're always trying to be the tough one. This Domenic guy sounds like an absolute nightmare, darl. Let us be there for you."

Liz smiled. "Thanks, and I'll try to keep you guys in the loop."

Jamie squeezed her hand. "It is doctor's orders that you express your pain as needed. Okay? And no excuses next time."

"Yes, Doctor. I know you're right!"

The ladies laughed until Liz's body trembled at the sound of a man's raised voice near the shore. He was swinging his arms in the air while a woman along the shore moved back and bowed her head as if ashamed. She hugged her body tight. "You are so fuckin' unbelievable and stupid. I don't know what the hell I saw in you in the first place."

The woman clasped her hands in front of her. The man grabbed her hard by the shoulders. "Please Jerry. I'm so sorry. So sorry. Please forgive me."

He shook his head and pushed her hard enough to cause her to slip on the ground. "It's fuckin' over, you stupid woman!" He walked off and left the poor woman trembling in the sandy water.

Liz stared, her heart going out to the woman and her mouth suddenly dry. Should she call the police? Maybe he'd threatened her life and she could stop this. But then again, he broke off with the woman so she should be safe.

Once the woman recovered, she brushed the sand off her body and scurried off in the opposite direction to her partner. She was crying and wiping her tears, continually looking back at the man. Maybe she would be safe without him now.

Bella touched Liz's knee. "Are you okay?"

"Sure." She put her hand across her chest; her heart was beating so fast she thought it might drop out of her chest. "It's so widespread, isn't it? The anger, violence, the pain. It never stops with the domestic abuse."

"It sure doesn't," said Jamie.

Penny fanned her face then put sunscreen on it. She was beginning to burn from the scorching sun. "You need to focus on more positive things."

Liz turned to Penny. "But how can I when Marco tells me there are no fingerprints on that rattle? And Domenic had an alibi for that day of the incident? I mean, knowing who the perpetrator is, is scary enough, but not knowing if it is Domenic is even scarier. I'd rather it be Domenic because I kind of know who I'm dealing with, but if it's not him, I don't have a clue who I'm dealing with. It's that much worse and I'm less prepared that way."

Bella's eyes softened. "Marco has your back. We all do. Just make sure you call us whenever you're spooked or something happens. No matter how trivial. We're not too far, okay?"

Liz smiled. "Thanks, Bella. After all you went through, this is nothing compared to that."

"Stop it," Bella said. "You've been through hell and back, so don't diminish it. Acknowledge your pain rather than distract yourself. That way, you'll heal faster."

Liz wanted the focus to be on something else. "So how's your mother doing in the nursing home, Penny?"

Penny's green eyes became a shade darker, her fringe covering her eye. "She doesn't remember me half the time, Liz. It's heart-breaking. I remember how we would go out for coffees together and walk along the beach, but now she thinks I'm a stranger. I struggle with that sometimes." She fought back tears. "I wish we could get a cure for Alzheimer's. It's a life sentence." She sniffed. "My mum would say to me that children should never die before their children, but now I know that her years are numbered."

"I'm sorry," said Liz. "No-one deserves that."

Bella shifted in the sand. "Hold on to those memories, Penny. That'll get you through this. But we're here to support you, day and night. I'd be happy to visit your mother anytime. Just say the word and I'll go visit."

Penny wiped away her tears. "You would do that?"

Bella nodded. "Of course I would."

Liz reached over and touched Penny's shoulder. "Me, too, girl."

Jamie lifted her body up. "Count me in for the great adventure too, Penny."

Penny gave a light chuckle, fixing her gaze on all her friends. "You guys are all amazing. Thank you."

Liz's heart broke for Penny, but they would all be there for her.

CHAPTER 21
FIREFIGHTERS' DRINKS

Matthew walked inside the club, with its dark and misty ambience. The lounge area was busy with couples kissing, holding hands, or talking into each other's ears while the beat of the music resounded loudly. The couches were close to the dance floor, with lights hanging down. A band of five performers were setting up equipment to play music. Strange smells and scents filled the air, with huddles of people dancing and singing along to the music.

It was a Wednesday night and Johnny shoved him on the shoulder. A few other firefighters walked alongside them as they headed to an empty table. Johnny ordered the first round of drinks and snacks then set them on the table. "Anyway, the next round's on you, Mattie boy."

Matthew nodded. "Happy to, but I thought I was the guest of honour after working at the firehouse for the past couple of weeks."

"Of course you are buddy, but fair's fair. We share it around," said Johnny.

The two other firefighters, Rowan and Pete, toasted to Matthew, welcoming him as the new staff member who had an impeccable record in the Queensland Fire Brigade.

Rowan, who was six feet tall and solidly built, gave a crooked smile. "So, Johnny, isn't this the club you usually meet with that chick? You never mentioned her name, though. She must be something special if you keep coming here."

Pete, who had a short stature and a smaller frame, smiled and shook his head. "Leave the guy alone. He's entitled to his fun. Not that he's married or anything."

Johnny slapped Pete on the back. "Thanks, Pete. Great you've got my back but she doesn't want to get serious. She's absolutely gorgeous but doesn't want a commitment. And not that I want to get serious either. Far too young, mate." He turned to Matthew. "And what about you? Anyone special in your life?"

Matthew shrugged, pushing down an image of Liz in his mind. Where did that image even come from? He barely knew the woman. "No, no-one in my life. Happy to get settled here with my niece and sister."

Johnny turned serious. "How is your sister going in rehab?"

Matthew shrugged. "She's due out any day now and, hopefully, she'll stay clean. She's been through a lot of crap but she'll continue to get counselling." He hoped her past wouldn't catch up with her again. He couldn't blame her as she'd been through a lot more with their father, simply because of her gender. In the end, the bastard destroyed them all.

Pete and Rowan rose to follow two young women that were staring them down while dancing on the dance floor. A Celine Dion song played, and patrons suddenly rushed to the dance floor. Obviously, she was very popular with her songs that, in his opinion, mostly appealed to women.

After further small talk with Johnny, he fiddled in his seat when his new friend's eyes distended. Johnny bowed his head. "Holy shit!"

Matthew was tempted to turn to look at whatever had shocked him. Or was it a who? "What is it?"

"That woman, Liz, I told you about. She's here and friggin' looks smokin' hot." He covered his face with his hands. "She's at the bar, getting a drink. I didn't think she'd come tonight. She normally comes on Tuesdays and Thursdays. Regular night owl, that one."

Matthew rose. "I'm happy for you to talk to her, Johnny." He turned around. Looking at the back of her, he bit into a peanut and took a quick sip of his beer. "Right. I'm going over there and inviting her over. You can't chicken out, man. She might be the love of your life."

He shrugged. "Whatever. Fine. I guess you can meet her, too. But remember, she's just a fling, nothing serious man."

Matthew ignored him, put down his drink and made his way to the bar. She wore a beaded peach dress that flashed her long, toned and tanned legs with slim curves and lean muscle. Her long, black hair framed her back nicely as one side of the dress was longer than the other with a low bare back. He swallowed, thinking that this woman was off bounds. She was Johnny's woman, not his.

He lifted his shoulders and took a breath. "Ah, excuse me, but this..." The woman turned. His mouth fell open, his fingers touching his parted lips. His vocal cords constricted. He took a deep breath. "Liz. What are you doing here?"

She jumped in her seat, almost falling off it. She blushed and averted her eyes. He steadied her in the seat, and he lost breath at her softly made-up face; her inviting red rosy lips and her sweet, hazel eyes that drew him into her gaze. "Matthew. This is a surprise."

His legs wobbled underneath him as his voice suddenly got caught in his throat. He noticed how much more beautiful she looked in this moment. His eyes briefly wandered to her open cleavage in the thin-strapped dress. He recovered himself. "Johnny said you guys are friendly."

Liz sat silent, her eyes roaming past him in the direction of Johnny. She swallowed and avoided his eyes again, dropping her chin to her chest. Her body started shivering, and he didn't know what more to say, so he waited. "We're friends, sure. Nothing serious."

He wondered why she added that 'nothing serious' part. "Anyway, I had no idea who you were and promised him I'd ask if you'd have a drink with us. Care to join?"

Liz slouched. "How do you know Johnny?"

"We work together."

Liz nodded, then pulled herself off the stool, grabbed her martini and followed him to their table.

A sudden nauseating sensation filled his stomach. Why did it bother him so much that she'd had a fling with Johnny? She was definitely off bounds now.

CHAPTER 22
GAME-PLAYING

Liz quieted in her seat as she sat across from Johnny, whose curious eyes remained fixed on her and Matthew. "Sorry to interrupt your welcome party for Matthew." She never in a million years expected to see Matthew. He looked breath-taking. He wore tight-fitted black pants and a silky-white buttoned-down shirt that showed his taut, tanned chest. She imagined herself rubbing her hands down his chest and beyond.

She had to stop having wicked thoughts about this man when Johnny was staring her down. If only she could crawl under a rock right now. The unease she felt between the two men were putting her on the spot. Normally, she loved the attention of people but not in this scenario.

"That's fine, Liz. So you two know each other?" Johnny asked. He crossed his arms.

Matthew turned to Johnny, his face blazing red. "She's the social worker I met on my sister's case."

Liz held up a hand. "I can't say any more about that, Johnny. It's a conflict of interest me even being here with Matthew, so I don't think I should stay."

Mathew's eyes darkened and his breath appeared to quicken. He sat beside Liz and leaned forward as if wanting to say something. He remained tight-lipped and leaned back in his seat, his eyes drifting. His fingers tapped on the table as if he was bored.

"I'm sure one drink won't hurt. Just between friends." Johnny watched Matthew with interest. Liz wondered if Johnny suspected her attraction to

Matthew. Liz's chest tightened as she turned to Matthew. His expression turned into a look of disappointment, almost as if he didn't want to be there. Not that she blamed the guy. It was an awkward situation, but it wasn't like he was her boyfriend, and she was free to do what she liked. But why was she having mixed feelings about Johnny tonight? She enjoyed his company and had fun on those two brief nights. But when she compared him to Matthew, he didn't appear as exciting to her. "I'm fine with the jug of water here."

Johnny faced Matthew. "Where are Rowan and Pete? They've been gone a while."

Matthew shrugged. "I don't know, but I'm going to get a drink at the bar. Are you sure you don't want a drink, Liz?"

Liz shook her head. "No thanks, Matthew."

"Johnny?"

"Nah, mate I'm good."

"Okay, then. I'll be sitting at the bar for a while." Matthew made his way to the bar, and Liz looked after him as he walked with a slouched posture. Her chest tightened.

Johnny sat in Matthew's seat and grabbed her hand. He put it to his lips but Liz kept looking over at the bar, the outline of Mathew's ripped muscles in his rolled-up white shirt, the tightness of his pants that showed a well-toned and worked-out body. "Liz. Are you alright?"

She faced him again. "Sorry. I'm probably going to go home. I'm tired after a long day, but you stay here with your friends. I didn't mean to rain on your parade, Johnny." As she looked over at the bar again, a towering woman with long blonde hair and a buxom outline leaned in towards Matthew. He smiled, moved closer to the woman and stroked her cheek. Why was he flirting back? Liz's chest stung. She drew back at this strange woman's overture and wondered whether Matthew liked those tall, gorgeous blonde-types. *Two could play at that game.*

Matthew looked over his shoulder at Liz who, in that moment, decided to stroke Johnny's face. She leaned into him and kissed him hard on the lips. Johnny reciprocated, their tongues colliding as her mind remained on Matthew. She had to get Matthew off her mind. He was obviously taken with this attractive woman.

When Liz pulled away from Johnny, Matthew turned away. She swallowed, a sense of guilt flooding her senses. Johnny touched her thigh and kissed her neck, but Liz's mind stayed on Matthew as she kept watch over him. Only a minute later did Matthew pull the woman close and kiss her on the lips with the woman reciprocating. A wave of jealousy swept over her, but what did she expect? A gorgeous woman had made herself available to Matthew, so why not take advantage of that? She didn't have any claim on him, and he was free to do as he pleased.

"Why don't you come over to my place?" Johnny asked.

When it was obvious he wasn't returning to his seat anytime soon, Liz made her excuses. "I'm not feeling well. I hope you don't mind us taking a rain check?"

Johnny frowned. "Not at all. But I want to ask, what is this thing between us?"

Liz shrugged. "This thing is not a thing. Simply friends who shared a few kisses. Nothing more. I'm not interested in a relationship and I know you're not either."

He shook his head. "I know, but we could have fun tonight. You smell amazing and you're gorgeous."

She gave him a reassuring smile. "Thanks, Johnny, and I'm sorry we can't have fun tonight, but I..." She stopped short when Matthew walked alongside the blonde woman. He followed her towards a couch that became empty. A pain deep in her stomach unnerved her.

He held up his hand. "Hold up! Just got a text from Matthew. Said he's otherwise engaged tonight and might be a while." He turned to her. "So I am free."

Liz's chest burned. She was fuming to the point that she almost wanted to play his stupid game. Maybe she should have sex with Johnny, but what would that accomplish? She had a lot more self-esteem than that and didn't want to put herself down this way because she was angry at Matthew. She had no claim to him and no right to be angry. No, she wouldn't have sex because of her pain. She was better than that. "Bye, Johnny."

She wandered to the exit, a sense of emptiness pervading her chest. She didn't need Matthew. She didn't need any man.

CHAPTER 23
A WORK VISIT

Liz sat in the staff room with her head bowed, nursing a headache. She pressed her fingers into her temples. She wondered if she should've even gone out last night. Going out at night always led to body tension and headaches at work the next day. Bella kept telling her not to burn herself out with too much fun, but she struggled to heed that advice. Maybe it was time to stop these distractions.

Thankful for the peace and quiet, Liz pondered her night with Matthew and what a mess it had been. She had considered going to Johnny's house out of anger and as a way to distract herself. Seeing Matthew's tongue deep into that other woman's throat pained her. She admittedly had been jealous. She shook her head at the guilt over poor Johnny who was a nice guy and didn't deserve to be treated that way.

But then again, Johnny knew where he stood. She didn't want a relationship and she had said as much at the club. But what were the odds that Johnny and Matthew recently started working together? The two hot firefighters who made women drool.

She jerked in her seat when a gentle hand touched her shoulder. Penny gave her a reassuring smile. "You look like you haven't slept, Ms Randiza? What's up?"

Liz rubbed her eyes. "Nothing, just went out last night and shouldn't have."

Penny chuckled and gave her a wide beam. "You need to rest some nights, girl. Some of us do need our beauty sleep, including you. But you need less beauty sleep than some of us, given the way you look."

Liz sipped her water. She set it down when it almost slipped out of her hand. "Oh shut up! You're way more gorgeous than I am, Penny."

"Middle-aged woman doesn't cut it. I am in my mid-forties and the wrinkles are starting to show." She touched her face, which didn't show any wrinkles. "Here they are." If only Penny knew how attractive she looked at her age. She didn't have any children or a husband but lived a full life as a single woman with many friends. She looked behind her. "Has Marco had any new leads on your case?"

Her mood suddenly changed. "No, nothing at this stage, but I still think Domenic might be involved."

"I really hope he leaves you alone, Liz." She huffed and gave Liz a reassuring smile. "But at least you've got a detective in your corner. Any time you need to talk, day or night, I'm just a phone call away."

Liz grinned. "I hear you, Penny. You're a great friend, but I don't want you involved in any of this. It's my issue, so please don't worry about anything. I'll be fine."

"Hmm," said Penny. She moved towards Liz and wrapped her arms around her. "As I said, I am here for you. Nothing's going to happen to you on my watch, girl."

Liz held back her tears. She loved Penny like a sister, as she did her other friends.

Gabriella walked into the room and intervened. "Sorry to interrupt, ladies. But, Liz, you have a visitor."

Was it Johnny? Maybe she shouldn't have kissed him last night, sending him the wrong message. In spite of being attracted to him, she didn't like him enough as a boyfriend. "Who is it?"

"It's Camilla's brother, Matthew. He was asking about his sister. I did give him the update that Camilla's coming out of rehabilitation tomorrow, but he wanted to talk to you."

Liz rose. "Thanks, Gabriella." She brought her glass to the sink, rinsed it out, and. eyed Gabriella. "If you wouldn't mind writing up that case note on Julie, I shouldn't be too long."

Gabriella nodded. "Sure, not a problem."

Liz headed out and approached the reception area, her heart thudding. A bead of sweat fell down the back of her neck and her headache heightened. Spotting Matthew made her speechless. He wore a tight-fitted t-shirt that showed great pecks, pleated pants, and shiny black Italian shoes. Was he going to a party?

She managed a brief smile. "Hi, Matthew. Let's take a walk to a private room."

"Hi, Liz. Sorry to come unannounced." He fiddled with his hands inside his pants pockets. "I hope I'm not interrupting you at work."

She shook her head, led him towards a conference room, and swung open the door. She ignored a tingle down her back "I was having lunch, and still on a break." She paused. "Is this about Camilla?"

"Partly," he said.

Clearing her throat, she led him to a seat opposite. His cologne smelled like a mixture of musk and flowers, and the plant scents caused her to relax on the seat. "Well, anyway, about Camilla. She's coming out tomorrow and has been doing well. We're keeping her engaged with a few support services like the local clinic that specialises in drug and alcohol counselling. She'll also link in with Narcotics Anonymous so she can get accountability and support. I know you've been preparing Mariana, so she must be excited to have her mother back."

"Definitely. She's with Joan, who's great with her. She's agreed to babysit her when I work my afternoon shifts at the firehouse. At least until Camilla returns."

"That's good. I guess now it's up to Camilla to care for herself and her daughter. Do you plan on staying there?"

He shrugged. "Only for a little while. I'll see how things go, and once I know she's fully recovered, I'll look for my own place."

Liz swallowed. "That's great." She hesitated. "I guess this means we'll be cutting ties soon. I'll probably see you tomorrow when Camilla gets home."

"Liz, I..."

She cut him off. "It looks like you had a great time last night."

Matthew avoided her eyes and fidgeted. He took a deep breath but still averted his eyes. "I can say the same for you. So you and Johnny, ha? I never would have guessed you were hooked up with one of my co-workers."

"We're not hooked up, but we've had fun."

His eyes looked unreadable. "I guess this is it."

"I guess so. At least as of tomorrow, we'll be finished."

"Can we be friends, Liz?" He looked hard into her eyes, with a worried expression.

She shook her head as she didn't need complications. It was best they went their own ways.

She couldn't commit to anyone since Domenic and didn't feel like she could now. It hurt too much to put her trust in a man, only to have him crush that trust. The pain of her past had been unbearable. She was happy to be free and single with no ties. She turned in her seat and took hold of his hand that was warm and rough. It sent shivers down her legs as his hand lingered in hers. She pulled away and began walking back to her office.

Matthew hid his disappointment. "Just friends at least. No harm in that." He followed her, his expression changing to a ray of hope lighting up his eyes.

"It's not a good idea, Matthew. We need to keep this professional." Her heart ached but she pushed it down. *No more complications.* "I'll see you tomorrow." She waved to him as he headed towards the exit. A numb sensation penetrated her chest as she approached her desk. Sickness permeated her stomach.

CHAPTER 24
CAMILLA'S RETURN

Matthew checked his watch and paced the floor while waiting for Liz and Camilla. Mariana kneeled in the living room, pulling a white apron over a Barbie doll's head, the doll looking like a mother. The poor girl was acting out the ideal mother with her toy. Matthew wondered if Mariana would get her mother back. Would Camilla stay clean and not relapse, or would she be triggered yet again because of her terrorising past? It was a precarious situation, given their sordid history. He had dealt with the past by helping others in dire situations while Camilla dealt with her trauma by blocking the pain with drugs. At least now she'd be getting regular counselling, on top of the counselling she'd had in the rehabilitation centre.

He joined Mariana in the living room and knelt beside her, squeezing her shoulder. She turned to him with a smile then pulled a dress over another Barbie doll. She brushed the doll's hair roughly, leaving strands of hair remaining on the small brush. "Are you excited?"

She nodded. "Will Mummy be here soon, Uncle Matthew?"

He swallowed, an uneasy feeling spreading in his chest. "Yes, any minute now, sweetie."

His mind turned to Liz, as he flashed back to the way she bit her bottom lip whenever she was nervous. How she frowned whenever she was in deep thought, and how she stood tall and strong every time she walked. But he'd seen the innocence and vulnerability in her eyes whenever she wanted to hide her feelings. A safety net. Her fiery eyes hid a deeper darkness inside her, and he so desperately wanted to know what had happened to her in the past.

Matthew's mobile phone rang. He rose from the ground and moved over into the kitchen. "Hey Mum, how are you doing?"

"Matthew, I'm good. How are you coping in Melbourne?"

"I'm settled, Mum. I've started my new job."

"That's great, darling. And your sister? How is she doing after rehabilitation? I assume she's back now?"

"Not yet, but any minute now. I can get her to call you once she's ready."

"That would be lovely. Thanks, son."

"And your operation is still scheduled for next week?"

"It is. After I've recovered, I might come down and visit. How does that sound?"

His heart warmed. He'd always been close to his mother. "That's great. And are you still getting counselling?" Silence. "Mum?"

"Son, I'll be fine. I'm more worried about Camilla. I just hope she recovers from this. At least you'll be there to keep a watch on her. Now, you don't go worrying about me, you hear? Take care of yourselves. I love you, Matthew."

"I love you too." He hung up with a heavy heart, his mind turning back to the past. Images of his father's heavy hand and non-stop drinking impacting the whole family. He calmed his breathing.

Matthew jolted back to the present when the doorbell rang. His stomach flipped, and he clenched his hands before opening the door. Rushing behind him was Mariana, who held on to his leg as she waited.

Camilla stood side by side with Liz, whose penetrating gaze stilled his breath. His sister gave him a reassuring smile then looked down at her daughter. Quickly, she bent down and wrapped her arms around her. "Oh, Mariana, I've missed you so much."

"Me too, Mama. I love you."

"And I love you too." She pulled away from Mariana and turned to Matthew with tears in her eyes. Liz stood behind Camilla as she hugged Matthew tightly in the foyer.

"Oh, Camilla, it's so great to see you after all this time," Matthew said.

"I love you, bro. Always," Camilla said with tears in her eyes.

They walked into the kitchen but Mariana reached for her mother's hand. "Can you play with me first, Mummy? Then you can talk to Uncle Matthew."

Camilla gave him an apologetic look. "Of course, darling."

Liz smiled. "It's fine, Camilla. I need to talk to Matthew about a few things anyway. Take your time." Camilla nodded and headed to the living room with Mariana.

Matthew sat across from her in the living room, his eyes drawn to her. She looked amazingly beautiful in a well-cut white cotton blouse and a tight-fitting skirt. He liked the way she touched her throat as if nervous. A rash lined her neck. Was she nervous talking to him right now? "So what did you need to talk about Liz?"

She took out a manila folder and handed it to him. "This is a record of Camilla's support systems. Her sponsor's number, counsellor, support group, and other legal details she needs to follow. I'll no longer be working with her, so I thought you should make sure she keeps up with her support systems. She mentioned that your mother'll visit once she recovers from surgery, is that right?"

"Yes, she wants to help and might even consider staying here. Who knows?" He rubbed his hand, suddenly obsessed with the colour of his skin. "So you and Johnny? You're not a thing?"

Liz cleared her throat. "Like I said yesterday, we had our fun. Nothing serious."

"Can I call you?" She stared at him, saying nothing. "Liz? I mean, to let you know how Camilla's doing at least?"

She nodded. "Of course. I'll contact Camilla in a few days to check in, but if you have questions about Camilla, that's fine."

"Listen, that girl from the other night. Nothing happened between us. I mean, we only kissed, but that was all. I wasn't really interested."

Liz drew back. "So do you usually kiss women you're not interested in?"

His face warmed. "And do you usually kiss men you're not that keen on? Because it goes two ways."

Liz started to rise out of her chair. "Listen, whatever I do is my business, not yours. And what you do is your business. I couldn't care less who you kiss." She stood up, arms crossed. "I'm leaving. I'll speak to Camilla myself. Goodbye." He watched her back as she made her way towards the living room in a huff. What the hell just happened? They were getting along when he had to be stupid enough to bring up Johnny. Why did he have to ruin things between them? She seemed to care about him, but why was she keeping her distance?

CHAPTER 25
PARTY PREPARATIONS

As Liz neared her car after work, she looked over her shoulder. She sensed she was being watched but couldn't see anyone suspicious around the parking space. The scuffle of feet in front of her caused her to face the front as she gasped for breath. Nobody there. She ran forward and almost tripped over a rock. Picking it up, she roamed the area, not surprised that only a few staff members remained. Prickles of fear ran down her spine as she crept around, scanning the work parking area. It was deserted, but she was sure she'd heard footsteps. Shaking her head, Liz stepped into her car, thinking how silly it was that someone was watching her. It was ludicrous. Domenic wouldn't come near her knowing the police were watching him closely. He'd be a fool to do anything. If it was Domenic who had vandalised her car, then he'd get caught eventually. Surely, he'd make a mistake eventually? At least she'd had had the car repaired and all traces of the vandalism removed.

Liz gripped the steering wheel and drove towards Bella's house to help prepare for her engagement party to Marco. All thoughts of Domenic vanished as she thought about them. It was amazing to find the kind of love they shared and she wanted it too, but was she worthy of it? She only knew dysfunctional relationships. Domenic was initially charming, as good-looking as a model, and had a great gift of the gab. He had drawn her in like a spider into its web, and then spat her out to create a fall-out of a million pieces. Not anymore would a man abuse her in that way. She didn't need a man to make her complete.

Turning off the motor, she took a deep breath and headed to Bella's front door. She passed through the open gate in the white picket fence and rang the doorbell. She eyed the pruned flowers and recently added hanging plants suspended from the eaves of the cottage-style, colonial home. She pushed in a few loose bricks from the brick wall, built at the side of the house to separate it from the home next door, then waited for her friend.

Bella opened the door and smiled. She leaned forward to kiss her friend on the cheek. "Hi Liz. Thanks for coming." She led her inside.

"Any time, girl."

"Jamie couldn't make it. She was on stand-by so she had to get to the hospital quickly. Take a seat."

"So what are we doing today?" Liz settled on the couch with Bella beside her. She spotted a box of bombonieres made up of salt and pepper shakers, and a roll of ribbons with some cut to size, sitting on the coffee table. A stack of invitation cards and RSVPs for her engagement lay to the side. They sat in the living room while Bella picked up a bomboniere and slid the metal of the scissors across the ribbon to curl it. "Curling ribbons I take it?"

"Ha ha. Marco's Italian and this is what Italians do at engagements and weddings, so I have to get this organised by next week."

Liz picked up a ribbon and tied it around the shaker then curled it with the scissors. "So how are you feeling about the engagement? Nervous?"

Bella's eyes lit up. "Of course nervous, but I'm excited too. I can't wait to marry that man. I love Marco so much. He makes me crazy." Liz slumped in her seat, and a soreness in her throat made her speechless. Of course she was happy for her friend, but the heaviness in her chest told her that a part of her wanted what Bella had. If only she didn't keep choosing the wrong men. "Are you okay? Liz?"

"I'm fine." She squeezed Bella's shoulder. "I'm so happy for you. After what you two went through, you both deserve it. And I hear his mother's been giving you a bit of a hard time."

Bella squinted, putting her scissors down. "And who told you that? Jamie, no doubt."

"Maybe, but I'll never tell."

"Don't get me wrong. She's lovely, but being a single mother with an only child means that he's her sole focus. And I get where she's coming from, Liz. She only wants the best for her son. But no doubt, she had to raise a son on her own after Marco's father died and did an amazing job. He's one of a kind, that's for sure."

"That he is." An image of Matthew flashed through her head, but it was quickly replaced by an image of Domenic. Her mind took her back to another dark time.

"Fuckin' bitch. All you women are only good for one thing."

Liz wrestled with him as he pulled off her skirt and underwear.

"No, please don't. I'm not up to it now, Domenic."

He groped her between the thighs, but Liz tried to push her legs together. Forcefully he pushed one of her legs out then undid his own jeans. "If you stop fighting

113

me, you might enjoy it. Now, fuckin' spread your legs
or I'll pound my fist into your face. Your choice."

Liz's body shook as she resigned herself to the
situation. She told him, "You might have my body but
you don't have my heart, Domenic. Not anymore."

"I don't want your heart. Only your submission. But
you'll always be mine 'cause I own you, bitch!" He
glared at her, and Liz stopped fighting him as she
imagined him to be someone else. He prodded his
manhood inside her while pushing his hand hard into
her face, causing it to bruise. Staring up at the ceiling,
she focused hard on the cracks. She was dead inside.

Liz turned back to the present. "Just give me a
minute, Bella. I need water."

Bella looked at her with concern. "Sure thing. Take
your time."

Liz scurried into the kitchen, wet her damp face,
and drank a glass of water. These flashbacks had to
stop.

CHAPTER 26
HALLUCINATION

Liz walked around the venue where Bella and Marco held their engagement a week later, savouring the space that had a New York style feel to it. A white curtain that had been parted to maximise space hung down. White leather footstools surrounded the dimly-lit function room that emitted its own light with an array of scented candles placed on mahogany timber tables. Timber stands centred the room, and white padded leather seating ensured comfort for the one hundred and twenty guests that had been invited. The brick wall and brown plush carpeted flooring ensured that no-one tripped on a slippery floor. A table filled with savouries and hors d'oeuvres whet Liz's appetite, but she refrained from picking at the food until all the other guests arrived.

A tall waiter, sporting a moustache and a goatee, approached and offered her a drink. "You look thirsty, maam. How about a drink?"

Liz nodded. "Sure, why not." She grabbed the flute of champagne and sipped. As the waiter left, she peered over at Bella who was giving Marco's mother a fake smile and nodding at something she was saying. Marco was talking to a few friends who just arrived, so Liz headed over there to attempt a rescue. "Hi, I'm Liz. And you must be Marco's mother?"

The woman had clear, blue eyes and strong, attractive features and was taller than both Bella and Liz. Even age didn't stop her naturally good looks. No wonder Marco was so good-looking. He took after his mother. "Hello, I'm Maria."

Liz put out her hand. "Nice to meet you, Maria. I'm Liz"

Maria turned back to Bella. "Anyway, I think those candles are a hazard. We should remove them. I mean, surely, Marco didn't agree to those?"

Bella sighed but clenched her hands. "It's part of the feature, Maria. And I'd like to keep them. Nothing is going to happen. I can assure you. It's perfectly safe."

The woman shook her head. "Well, I think I'll speak to Marco about that. He would definitely not agree to having those candles. And what about more light? It's too dark in this place. Someone might trip." Without waiting for a response, she huffed and headed towards her son.

Bella grabbed Liz's hands. "Oh, save me from that woman. I've been arguing with her for the past fifteen minutes, and she's doing my head in."

"I'm sorry, Bella. You don't need this kind of stress on your special day. Is there anything I can do?"

"No, you already did it. You rescued me." Jamie arrived and a few other people ambled in behind her. "Excuse me, Liz. I'd better go greet the guests as they come in."

"Of course, darl. You go. I'll be around." She headed over to Jamie, and together they made their way to the food table and nibbled on a few snacks. She downed her drink and realised she needed a top-up. Her head began to swirl, and the room seemed to close in on her as she wiped her mouth. *Strange!* She only had one glass of alcohol.

Jamie fixed her gaze. "Are you okay?"

"I don't know. I feel a bit dizzy." Jamie pushed her over to the leather seating while Liz bowed her head for a moment and took deep breaths. Her vision was somewhat blurry, and in the distance, more and more guests arrived. The muffled sounds of voices and the blaring music sounded heavy in her ears. Throbbing pain pressured her eyes and head.

"How much have you had to drink?"

"I only had one glass of champagne. That's all."

Penny headed over to them and wrapped her arms around Liz. She started feeling better. That brand of champagne must've been strong. Liz took deep breaths and pushed down her pain. She wouldn't ruin Bella and Marco's special night. She could fake it.

Later in the night, Marco and Bella toasted to their engagement and cut the cake. But Liz was desperately thirsty and needed another drink. There were a few other waiters floating around, and she had stuck to water all night. But now she craved a glass of alcohol. A different waiter came by and held out the tray of drinks with glasses of wine and champagne. She took the proffered glass of champagne and was about to sip it when Jamie grabbed the glass off her.

"I'll take that glass." Jamie set the glass down on the table and shook her head. "If you're not feeling well, I'd suggest you keep drinking water." She frowned.

The same waiter with the moustache and goatee offered them cake. They grabbed a plate and Liz savoured the spongy vanilla and coffee taste as some of the cream dripped down her lips. She had the last bite and wiped her mouth with a napkin while watching the scene before her with Marco's mother, Maria.

Liz laughed at Maria who was talking with her hands up in the air. She was standing beside another woman who Bella had introduced as Marco's aunt. Maria flailed her arms as if she was enraged about something. No doubt, complaining about some other aspect of the party. Poor Bella!

Jamie and Penny were talking to her, but their voices sounded distant.

"Sorry, what?"

Penny touched her on the shoulder. "I said, what time are you planning to leave? I've got an early start tomorrow. I have to go into work."

Liz tilted her head. "On a Sunday?"

"You wouldn't believe the ton of work I've got. I have no choice."

Liz's head throbbed again. It was as if Penny was miles away, her voice fading out. "Is there anything I can do to help? I'm happy to come into the office too and share the load."

Penny looked at her strangely. "No, of course not. I've got it covered. Are you okay? I can drive you home if you're not feeling well, girl. Say the word and I'm your driver."

Liz swallowed and lied. "I'm fine. You go."

Penny nodded and turned to Jamie. "Look after this one. Anyway, I'd better go. See you, ladies."

Jamie smiled. "It was great seeing you, Penny. Take care."

Liz waved but her energy waned. "See you Monday, girl."

As Penny walked off, Liz turned to Jamie but her face looked hazy. Then beside Jamie, a young woman stood beside her. "Who's this?"

Jamie faced her. "What?"

"That woman beside you. Who is it?"

Jamie looked at her like she had two heads. "Who are you talking about? There's no-one beside me."

Liz drew back. "What?" She closed her eyes then opened them again. The woman stood frozen in her spot, with a neutral expression. "But I can see a woman, Jamie. Can't you see her, standing right beside you? Blonde hair and the deepest hazel eyes. Very young and pretty."

Jamie grabbed Liz's hand. "Liz, look at me." She stared into her eyes and put her hand over her heart. "My God! Your heart is racing like anything and you're burning up. I'm taking you to the hospital, Liz. You're not well."

Liz shook her head. "No, no, I'm fine. Just a bit tired and sleepy, but I'll be okay."

Jamie pursed her lips. "No arguments. We are leaving right now."

Liz had no energy to fight her, so she stood up with Jamie and they made their excuses and left the party. "Fine, but take me home. I need to rest." The last thing Liz remembered was falling in a heap once they reached the city street.

CHAPTER 27
MYSTERY CALL

Several days later, Matthew was in the firefighter's gym as he pondered their recent call-out. He had recently returned with other firefighters from a rescue of a victim in a cardiac arrest. They had managed the unconscious and non-breathing victim to provide life-saving emergency care until the ambulance arrived. Luckily, they had started the man's heart again and kept him stable until the ambulance officers walked inside the door. It was a close call, but necessary, as waiting even a few seconds was the difference between life and death. Early CPR was crucial if they were the closest in the vicinity and the first to respond on a call-out.

His heart beat fast as he increased his pace on the treadmill, wiping his brow as he ran and focused on his breathing. After ten minutes, he turned off the machine and wiped his face with a towel, then proceeded to grab some weights. He completed a round of weights then left the room and headed to his locker. His shift was over so he reached into it and took out his casual clothes. As he was getting dressed, Johnny appeared beside him, beaming.

Johnny tapped him on his shoulder. "A close call today, Matthew. And great work."

"Thanks, but you did most of the hard work."

"A team effort, man. Team effort." Johnny pulled a t-shirt on. "How about a drink?"

Matthew's energy was depleted. "I'd love to, but not only am I bushed, I promised my sister I'd be home in time for a late dinner. Rain-check?"

"Sure, no worries. Any time."

Matthew took off his uniform and dressed himself. Johnny's phone rang. His new friend replied, but the look on his face was one of pallor and shock. Whoever had called him was obviously someone he didn't want to speak to. He moved his phone away from his ear and peered at Matthew. "Excuse me, but I've gotta take this."

"No worries," said Matthew. He'd noticed a couple of times before that Johnny seemed to get the same kinds of calls where he'd rush off and talk in private.

As he walked off, Rowan and Pete walked in. "Hey, guys. Great teamwork today," said Pete.

Rowan hovered over him with his tall stature and started to take off his uniform. "I just saw Johnny. Who was that on the phone? He looked a wee bit nervous."

Matthew shrugged. "Haven't a clue."

Pete, who was shorter, said, "I'm guessing it was his wife. They've been divorced for a couple of years now, but she still rings him for whatever reason."

He lifted his eyebrows, surprised he'd been married. "Do they have children?" Matthew asked.

Rowan chuckled. "Nah, as much as I love Johnny, he has a bit of growing up to do."

Pete shook his head and shoved Rowan. "Oh, cut that out, Rowan. Johnny's our friend. Have some respect."

Rowan put up his hands in surrender. "Sorry, man. I didn't mean any disrespect, but we've known him for a few years now, and I get the sense that something's going on with him. More than what we already know. Not that he'll ever admit to anything. And someone with possible secrets means they're not damn ready to have a kid."

"What secrets?" Johnny obviously didn't want anyone hearing his phone conversation, so maybe there was more to the story.

"Haven't the faintest," said Pete. "But we've asked him countless times about whether he needs help or if he's in some kind of trouble. He fobbed us off with a story about wanting to get back with his ex-wife, but I think there's more to it." Matthew locked up and gazed seriously at Rowan who looked as if he was itching to say more.

Pete shoved him hard. "Don't say anything, Rowan. He's our friend, remember."

Matthew tilted his head. "Listen, guys. Whatever it is, I won't say anything. If there's something we can do to help Johnny, then shouldn't we be helping him?"

Rowan stared at Matthew as if considering it while Pete stayed silent, shrugging. "About a week ago, we noticed a prescription in his pants pocket that accidentally slipped out while he was getting changed. It was a prescription for some kind of medication, but we don't know what kind."

Matthew gave him a questioning look. "Was it for him?"

Rowan slipped a white t-shirt over his head and his eyes darkened. "He said it was for his ex-wife, but we wondered why he'd have her prescription when they're divorced. I know they're not back together. We asked him that very same thing, but he said that he felt he still had to look out for her. But we got the feeling he was lying." He sighed. "And I don't think it's for him."

Matthew peered into the distance. "He would've had all the medical tests, so surely if he had a prescription, it was probably for a common cold or something acute. Maybe it's for sleep issues or for his wife." He exhaled. "I don't think a prescription is a big thing."

Rowan looked to Pete again. "Maybe. But, why did he look guilty when we asked him about it? And I wonder about these secret phone calls. It's strange."

Pete turned to Matthew. "Please don't say anything. He told us not to mention it to anyone."

Matthew shook his head. "I won't, don't worry."

He wondered what those phone calls were about and if there was more to the story.

CHAPTER 28
PANIC ATTACK

Matthew stood in the grocery aisle with his sister and Mariana the next morning, picking up a box of Milo for his niece. He turned to his sister, who put the box into the trolley and held her daughter's hand. She was looking healthier these days and was getting along well with Mariana, which was a possible sign that she'd finally received the right help. Her skin glowed and her blue-green eyes lit up each time she spent with Mariana.

As they swept down the aisle and entered the next one, he pondered about Johnny for a moment and wondered whether the prescription belonged to him or whether it was really for his wife. It couldn't be anything chronic for him as he wouldn't have been able to be recruited with the fire brigade, given the high stressors of the work. There had to be an explanation, but when he questioned Johnny randomly about whether that phone call was bad news, he said it was his ex-wife. But Matthew could tell he was lying.

"Matthew, wake up."

He turned to his sister. "What?"

"I said get the tin of beans, please. I can't reach it."

He looked straight up the shelf and reached for the beans. "Sorry, sis. I was out with the fairies."

"It's all good. Thanks for coming with me. I'm still getting used to things and get a bit anxious going out on my own sometimes."

Mariana grabbed her mother's arm. "Mummy, what's 'out with the fairies' mean?"

Camilla bent down to her daughter's level and squeezed her cheeks. "It just means he was thinking about something else, darling. Now, let's get moving."

Matthew and Camilla headed over to the delicatessen section of the supermarket, and Camilla grabbed a ticket to wait for her turn.

"What do you need here?" Matthew asked.

"Oh, just chicken pieces and sausages." She looked over at a middle-aged, bulky man who stood, arms crossed beside a petite woman of the same age. Her hunched shoulders made her appear smaller than him.

The server asked, "What would you like?"

The woman looked at Camilla who held a ticket, but she didn't have one. "It's okay. You can serve this lady."

The man grabbed the woman by the shoulder and moved her closer to the counter. "We were here first," said the man. He glared at the woman. "You forgot to get a ticket, you silly woman, but we were here first. Say something." The woman grabbed a ticket, shook her head, and smiled to Camilla.

Camilla turned to the woman. "It's okay. You can go first."

"No, I've got the next ticket number. I can wait," the woman said.

The man kept glaring at the woman, "Fuckin' hopeless. I'm in a hurry and you can't speak up, woman. What the fuck?" The server shrugged and turned to Camilla.

Matthew walked over to the man and spoke to the server. "You can serve this wonderful lady. We can wait, thanks."

"Who you calling wonderful? That she aint," said the man. He smirked, his fingers pressing hard into her shoulder. "She's too much of a mouse to speak up about anything. Fuckin' stupid and hopeless."

Matthew whispered into the man's ear. "If you don't want me calling the police, I'd have more respect for the lady."

The man closed his mouth but the damage had been done. Camilla gasped for air, her face as pale as a ghost, holding a hand to her chest.

Mariana stared at her mother. "Mummy, you okay? Mummy? Mummy."

Matthew moved Camilla away from the counter, towards the other side of the delicatessen section. "Sorry," he said to the server. He pushed Camilla down into a sitting position with her back leaning against the freezers. "Look at me, Camilla. You're safe. Now take a deep breath. In and out. In and out. You are safe. Do you hear me? No-one can hurt you anymore." The server later came by with a cup of water and handed it to Matthew. "Thank you." Turning to Camilla, he propped the cup underneath her lips. "Now, drink this. You'll feel better." He brought the plastic cup to her lips and she settled, looking into Matthew's eyes. He held her hand and put it against her cheek. "I love you, sis, and you're safe. You know that, right?"

Camilla nodded and a single tear fell down her face. "I'm sorry. So sorry."

Mariana sat close to her mother and lay her head against her mother's shoulder. "Are you okay, Mummy?"

"I'm fine, darling." She continued to take deep breaths. "Mummy was just feeling a little sick, but now

126

I'm fine. It's all good." She managed a fleeting smile. "Sorry to scare you both." Mariana's eyes darkened but she said nothing and held Camilla's hand.

He took out his phone and called Liz. She needed an update even though Camilla was no longer linked in with the service. She had experience in dealing with these issues. Besides, he needed to hear her voice. "Hi, Liz. It's Matthew." Silence. "Liz, are you there?"

"I'm here. What's up?"

"It's about Camilla. I think she needs your help."

"Tell me where you are and I'll be right over."

"We're heading home now and should be there in about ten minutes or so."

Matthew hung up, reassured that Liz would be Camilla's saving grace, or at least a great liaison with her counsellor. His heart ached for Camilla after what that bastard did to them.

CHAPTER 29
A NURTURER

A week after the engagement party, Liz stood in front of Camilla's house. When Matthew called, she was inside her local cafe, drinking a strong cappuccino. She'd needed the caffeine hit after the crappy way she was feeling. She rang the doorbell. Her mouth was dry and she had a rolling feeling in her stomach that kept her unfocused at the thought of seeing Matthew again. She needed to be there for Camilla and forget about her own sensations whenever she was around Matthew. She could do this.

Matthew opened the door, his gaze lingering on her eyes and sweeping down to her mouth. He cleared his throat then swung the door wide open. "Thanks for coming."

Liz stepped into the foyer. "No worries. How is she?"

"A bit rattled, but resting on the couch." She walked over to the living room where

Mariana was flicking through a storybook beside her mother. Camilla was holding a mug of a hot beverage in her hands, seemingly in space until Liz called her. "Hey Camilla, Mariana. Great to see you both." She settled on the couch beside her and smiled.

Matthew alerted her to his presence. "I'll take Mariana for a walk."

Liz nodded. "Thanks." She gazed into the woman's eyes that spoke volumes about her anxiety levels, and her heart went out to Camilla. "So tell me what happened, Camilla."

She nodded then recounted today's incident while Liz listened with a heavy heart. She knew her trauma history with a man who should have never been a father. She had obviously been triggered. "Oh, Camilla, I'm sorry you had to go through that. I think you should call your counsellor and schedule an earlier appointment. Perhaps you need to have more frequent sessions. What do you think? Would that help?"

Camilla wiped away a single tear. "I think it would. Thanks."

Liz nodded. "And you're doing your relaxation exercises?"

Camilla wiped her red nose with a tissue. "I am. Sometimes I wish I could take an anti-anxiety medication, but it'll be another addiction."

"So long as you have the anxiety strategies you're learning, anxiety should be manageable. I mean, we all have anxiety to some degree. It's a matter of continuing on with your daily activities in spite of it."

"I know, but it's an effort to get out of bed sometimes. I panic that I might have another attack. Or I worry that I'll meet someone as violent as my father. It's a cycle you know?"

Liz pressed hard against her forehead, a headache coming on. She ignored it. "When you're dealing with trauma, it's a bit of a process." She smiled reassuringly. "Whenever you feel you're being triggered, you can identify the trigger and challenge your thoughts around it. But to do that, you need to re-experience the trauma in a safe space. And the psychologist you have is experienced in that sort of thing. It's about giving it time and realising it's a process. Do you feel connected to your psychologist?"

"I do. She's amazing." She frowned. "And I know I need to give it time but it's hard."

Liz stroked her hand, the coldness evident. "I know. Nothing worth doing is ever easy, but so long as you have the support and willingness to stay off the drugs you'll get there. You need to believe in yourself, Camilla."

"The drugs were a band-aid affect that gave me that short-term relief, but in the end, it stuffed up my life. I can't go back to that. I damn well won't."

"Of course you won't." Liz gave Camilla a soothing smile. "And I'm happy to ring you every now and again even if you're no longer with the service."

Camilla nodded, her eyes shining. "Thanks, Liz. I'd like that."

Half an hour later, the front door opened and Matthew and Mariana returned. Her daughter rushed over to her mother and fell into her arms. Camilla twirled her daughter's hair strands in her fingers in silence.

"How is she doing?" Matthew asked.

Liz smiled. "Better. She'll be fine. She'll call her psychologist and get her in to see her earlier than her next scheduled appointment. She'll hopefully have the space to give Camilla more regular sessions." She hesitated. "I'm happy to check in from time to time. I don't mind." Why was a part of her tingling inside?

"Thanks, Liz." He turned to his sister. "Listen, Camilla. Will you be okay with me going in to work in the next hour?"

"Of course, Matthew. You're new there so you can't start taking time off. I'll be fine. I have to learn to do this on my own."

"I'll get the neighbour to check in on you later."

Liz fought back her blurred vision and unsteady legs. What was going on with her? The last couple of days she'd been feeling queasy and weak, but she didn't know why. "Anyway, I'd better go. Take care, Matthew."

He nodded. "Are you okay? You look a little pale." He squeezed her shoulder and she ignored the tingle.

She gave him a reassuring smile. "I'm fine. Just a little tired, that's all." She walked out and headed to the car, taking a deep breath.

CHAPTER 30
A CRY FOR HELP

Two days later, after grabbing her favourite cappuccino from the usual local cafe, Liz rested her hands in her lap and listened to a young lady at her desk at work. The client named Anne sat, cowering in her chair with quaking hands. Her eyes were bloodshot, her hair was dry and dishevelled around a pale and gaunt face, and she appeared malnourished. Her lips trembled, and with each passing minute, she turned to look over her shoulder as if expecting someone to be there. She jolted at the sounds of footsteps and doors closing and gasped at the questions Liz asked. She didn't offer much detail about her history. Anne was eighteen years old and wanted help with substance abuse in order to regain custody of her daughter. Gabriella looked on with a keen eye and took notes in a pad.

Liz smiled, conscious of the woman's wandering eyes. She barely focused on Liz or Gabriella. "We provide support services and early intervention to avoid legal involvement if possible. Luckily, your daughter's in the care of your mother. She's in good hands, but if your mother's not able to help in the future because of her health, we'll need to explore foster care options. Custody depends on your recovery from substance abuse." She turned to Gabriella and ignored a throbbing headache. "Gabriella here will ask you further questions and invite you to ask questions at the end."

Anne's eyes darkened and her hands began to flutter. She nodded. "Thanks, but I think I'll be good before you know it. I need to get out of this place. Can I go to rehab far from here? Say, interstate? I have to get away. Please."

Liz got an uneasy sense. What was going on with this woman? "Anne, are you in any kind of trouble?"

Anne laughed nervously. "No, no. I just meant I need a fresh start. Too many memories 'round here. The country air would help."

Liz ignored her still-pounding headache. "Are you telling me everything here? I can't help you if you're not totally upfront."

Anne stiffened. "Yes, I just want my daughter back. Please help me with that. I need rehab in the country."

Liz smiled. "We'll talk about rehabilitation later, but for now, Gabriella will ask you questions so we can work out how to best help you." The woman frowned and fidgeted again.

Something about this woman was wrong, but she didn't know what it was. The woman appeared afraid of something or maybe she was she high. Liz's headaches and blurred vision were making her see things that weren't there. She would see the doctor after work tonight.

Gabriella changed seats with Liz while she observed. "I'll be asking questions about your background. I'll need to know your medical history, current family members, your environment, previous treatment, and any links to current support services." The woman flinched. Gabriella opened up a new page in her notepad and crossed her legs. "Do you have any current physical or recently diagnosed mental health conditions?"

Liz's attention shifted fifteen minutes later as the room spun around her. The voices faded in and out, and her surroundings looked fuzzy. She missed most of the session, and at the end, Anne left with her head bowed down. Did she grab a pen from the desk or was she imagining it? Gabriella mustn't have seen anything so she might've been seeing things again.

"Can I use your bathroom?"Anne asked.

"Of course," said Gabriella. "I'll show you where it is." Before leaving, she looked at Liz strangely, whispering, "Are you okay? You don't look well."

She focused on her lap and nodded. "If you wouldn't mind taking her, that'd be great. Thanks," said Liz.

"No worries," said Gabriella. She was gone for a few minutes, and when she returned she jotted down case notes in her exercise book. "Anne's taking a while. I'll go back in a minute." She tilted her head. "Are you sure you're okay? You don't look well."

Her eyes were slowly closing as she bowed her head, clasping her hands. "The woman. You should be...supervising...her."

"I'll go in a minute, but I am worried about you. Should I call a doctor or Penny, maybe?"

Liz's throat dried up, then the woman from Bella's engagement party showed up again. "Who's that woman sitting next to you?"

Gabriella tilted her head. "What woman?"

Oh crap! She was seeing things again. "Nothing."

Gabriella rose and returned with a glass of water. "Here, drink this. You're probably dehydrated, Liz. Just rest a minute and I'll be back." She walked back to the bathroom.

A few minutes later, Liz's clear vision returned after the water when Penny called out. "Liz, get to the bathroom now. I need to get these clients out of here. I'll have to reschedule their appointments for today."

Liz jolted in her seat, ignoring the accelerated heart rate and tension in her head. "What happened?"

"Just get to the bathroom. Gabriella's in there now, but she can't stand the sight of blood. Help her out." Penny rushed ahead and turned back to Liz. "The client you just saw. Anne. She stabbed herself with a pen." Liz stood up, ignoring the light-headedness and rushed over to the bathroom. The strong, tangy smell of blood made her nauseous. She bent down and sat beside the woman whose wrist was covered with a blood-soaked bandaged. "I've got this. You go, Gabriella."

"Are you sure?"

"Yes, I've got this." Gabriella scurried out with her hand over her mouth.

Liz stayed with the woman for ten minutes, reassuring her and trying to get her to talk about her pain, but the woman stared into space. She kept pressure on her wrist, the blood seeping through the bandage.

"Please tell me why you did this. We can help you," Liz said.

A look of terror filled her eyes. She remained silent as her eyes opened and closed. It was a cry for help to harm herself with staff present. Why didn't she pick up on this before, and why did she not think that the pen could be a deadly weapon? This was a grave mistake and could cost her her job or reputation.

Once the ambulance arrived, a female paramedic and male paramedic asked Liz questions while assessing Anne's injuries.

"Will she be alright?" Liz asked awkwardly.

The female paramedic gave her a reassuring smile. "The stabbing's superficial, not very deep. She'll be fine, at least physically. But she will need a psychiatric evaluation."Both paramedics lay her down on a stretcher and lifted her into the waiting ambulance outside. They drove off to the nearest hospital.

Liz wandered over to the staff room and grabbed a glass of water. She sat with her

head bowed, the weight of her shoulders burdening her. She turned at the sound of Penny's voice.

"Why did you let her leave without knowing she'd do that? And you let her grab a pen on top of that. She should've been supervised, too. What were you thinking, Liz?"

She shrugged. "I'm sorry, Penny. I wasn't thinking, and it won't happen again."

Penny sat across from her. "What is wrong with you? You've been making grave mistakes at the office. Yesterday, you called the wrong doctor, and earlier this morning you added the wrong case notes in someone else's file. Later this morning, you let this poor woman harm herself. What's going on, Liz? This isn't like you."

She pressed her temple and sipped water. "I don't know. I've been feeling sick and dizzy, and having these massive headaches. I've even hallucinated a couple of times. Seeing this woman that doesn't exist, but existing only in my mind."

Penny leaned forward, touching her forehead. "You're a little feverish." She stood and looked at her watch. "Why haven't you seen the doctor?"

Liz sighed. "The symptoms come and go. Mostly, I've been okay and managing."

"But you're not managing. You're making mistakes, and in our line of work, it can mean the difference between life and death. I'm taking you to see the doctor now." Penny's phone rang. "It's my Mum."

Liz watched her face turn pale as she gripped the phone. "What's wrong?"

"My mum's hit her head in the nursing home. She's with the nurse now. She said she's okay, but I have to go see her." Penny fought back tears.

"Of course, go." She touched her on the shoulder. "Is your mother remembering you, sometimes?"

Penny shrugged. "A few times she'll remember me. But, lately, she's been talking about being with my father. It's gut-wrenching. I'm not ready to lose my mum. And it's bringing up memories of my dad. He was a good man and didn't deserve to die that way. That good Samaritan work can be way too risky at times."

"I remember you telling me about your dad. How he tried to help that poor woman who was being threatened with a gun."

Penny nodded. "Yeah, he tried to take the gun off that drug-affected guy, but instead, the man ended up shooting my dad. I get angry with him sometimes, questioning why he would risk his life like that when he had a family to think about. It will never make sense to me."

Liz's heart warmed. "I'm sorry about your dad, Penny. You've had a rough life."

Penny ignored her comment. "Listen, enough talk about this. You need to rest and wait for me to come back. Let Gabriella do the bulk of the work. I will be back soon and I'll take you to the doctor."

"Don't worry. I'm a big girl and will go to the doctor myself. I don't need baby-sitting. You shouldn't get back here if you can't."

"I'm still taking you to the doctor. Are you sure you'll be alright?"

"Of course. It's passed now. In fact, I'm going to eat my lunch early then I'll go see the doctor myself. Most likely, I'm dehydrated and not eating well. I'll be fine after I eat." She rose, headed to the fridge and grabbed her salad wrap. She sat back down and took a bite. "See, I'm eating. Now go!"

Penny smiled. "Okay, I'll call you later if I don't get back."

CHAPTER 31
INCIDENT

Liz walked outside to her car earlier than usual from work so she could see her regular doctor. Gabrielle was shadowing another social worker, and Liz was feeling better as she stepped inside her car.

Liz drove in the school traffic until she started experiencing a dry mouth. Her head spun with a slight tremor and her hands tingled. Body fatigue set in bringing her to the point of drowsiness. She had to stop the car, but the wave of light-headedness made her eyes droopy and her vision blurry. Sleepiness set in, but she was fighting it off. The main road was busy, and she couldn't find anywhere to stop. A parking space came into her view up ahead. A few more minutes and she'd be able to stop. She could hold on until then. A large reserve came into view so she could turn in there and stop.

Liz had a cup of tea in the morning then a wrap for lunch. Surely the wrap wasn't what made her sick? She'd had a cappuccino in the morning before work too.

Slapping her cheeks with one hand, she was fighting to stay awake and had slowed down. The car behind her beeped its horn as she was driving down to thirty kilometres per hour. She couldn't risk driving faster. The car up ahead suddenly braked and she stopped just in time before smashing into it. Her head weighed her down and blurred vision led to a struggle to stay alert. Bouts of drowsiness made it hard to keep driving. She closed her eyes for a minute before seeing a car turn right. She gave way and spotted the reserve with large trees surrounding it on her left. She could turn in here. The car up ahead suddenly stopped without her anticipating it when she steered the car to avoid a collision. Turning the steering wheel to her left, she gasped and smashed straight into a tree. The moment the airbag hit her squarely in the face, she blacked out.

***

Matthew's heart hammered in his chest as he yelled to Rowan. "Get me that damn neck brace, will you. We need to support her neck while we get her out."

Rowan handed over the neck brace and watched Matthew. "Easy, now."

He turned to Rowan. "I got this, man."

Johnny pushed Rowan out of the way. "Shit, there's bruises on her chest and it looks like her wrist's fractured. Let's get her out of there, Matthew."

Matthew nodded and gently pulled her out after attaching the brace. "Be easy with her. We don't want to risk further fractures." Johnny and Rowan reached for her and placed her on the stretcher. The ambulance pushed her in the back.

Matthew struggled to breathe. A nauseating sensation made him wince. He turned to the ambulance officer. "I'm coming with you."

Johnny's head angled. "No, I'll go. You stay here."

A tinge of jealousy overcame him. "I'm going. Liz is a friend so no arguments."

Johnny frowned and held up his hand. "Okay, we'll both go."

The back doors closed and the driver headed to the hospital. Matthew held on to her hand, his eyes glazing over her while Johnny looked on with interest. If he lost her, he didn't know what he'd do, but she was going to be okay. He wondered how she had managed to hit a tree.

Matthew and Johnny sat in the waiting area later that day for what felt like hours until the doctor arrived with news.

He clasped his hands and sported a beard and casual attire. "I take it you're the firefighters who helped Ms Randiza out of the car?"

"Yes, how is she doctor?" asked Matthew.

"Well, luckily for her she wasn't driving very fast at the time. The airbag caused small abrasions, and the seatbelt led to some bruising on the chest and abdomen. She has a fractured wrist and grazing around her face. She'll be fine, but we'll need to keep her overnight for observation should anything else be affected. We completed scans to her head and neck, and that looks okay. We also found traces of an antipsychotic medication known as Zyprexa in her blood work. Nothing in her medical history suggests a mental illness." He checked his watch.

Matthew's heart hammered. "So how would it get into her system?"

The doctor cleared his throat. "The police are currently speaking to Ms Randiza. They'll need to investigate if they suspect foul play. Is there next of kin that can be reached?"

Matthew wished he knew her family. "Not sure about her family, but there's a co-worker, Penny. I can ring her and see whether she can notify Liz's family."

"Great. Thank you." He nodded then scurried away.

Matthew gasped. "What? That can't be right. How the hell did that happen?"

Johnny's face paled. "I don't know, but maybe the doctors missed something in her history. It's been known to happen. An undiagnosed mental illness."

Matthew could barely breathe to think of the possibility that Liz would have an undiagnosed illness. It couldn't be true.

Matthew placed a call to Penny. He later turned to Johnny who looked stricken. "Are you okay, man?" His hands fidgeted and his eyes roamed as if he was looking for something. "What's going on with you?"

"Nothing. I'm just glad she's okay."

If she wasn't belted or had no airbag, she'd be suffering from very serious injuries. Matthew was thankful that she'd be okay. But why did she have traces of an antipsychotic medication in her system?

CHAPTER 32
A WARD VISIT

Matthew snuck into Liz's room as Johnny walked out of the ward. His eyes were dark as he nodded to him in the corridor. As he stood there, watching her, he cringed at the bruises and grazes around her face and arms. She had a cast around her fractured wrist and looked fragile and weak as she sat up, her back leaning against a stack of pillows while her eyes appeared drowsy and worn-out.

Liz's eyes lit up at the sight of Matthew. He took a seat across from her. "How are you feeling?"

She shrugged. "I've got to wear this stupid cast for at least the next four weeks. But other than that, I guess I'll live."

He ignored the tingly sensation in his stomach, realising she looked more beautiful each time he saw her. He brushed those thoughts away. "I'm sorry. I know it's hard, but it could've been worse. These are conditions that will get better, Liz. Hang in there."

She nodded. "I'm not used to being an invalid. I can't do anything without the use of my arm. One-handed Liz."

He took a relaxed breath with a shake of the head. "I've called your co-worker, Penny, at the centre you work, but she mentioned your parents are on a cruise. She's coming by later and wasn't sure whether to notify your parents. She'll speak to you about it." He sighed. "She said she'll also ring your friends, Bella and Jamie." He paused. "So what happened?"

Liz frowned then turned the other way. "I spoke to the police and told them I was feeling sick and smashed into a tree. Obviously, the effects of this medication. There was no other car involved."

Matthew was curious. "Zyprexa."

Liz nodded. "I was feeling dizzy, feverish, and drowsy, had the worst headache, and couldn't see clearly. I was falling asleep at the wheel. And now I know why." She sighed. "I guess the doctor told you guys. Johnny looked really upset about it." She chuckled. "I mean, we're not even a couple, so I don't know why it's affected him so much."

"Do you know how that got into your system?"

She shook her head. "I don't have a clue but I plan to find out. I...I...Oh never mind."

"What?"

"Nothing." She averted her eyes again and remained silent.

Matthew leaned forward and gazed into her sad eyes, feeling the need to light up those beautiful eyes. "When I saw you in that accident, your car colliding with that tree, I didn't know if you were alive or dead and I was so damn scared, Liz. I'm really glad you're okay." He pressed his lips together and yearned to kiss her, but he pulled back. Liz blushed, and he wondered whether he'd seen that same yearning in her own eyes. "So I gather the police aren't doing anything if there's nothing suspicious?"

"No, but my friend, Bella, has a fiancée who's a detective and he's got my back. He's there for me if I need anything, and I'm sure he'll look into this."

Matthew frowned, wondering what was going on. "Why would he need to have your back? What's going on?"

She avoided his eyes again. "Nothing. Like I said, it's all good."

Penny interrupted, accompanied by two striking young women Matthew had never seen before. Quickly, he nodded in their direction then moved back to make room for them. All three women wrapped their arms around Liz, and one of them, who was tall with brown hair, started crying. The other woman with red hair looked concerned but remained stoic. Complete opposites.

Liz faced him. "Oh Matthew. Sorry. These are my friends, Bella and Jamie. And you know Penny from the centre."

He neared both women and shook their hands. "Nice to meet you both."

"Thank you so much for saving Liz," said Bella.

He smiled. "It's my job."

"And an important one at that," said Jamie. "I take it you were stationed near the car accident?"

"Yep. I'm at the Northern district office so we were close to the incident. Luckily, she wasn't driving fast."

Bella turned to Matthew and gave him a cheeky grin. "It's not great to meet under these circumstances, Matthew. Aren't you and Liz friends?"

Liz cleared her throat. "Yes, we are friends."

Matthew smiled. "I guess it would've been ideal to meet in a different place, but I'm glad I could be there for Liz."

Liz looked up at Jamie. Normally, she didn't mind the spotlight, but not with Matthew in their presence.

Her friends were being a little nosey. "You're not on duty today, Jamie?"

Jamie shook her head. "Day off today."

"I'm sorry to bring you into work on your day off."

She frowned. "Not to worry, Liz. I'm glad you're doing well."

Penny's body shook. "I should've taken you to the doctor myself. This is all my fault. Why did I agree to let you go to the doctor alone? Pure madness."

Liz looked up at Penny. "How's your mum, by the way? After her fall?"

Penny smiled. "She's fine. A little shaken up." She lifted her shoulders. "You could've waited for me. I was planning to go back to work but Mandy mentioned you left."

Matthew's body stilled as he turned to Liz. "Were you going to the doctor because of those symptoms or for another reason?"

Liz hesitated and stared hard at Bella and Jamie. "Because of the symptoms."

Bella looked clueless as she questioned Liz who explained how she'd been feeling for the past week and a half.

"Since my engagement, you've had these issues and didn't tell me. Why not?" Bella said, her eyes squinting in her direction. Jamie gave her a reassuring smile.

Liz shrugged. "I didn't want to worry you guys. Besides, Marco's been there for me."

Bella drew a slim hand through her hair. She moved further back to include Matthew in the conversation and smiled at him. "Jamie told me what happened after the engagement party. That you weren't feeling well but not that you were hallucinating." She took a breath.

146

"And I'm sorry for not coming to see you sooner. I've been so busy with work and the preparations for the wedding. But you still should've told me. I'm your friend and I should've known."

"I know, but you have been calling me every day. I didn't tell you the whole truth about how I was feeling. You have enough going on as it is without me adding to it."

Matthew walked closer to the edge of the bed. "I think you guys need to start telling me what's going on before I get back on shift. I have a few minutes."

He had a feeling he wasn't going to like the full story, but he would be there for Liz because he cared for her a lot more than he wanted to admit. It frightened the hell out of him.

CHAPTER 33
OFFER OF HELP

Liz winced at the ache in her wrist as she rose from the hospital bed, taking a deep breath. She thought about her client Anne, who had stabbed herself in the bathroom, and had asked a nurse earlier about Anne's ward number. She made her way over there and ignored her aches and pains. She was only a few minutes away from her room, and once she entered her ward, the poor woman stared up at a television screen, her arm bandaged and her eyes blood-shot. The look of sheer despair flashed across Anne's face. She jolted in her bed when spotting Liz.

"I'm sorry, Anne. I didn't mean to scare you. I wanted to check in. I guess you remember me from the centre. I'm Liz." Marie hugged the blankets tight against her chest, nodding. "Can I sit?"

Anne shrugged. "Free country." She looked at her closely. "Were you in an accident?"

Liz nodded. "I wanted to see how you're doing and offer to help you. Have you seen a psychologist yet?"

Anne's eyes wandered. "Yep." Liz would hopefully get a copy of the assessment report.

"Is there anyone I can call for you? Family? A friend?"

Anne shook her head rapidly. "No-one supportive. Please don't call anyone. I'm fine."

"Okay, I won't. It's okay." This woman was spooked as Liz watched her eyes steer over towards the entry. What was she so afraid of? "Listen, just hear me out and then you can make a decision." Anne nodded.

"If you're in some kind of trouble, we can get you into a homeless shelter and keep you safe. We can look at other support services, too."

Anne's eyes dilated. "No, I'm fine. I have somewhere to go."

Liz didn't want to give up on her. "I know you didn't answer many questions when you were at the centre, but are you willing to answer a few of mine?"

Her bottom lip quivered. "I can't stay here, Liz. It's not safe. Please get me out of here."

Liz was helpless in that moment. "I'm in the hospital myself now, but once I get released, we can leave together. What do you say? We can go straight to the police. They'll keep you safe." She had to tread carefully. "Tell me about yourself."

Anne shrugged. "I have no-one. Most of my family was abusive so I ran away. I got pregnant and then lost custody of my daughter because of drugs." She breathed heavily. "My dad was abusive and then died. My older brother was trouble too. But my mother was great, and I trust her with my daughter." She winced. "I have to look after my daughter and keep her safe."

"Safe from what? I thought you trusted your mother." The woman remained tight-lipped. "Anne, please tell me what's going on. I can help."

She shook her head. "I just want my daughter back."

Liz nodded. "Okay, we'll get you the help you need. So why did you hurt yourself?"

Anne swallowed, her eyes darkening. She peered into her lap. "Don't know."

What was the woman hiding? Something had triggered her to self-harm, but the cost of opening up obviously overrode the help Liz could provide. "Okay, Anne. That's fine. We don't have to talk about that." Anne offered a half-smile as if to say 'thank you' then tears swam around her eyes. She looked towards the window. "But I have helped a lot of women in your situation and I won't give up on you. I'm here for you, and when you're ready to tell me more, I'll still be here for you. Okay?"

Anne smiled again and wiped her tears. But when her eyes lingered back towards the entryway, her body stilled. She shook her head again, her eyes blinking rapidly. Her hands clenched and her lips pressed hard together. "Just leave. Go."

Liz looked behind her, but nobody was there. She was looking at something behind her. "Anne. I'd like to help. I can keep you safe. Please tell me what you're afraid of."

The woman started screaming and her body shivered. "No, get out . Get out!" Two nurses rushed into the room and held her body down. One of the nurses gave her an injection that suddenly knocked her out. She turned to Liz. "You'd better leave. You should still be resting in your own room."

Liz nodded, her mind churning at all the possibilities. Whatever she was afraid of was probably deeper than anyone could imagine. But had someone passed by her room, scaring her. She had to ring Marco and get him to keep her safe.

Getting back inside her own ward, Liz rummaged in her bag for her phone and dialled Marco. He answered on the second ring. "Hey, Marco. I need your help. This woman, Anne specifically, needs your help." She recounted her story.

"No problem, Liz. I'll get to the hospital now and get her somewhere safe. I should be there in the next hour or so."

"Thanks, Marco. And hurry."

***

Liz had roused from sleep at the sound of shuffling feet and muffled voices in the hospital. She slowly opened her eyes and realised she'd fallen asleep, obviously more tired than she thought. Peering at her phone resting on the bedside table, she was surprised at the time. It had been five hours since she'd spoken to Anne. Marco probably came by and she'd been asleep.

A familiar figure stood before her. It was Marco gazing at her glumly with a flat posture and slow feet as he made his way inside the ward.

"You look like your cat died. What's going on?"

Marco hesitated. "Make yourself comfortable, Liz." She lifted her body in the bed and again, fought the aches and pains. This had to be about Anne. Surely she was okay?

Liz stopped breathing for a moment, watching Marco's hands clench tight. "You're scaring me, Marco. It's not Anne, is it?" She waited with clammy hands and he slowly nodded. "What is it?" He looked spooked so it must've been pretty bad.

"Your client, Anne. She's dead."

Liz slumped in her bed as she recalled her sweet, sad eyes as if she wanted out of her current life. "What?" A sense of guilt rushed through her. Maybe she could've done more to stop this. Maybe she made things worse by talking to her. "How did she die? Did she kill herself?" Maybe she should've taken more preventative measures.

Marco hesitated. "She escaped from the hospital before I got here with an officer. We searched the hospital grounds but couldn't find her. We looked further into her background and searched the streets she frequented, being homeless. We found her belongings close to an abandoned warehouse underneath a pitched tent. We found Anne inside this tent. But it wasn't suicide. She was beaten to death."

Liz's head spun and she grasped the edge of the bed, digging her nails into the sheet. No, she wouldn't go back there. She wouldn't think about her own trauma. "How exactly was she beaten? I need to know."

Marco bowed his head. "Liz, no."

Liz glared. "I have never had this happen to any of my clients, and not long after Domenic is released, one of my clients dies this way. Please tell me what you saw. I can tell you if that's Domenic's style. Please. I can take it." She steeled herself for the news. Detach herself. Liz was able to compartmentalise. The psychologist was teaching her strategies to keep herself grounded. She could do this.

"Her face was bashed in beyond recognition. Her head was kicked in with some kind of hard shoe. One eye was gouged out, but that one was post-mortem, thank God, and multiple bruising and scarring lay around her abdomen."

Liz sat frozen, imagining all the blood. "Dear God, Marco. That sounds like something Domenic would do. He told me once that he can hurt other people if they don't do his bidding."

"But what's the connection? As far as we know, she had no known connections with Domenic, unless he's gone back into the drug and escort business."

"Maybe revenge against me? Getting me to feel this poor girl's pain. It could be a message. I don't know. But don't you see? He was arrested all those years ago because of drugs, but he got a longer sentence because of attempted murder against me. He wants revenge for my testifying against him. He won't kill me, but he wants me to suffer long enough until he can kill me. Not only for testifying against him, but because I wanted to leave him with our child. He could no longer control me then, but he is damn sure controlling me now."

"Don't worry, Liz. We'll look into this murder. But I have a few questions about your encounter with Anne."

She nodded. "I can tell you what I know. But Gabriella could tell you more about the day she visited my work. I was drugged on Zyprexa that day, and can't remember much."

"Sure. We'll question her, but first, give me your recount."

As Liz divulged the day Anne had attempted suicide, she wondered if Domenic was involved. It had to be more than her connection to Liz.

CHAPTER 34
A WORK SEMINAR

Liz had taken time off from work and was still tense about Anne's death. That poor girl didn't deserve such a horrible death. No-one did. At least Marco was investigating, but this situation had become more complicated, and she wondered if Anne was dealing with partner abuse or something more. She might've escaped the hospital because she was terrified of something.

Liz returned to work on Monday, and in the afternoon, she'd agreed to attend a work seminar with Gabriella. They roamed a large conference room until they found two empty chairs, and watched as Gabriella's boyfriend, Nick set up his computer, projector, and lecture notes. Liz had arranged it with Penny to listen in on this talk about domestic violence and crime in general, as it was relevant to their work. Gabriella had mentioned the seminar, and now here they were. Apparently, her boyfriend was a prominent forensic psychologist who had done amazing work with victims of crime and violence.

Liz rummaged through her bag for a notebook and pen and watched as Gabriella held her hands clasped in front of her with eyes lit up towards the front. She was so in love, appearing oblivious to the jam-packed room of about one-hundred women and a few men in the mix.

Nick's eyes roamed as he smiled and turned to the group. He was average height with a robust physique, large hands, and black, short hair with a long fringe that he flicked over his eyes. He wore black pleated pants over black leather shoes and a tight-fitted red shirt. His underarms were sweaty already and he hadn't even started. He must've been nervous, given the stain underneath his shirt.

Gabriella faced Liz. "He's going to be amazing. I've listened to him before and he has a way to reel you into his speaker world. He's inspirational."

Liz nodded. "Looks like he's starting."

Nick cleared his throat. "Thank you all for being here today. I appreciate the distance some of you might've travelled, and I do believe I have a lot of value to offer. We can cover a lot of ground in two hours, and I am happy for questions in the last half-hour or so. I'm sure that some of you will most likely know more than I do about family violence and crime in general. Particularly with any experiences you might've had. Now if anything is too distressing for you, I'm happy for you to leave the room. I promise I won't take it personally."

Muffled voices filled the room, with a few women laughing quietly. Faces stared straight ahead, and Liz waited until he started his talk. After general introductions, Nick cited statistics.

"Now, here are some interesting statistics about violence in Australia." He looked up at the big screen. "At least one woman a week is killed by her partner or former partner. Women are at least three times more likely than men to be abused by their partner, and one in five women have been through sexual violence."

Liz swallowed as she listened to further statistics about Australian women, which put a damper on her spirits. She knew the facts but to hear it so articulately detailed by an experienced speaker in her world brought it closer to home. Liz shifted in her seat after twenty minutes, turning to the subject of restraining orders.

Nick swallowed and turned his head to face the entire group around the room. "Intuition is best used when you believe you might be abused. If you get the feeling that something doesn't feel right or that you're not safe, get the help you need. Restraining orders can sometimes aggravate a partner's behaviour to the point of injury or death. So women need to think carefully about taking that kind of action. If your partner says he has a gun, consider the possibility that he might use it on you. Don't believe it's a scare tactic. Women need to take that kind of thing seriously."

Liz took a breath, thinking about how her psychologist planned to delve more deeply into a safety response plan, should Domenic turn against her.

Towards the end of the session, Nick invited the group to ask questions that lasted for half an hour until he thanked the group. He handed out information brochures about support services to use for clients.

Gabriella waited until most of the group left before pushing Liz along to the front of the room to meet her boyfriend. "Liz, this is Nick. Nick, Liz, the social worker I work with at the agency."

Nick beamed widely and shook Liz's hand. "Great to meet you. Gabriella's spoken a lot about you. I know you do great work."

Liz smiled back. "Thanks, Nick. I enjoyed your talk. That'll definitely inspire those in our industry to give even more to our clients."

He nodded. "Thank you." He turned to Gabriella. "How was it?"

Gabriella leaned in closer towards him. "You were just as great as last time, honey."

He winked at her, then turned to Liz. "Listen, why don't you have lunch with us sometime? I'd like to talk to you about your cases, without divulging names of course, as I'm investing in another women's shelter. I have one set up already and plan to start up another one, but I need to finalise the legal documents. This is what'll keep women safe."

Liz was speechless. What an amazing thing to do. "I'd be happy to talk to you in general terms. That sounds great. Organise the lunch with Gabriella and I'll be there."

He nodded. "Fantastic. I guess we'll see you soon."

Gabriella leaned in and kissed him briefly on the lips. "See you later, hon."

Liz and Gabriella walked out of the conference room with smiles on their faces. It had been a productive afternoon, and she was looking forward to picking his brain about the women who had nowhere else to go but the streets.

CHAPTER 35
JOLTED BY THE PAST

Liz sat in a taxi with Gabriella. Her arm was in a cast so she couldn't drive. They headed back to the office after the conference with Nick. The police were still investigating who had drugged Liz, and she was cautious not to eat or drink anything she didn't deem safe. It was a horrible way to live, but necessary.

She turned to Gabriella whose face looked pale and sickly. Gabriella put her hand over her mouth as if she was about to be sick, but then it appeared to settle. "You don't look well, Gabriella. Are you okay?"

"I think I'm coming down with something."

She clenched her hands. "What brought this on? You were fine at the conference. You did have lunch before we left, didn't you?"

Gabriella nodded. "I had a sandwich, but I haven't had much to drink today. I'm probably dehydrated."

Liz drew back. "I'm happy to take you to the doctor."

She shook her head. "No, it's fine." A single tear ran down her face and she whimpered, turning her head away. "I'm alright, but this headache's pretty intense. I wouldn't mind a strong coffee. That usually helps."

Liz nodded. "We'll stop at a cafe that I've been to a few times. We can stop there before going back to work." She told the driver who parked in front of a cafe in Heidelberg. They got out and headed inside. It was a cramped cafe with only a few tables near the counter, but she found a table that was empty and sat opposite Gabriella. Liz ordered them hot drinks and sat down, placing the table number on the table. She looked at Gabriella who still appeared pale but managed to give her a reassuring smile. "So are you sleeping well?"

Gabriella shrugged. "I think it's the late nights I have with Nick sometimes, and probably not drinking enough. I worry about my mum too. I guess with Domenic out and about, it doesn't make me feel all that secure."

"Has he contacted your mother? Is she safe?" The waiter brought over their cappuccinos, and Liz sipped it slowly, watching the steam hover.

Gabriella drew a hand through her hair, with eyes turning over towards the dribs and drabs of patrons entering the cafe. "She's fine. My mum has a new boyfriend who was in the military, and he gives her pointers to keep her safe. He taught her how to use a gun, and she keeps one with her at all times."

Liz's heart tightened, thinking what a horrid but necessary way to live. Maybe she needed to do the same in terms of learning how to fire a gun. But then again, she had the police protecting her. She would be fine, wouldn't she? "That's great she's taking precautions."

"And how are you doing?" Gabriella asked. "I mean, I still cannot believe that Anne's dead. I only saw her that one time, but I wonder who would do that to her. An ex partner, maybe?"

"I don't know, Gabriella. But do you remember anything about your dad's side businesses when you were little?"

Gabriella's eyes distended. She touched the base of her throat and instantly her face turned beetroot red. "I can't remember. Sorry." Her hands were shaking.

Liz tilted her head. "Are you sure?"

"Nothing. Nothing. Can we go now? I want to get on home, but I can't do that until I collect some of my stuff from work."

Liz didn't want to pressure her. In her own time, she might open up about her past. They headed back to a waiting taxi. Gabriella was in her own world as she entered the backseat. As Liz looked in the opposite direction, Domenic lay back against an old, rusty car with his hands on a woman. She gasped, her feet unable to move. Staring at the scene, Domenic was touching this short woman's breasts and kissing her hard on the mouth. The woman walked off as Domenic slapped her hard on her bottom. He turned to Liz without looking surprised and waved with a smug look on his face. When he stepped into his car, he skidded across the road. She was startled by Gabriella who hadn't seen her father.

Her reverie broke. "What's wrong? You look like you've seen a ghost."

Liz squeezed her hands tight, the white of her knuckles showing. She managed to get her circulation going again and reached for the car's door handle. She didn't want to worry Gabriella as she'd been through enough with her father over the years before prison. "I'm fine. Let's get back to work. We need to finish up case notes then we can go home."

Gabriella nodded as she sat in the car, staring at Liz with concern in her eyes.

CHAPTER 36
TROUBLING NEWS

"The fuckin' bitch is getting too close. Starting to investigate things. We need to get rid of her. And soon. Do what you must, but make it clean. No ties to either of us. Just make it quick.

"Fuckin' oath. I'll take care of it. No ties. You taught me well."

They both chuckled.

***

A week later, Liz walked inside the Italian restaurant on Lygon Street to meet Bella and Jamie. She was tired of her splint and was counting down the weeks. The pain was still unbearable at times, but her wrist was slowly improving.

She struggled to do things with one hand at work and at home. Luckily, Gabriella had taken on some of the load at work and was amazingly efficient. She had a special way with children, and she empathised with those mothers who continued to relapse into drugs. She never mentioned much about her life with Domenic, but Liz got the feeling she was hiding something.

Liz found Jamie and Bella sitting in the far corner of the restaurant and headed towards them. Taking a deep breath, she kissed Jamie then Bella on the cheek and sat down between them. A bustling waiter soon arrived and took their food and drink orders. Once he left, Bella leaned forward with a cheeky expression.

"So, Matthew ha?"

Liz cringed. "What about him? He saved me."

"Hmm," said Bella. "He looked quite smitten by you, and he's absolutely gorgeous by the way. Such a sexy firefighter." She beamed. "If I wasn't so in love with Marco, I'd go after him."

Jamie chuckled. "Oh, leave Liz alone, Bella. She is obviously not ready for a relationship with a man who is handsome, sweet, giving, and has an amazing physique."

Liz couldn't believe her ears. "Stop it, you guys. Matthew and I are just friends, and he's way out of my league. I mean, he might be a firefighter but how do I know he won't end up being just like Domenic? The stats on these kinds of crisis jobs are high on those who get violent and angry. You can't trust anyone these days."

Jamie grabbed Liz's hand. "Did you did tell Marco about seeing Domenic near the cafe a week ago? He is taking a lot of risks."

Liz nodded. "I told him, but he wasn't very close and he didn't approach me. There's nothing they can do unless he's a threat."

Bella shook her head. "Listen, girl. Use your intuition to guide you, but ultimately, I think you should stay with me for a while."

Liz's hands turned clammy and her stomach was rock-hard even thinking about that creep. She intuitively knew that Domenic was bad news back then, but she ignored her sense. Surely, she could learn to follow it more closely this time? "I'm fine, Bella. I just need to ignore that he even exists, but I worry, too. I still don't know how I got traces of Zyprexa in my system. I'm making sure I don't accept drinks from waiters I don't know."

Bella scoffed. "Anyway, I was going to tell you. Marco's not meant to tell me anything about your case, but I have ways to get things out of him. Mum's the word about you hearing it from me." She frowned. "Anyway, Marco looked into that, and surprise surprise. That waiter you spoke about is missing. He cannot be found," said Bella.

"What do you mean he can't be found?" asked Liz.

"Well, the catering company we hired had no record of the waiter you described."

"Oh God!" Liz had an uneasy feeling about the missing waiter. Most likely an innocent man caught in the crosshairs of danger and manipulation.

Jamie turned to Liz. "But the fact of the matter is that this type of medication can still be in your system a week or a few weeks later. At least the hospital flushed it all out."

"So you're saying that whatever dose of medication I got at the party, that that's what's made me crazy for a week and a half?"

"In some cases, yes, but...."

Liz intervened. "But that's not the story in my case, is it? What do you know?"

Jamie leaned forward. "The amount that was found in your system suggested high doses of the medication, so it is likely that you were dosed several times."

She trusted Jamie as a doctor who obviously knew medications. "Are you serious? I thought that maybe Domenic had been dosing me in some sick way. Although, I don't know how he'd manage that."

"Liz. You will need to take precautions," Jamie said. "Think back to all the foods or drinks you've taken over the past week. Even from take-away stores. Make a list and show it to the police. They might be able to track its origin."

The waiter arrived with their meals; a medium-rare steak for Jamie, a Caesar Salad for Bella, and a vegetable risotto for Liz.

Liz sipped on her wine and relished the warmth of it inside her body. She briefly closed her eyes, sickened by the fact that she was most likely drugged a few times. But was this waiter hired by Domenic or was he someone entirely different?

Liz alerted herself to the present when Bella's phone rang.

She looked at the screen and said, "Sorry, I need to take this. It could be important." The look on Bella's face looked sallow after ending the call. "Sure, honey. I'll tell them."

Liz stared. "What is it?"

"Marco has news. He wants us to go to the station in the next hour or so."

"What news?" asked Jamie.

"Something he can't tell us over the phone, apparently."

Liz refused to think of the worst. Maybe Marco had something good to relay and preferred to share it face to face. She needed good news right now.

CHAPTER 37
BREAKING NEWS

Liz arrived at the police station and watched the comings and goings of citizens and members of the police force. A range of cubicles and closed offices surrounded her as Marco led her to an interview room while other detectives ushered Bella and Jamie to separate rooms. Why were they going into separate rooms?

She sat across from Marco whose look of despair caused her to shake and hold her breath. Crossing her legs, Liz shifted her posture and waited. The dank smell almost made her gag, so she assumed a person with bad hygiene had been in this room last. An uneasy sense permeated her whole body, and she suddenly knew this was bad.

"I'm afraid I've got some bad news, Liz." She braced herself and averted her eyes, not wanting to see the darkness in Marco's eyes. "I'm sorry to say that Penny is dead."

Liz's mouth fell open and her fingers touched her parted lips. She closed her eyes and jerked her head back. Tears automatically ran down her cheeks. A deep pit of emptiness in her stomach detached her from her body. This had to be a dream. "Please tell me I didn't hear correctly."

Marco turned away briefly. "I'm sorry, Liz. Penny died from a morphine overdose." Marco rattled on about his condolences, but his voice sounded distant and muffled. She wanted to give a sharp scream as she clutched her chest. Her muscles tightened and she rubbed at more tears sliding down her flushed cheeks.

"How? I mean, what happened?"

Marco leaned forward and clenched his hands. "She injected herself and left a suicide note."

Liz flinched. "She'd never kill herself. Can I see the note?"

He shook his head. "Sorry, it's with forensics at the moment as we're obliged to investigate it to get more information. We also have to question everyone in her friendship circle, and that includes you, Bella, and Jamie." He took a breath. "Now, are you okay if I ask you some questions, Liz? I promise it won't take long, but it's got to be done. For the sake of protocol, we have to rule you guys out. I'm sorry."

Liz nodded. "Of course. I understand." She fought back further tears as her arms crossed over her abdomen. She pushed her emotions aside and focused on the man in front of her. He'd make a great counsellor.

Marco's hands clasped in his lap. "First of all, did Penny ever mention being lonely and lost without having children or a husband?"

Liz cringed. "Of course not. She was happy with her life, had great friends, and a supportive family. She would never kill herself. Never."

"So you don't know why she'd inject herself?"

"No, she never would. This doesn't make sense."

"Could it have been an accidental overdose? I mean, something she engaged in to help with pain, or maybe for some other reason?"

Liz's shoulders ached. "By other reason, you mean indulge in it for a rush. Is that it?" Marco shook his head. "I'm not saying that, Liz. But go on."

Liz's chest squeezed hard. "Well, no. As far as I can tell, she never took drugs and was always there to help people fight against them. She didn't have a medical condition either, and I'm sure you would've checked her medical history."

Marco leaned forward. "We've done that, but we do need to ask the tough questions. If we don't, we can't determine if it was suicide or something else."

Liz swallowed, unable to fathom that someone would want to kill a woman with a big heart. Someone who would never hurt anyone. "So you think she might've been murdered?"

"The body's being held by the coroner at the moment, but it'll take time for their findings." He shuffled and moved in his seat. "Did Penny have any known enemies?"

"No, none that I know of."

"And when was the last time you saw Penny?"

"A few days ago, at work. It was Wednesday, but she'd called in sick for two days."

"And what was her state of mind at the time?"

"She was fine and had a bit of a cold. Nothing major." A new tear fell. Marco handed her a tissue box, and she pulled one out. She wiped her nose and fought back more tears. "So when did she actually die?"

Marco cleared his throat. "Her neighbour checked in on her on Thursday and found her body then."

If only Liz had gone to see her on Wednesday, she might still be alive. A sense of guilt punched her in the gut. If she was suicidal, she would've known it, but

167

something about this didn't feel right. Who would kill Penny and why?

"So what happens now?" Liz asked.

Marco swallowed. "We need to prepare a report for the coroner who will investigate the cause of death and do their own research. It'll take a number of weeks to get a finding, but it has to be thorough and accurate." Marco asked a few more questions then rose. "I'll be in touch once I get more news." He shook her hand gently. "And again, Liz, I'm so sorry for your loss."

Liz nodded. "Thanks, Marco." He led her out of the room and towards the waiting area where Bella and Jamie were. They both stood up, shaking and crying, into each other's arms.

CHAPTER 38
GRIEVING

As Liz and her friends ambled towards Bella's car in silence, Johnny walked towards the entrance of the police station. She turned to Bella and Jamie. "Can you guys give me a minute. I need to speak to someone. I won't be long." She rushed over to Johnny who ignored her, putting his hand over his chin as she scurried towards him. She wondered why he was seeing the police. "Johnny, wait. What's going on? What are you doing here?"

He avoided her eyes. "They want to question me about something, but I don't know what it's about." Surely, he could be seeing the police for any number of reasons, but what? "Anyway, I better go in. See you later."

She held her hand up. "Wait."

He turned back around, a few steps from the entrance. "What is it, Liz?"

It couldn't be, could it? "Is this about my friend, Penny?"

Johnny's eyes looked blank as he angled his head. "Who's Penny?"

Before Liz could respond, Marco rushed out and ushered Johnny away, pushing him inside. "Liz, leave the investigating to us. We're only questioning him as we are everyone else." He waved to Bella and Jamie then led Johnny inside.

Liz looked to her friends for support, but they looked confused. "Thanks for waiting." They got into Bella's car, and Liz dropped into the passenger seat.

Bella turned to her. "Who was that guy?"

Liz realised she had to tell her friends the truth about Johnny. She knew they wouldn't judge, but now, she felt ashamed of how she'd strung him along without wanting more. "He was a guy I kissed a few times, but nothing more than that. He said he was called in for questioning. He doesn't know why. I mean, he's a good guy and works with Matthew."

Bella's eyes widened. She started the motor and drove away. "So he was the nightclub guy? The distraction guy?"

"Yes, he is," Liz said with a sense of shame.

"He is probably being questioned in relation to your car accident. It could be for a multitude of reasons, Liz," said Jamie.

"I guess so," Liz said.

Bella touched Liz on the shoulder as she drove one-handed. "Marco will get to the bottom of this. He's good at his job."

Jamie spoke from the back seat behind Liz. "Marco is an amazing detective, and he will not stop until he finds out what's going on, okay?"

Liz nodded. "I guess I shouldn't jump to any conclusions, but I'm aware of who might know more about this."

"Who?" asked Bella.

"Matthew, but I don't have the energy to ring him. I just want to go home and do nothing."

"That's healthy," said Bella. You need to give yourself time to grieve and not distract yourself right now. Do you want us to keep you company?"

"I know this is unusual for me, but I don't want to be around anyone right now. I have this anger that's threatening to explode inside me, and I want to hurt whoever killed Penny."

"I hear you, Liz. And we're here if you want support. A phone call away and we're by your side in a moment," said Jamie.

Liz peered through the window, her throat dry, and fatigue threatening to engulf her. It was too much. First, the damn medication that made her hallucinate, then Anne dying, and now Penny's death. Her head threatened to explode, and she couldn't wait to go home to relax and hide away from the world.

CHAPTER 39
CONDOLENCES

Liz lay back against the couch, wiping her nose with a tissue after crying into her lunch the next day. It was a lazy Sunday morning and she didn't want to go out. Her heart ached and yearned for Penny, who was an amazing woman and didn't deserve this. She refused to believe she had killed herself as she was not that way inclined and hadn't been depressed. She was sad about her mother, but she would never have hurt herself.

Her whole body ached and her skin felt splotchy. She hadn't showered this morning and had no desire to clean herself anytime soon. Her shoulders drooped, and she stared down at her hands as she brought up the beautiful memories she'd had with Penny. She was reminded of the time when Penny supported her and Bella at a masquerade party, when she'd listened to her terrifying details with Domenic, how she'd cried when her cat died, how she nurtured her with her controlling ex-boyfriend, and how they'd shared fun on spending sprees at the high-branded retail stores. She'd always been there for her, and now she had lost a pivotal person in her life. She was determined to find out who did this to poor Penny and started to wonder if Domenic had a hand in this. Did he want to hurt her this much?

She moved more comfortably on the sofa, her back relaxing. Clearing her throat, she sniffed then grabbed her glass of water on the coffee table. When her doorbell rang, she answered it with a deflated posture, one arm resting across her chest. Opening the door, she drew back at the sight of Matthew standing with a soft look in his eyes.

"I'm so sorry for your loss, Liz. I wanted to see how you were doing."

She swallowed. "How did you know where I lived?"

He tilted his head. "When I called you last night, you gave me your address."

She suddenly remembered their conversation, but everything she said and did now was hazy. She was struggling with her day to day tasks and couldn't get poor Penny out of her head. It had been three days since her death, but she'd only known about it for almost two days. "Come in." She swung open the door and invited him inside. He followed her to the couch and sat beside her. She rested back on the couch and folded her legs underneath her. "Would you like a drink or something?"

"No, I'm fine. But I'm happy to get you a tea or something else."

She shook her head. "I'm okay." He took hold of her hand and stroked it as his thigh brushed hers. Their eyes lingered until she broke the gaze. "What happened with Johnny?"

Matthew shrugged. "All I know is that he was free to go yesterday, but he didn't mention anything else."

"Was it about Penny?"

Matthew scrunched up his face, his eyes looking into the distance. "No, as far as I know. He didn't know her. I don't know what to tell you. I mean, we're friends, but I don't know him that well." He averted his eyes, fiddling with his hands.

"You're hiding something, aren't you? I can tell."

Matthew avoided her eyes. "Nothing, Liz."

She was itching to know his truth. "Please, Matthew, I know there's more to this story so just spill it." He shook his head. "You don't understand how close Penny and I were. We shared a history together and I loved her like a sister. She didn't deserve this, and if you know something, you have to tell me now."

"You have enough to worry about, Liz. I'm not adding to that burden."

She fought back her frustration. "If the roles were reversed, wouldn't you want to know? Believe me. I'd tell you so that it might help. Please, Matthew." She begged him with her eyes and his gaze weakened.

Matthew sighed. "Nothing that I can really tell you as a fact."

"Okay, then give me your observations. Your opinions. That'll do just fine."

Matthew lifted his head and stared deeply into her eyes. "I've noticed Johnny acting strangely at work. He keeps getting these mystery phone calls but tells us it's no-one important. Then he mentioned his wife takes medication, and that he sometimes buys it for her from prescriptions. I think there's something going on with him, Liz. But, until we have the facts, we cannot assume he's guilty of anything."

"What type of medication?"

He rose. "I have no idea. Probably for a common cold. Who knows? I should get going. And give you time to grieve. Again, I'm so sorry."

Liz wondered whether there was more to Johnny being questioned by the police. But unless she had facts, she wouldn't speculate. "Thanks for coming, Matthew."

"I don't want you to worry, Liz. The police are on your side, and I've got your back. The police will find out what's going on. They're pretty resourceful these days, and I'll be around."

She changed the subject. "So how's Camilla doing?"

His posture relaxed. "Great. She's going to see the counsellor more often and is managing her panic attacks better."

"And Mariana?"

His eyes lit up. "She is so clever for a five-year-old, and I love her like my own." He beamed. "I'd love to have my own kids someday."

Liz said nothing and watched his ponderous expression. She wanted children too, but maybe that would never happen. Given her track record with relationships, she doubted it.

Liz stood up from the couch, but she didn't want Matthew to leave. "Listen, why don't I make you a coffee. I could use the company right now. If you're free, that is."

Matthew's eyes lit up. "I'd love to, Liz." He followed her into the kitchen and watched her prepare coffee. The silence between them was comfortable.

They sat in the kitchen in silence, sipping their hot drinks while Matthew reached out and held her hand. She smiled then bowed her head, letting her tears fall gently down her cheeks. He moved closer to her side as he wiped away her tears and tenderly wrapped his arms around her. His hands smoothed out her hair that swept over his arms.

"Let it out, Liz. It's okay to grieve. Let it out," he said.

Liz's tears suddenly streamed heavier and she cried in his arms, wishing her pain would leave her.

CHAPTER 40
EASY PREY

Liz stared at the ceiling as she settled into bed that night. Domenic had been close to her twice now. He wasn't meant to be close to her after his prison release, but what was the point of calling the police? He hadn't harassed her, and he was in a public place.

Tossing and turning in bed, Liz sighed and placed her hands over her head, thankful to have her wrist fully healed and the cast off. She closed her eyes for twenty minutes but struggled to sleep. The digital clock displayed midnight. An uneasiness settled around her but she didn't know why. She slipped out of the covers and got out of bed, bare feet temporarily comforted by the softness of the carpet as she walked over to the kitchen. She turned on the tap for a glass of water, the sound of the water sounding loud in the silent darkness of the night. Prickles of fear tingled up her back as she ran through her sightings of Domenic. It unnerved her to know that he still lived in the same city. Why couldn't he just rot in prison? He didn't deserve to get out after what he'd done to her. She had lost her baby and was badly wounded because of him. She was lucky he didn't disable her permanently with that final beating, and the multitude of beatings before that.

She drank down her water while peering at the glass sliding door to the balcony. Liz was sure she'd locked it before bed. She looked at her sofa. The pillow had been out of its usual corner on the couch. Her heart began to race and her body shook. Had someone been in her home or was it her mind playing tricks on her again? As far as she knew, she hadn't ingested more of the Zyprexa. The police still hadn't tracked down that waiter from Bella's engagement party. Maybe the waiter knew about the police search and was in hiding. Maybe he was closer than she thought and would slip her the medication again. Shaking her head, she refused to think the worst.

Creeping into the kitchen, Liz picked up a knife and gripped it with all her might. Moving over to the laundry, she turned on the light and held her breath, but no-one was in there. Turning back, she headed into her bedroom, her hands sweating on the knife, and a cold sweat rising on the back of her neck. Her elbows pressed into the sides of her body and her shoulders tightened. She slid open her closet but it was empty. Bending down, she peered underneath her bed but nobody lay there. Maybe no-one was here.

A sound alerted her. Shuffling? Footsteps? It came from the living room. With her sweaty hands, she held on to the knife and headed back to the living room. A shadowy figure that looked like a man stood in a dark jacket, but all he did was stand there. She couldn't see his face as it was covered by a mask.

"Who are you?"

The figure didn't move.

She held back a scream and her heart nearly exploded into her chest. She gulped down breaths and assessed the situation.

"I have a knife, and I'm calling the police right now." She reached for her phone on the coffee table, and that few seconds of distraction made her easy prey. The intruder rushed towards her, a bat in his hand, and swung it at her face. The stinging pain made her light-headed as she fell back and hit her head against the edge of the couch. He was about to swing the bat at her face again, but she lifted up her leg and kicked the person in the stomach.

She ran for the door, but the man pulled her down by the legs, and she fell back against him. He swung punches into her chest, and she almost lost her breath. The knife! Where was the damn knife? She fought with her attacker by biting his cheek and he screamed out in pain. "Fuckin' bitch! You'll pay for that." It wasn't a voice she recognised. It didn't sound like Domenic's voice, so who the hell was in her apartment?

The shiny glint of the knife cast a glow near the couch. She ran for it, but the man kicked her in the back and she fell forward on her face. He lay on top of her back and pulled at her hair, the pain searing into her scalp. The knife was within inches of her, so she extended her arm but couldn't quite get it. With all her energy, she shifted her body and stretched out her arm until the handle lay in her grip. Picking it up, she swung it behind her, attempting to stab him in the arm to deter him. She missed and he wrestled for the knife, but she managed to swing her head back and knock him in the face. He fell to the side.

Liz swung the knife into his arm. The knife connected and the blood poured out. The intruder scrambled to his feet and raced out the sliding door and over the balcony. She quickly locked the door, gasping for breath then called the police.

CHAPTER 41
A POSSIBLE LEAD

Liz sat visibly shaking with a blanket wrapped around her on the couch. After a police officer took her statement, she looked over at Marco who was shouting instructions to other officers.

"It looks as if the perp came inside from the balcony. Let's dust for fingerprints on the balcony door first. He climbed down the balcony too. Not that it's too high, but it's still, fairly gutsy. And I guess at night, he's less visible." He sighed. "Check all CCTV cameras and canvas witnesses on all sides of the building. We'll wait on forensics so let's cordon off this area. Marco held a camera and took photographs.

Liz turned to Marco. "I bit the guy so you can check my mouth."

Marco beamed. "Fantastic, Liz. Well done. I can arrange a mouth swab for you. Do you consent to the DNA sample?" She nodded. "We'll also get a sketch artist at the station to do a composite sketch of your attacker. It's best to get it done today so it's fresh in your mind."

"Of course. Whatever helps." She took deep breaths as a stocky male paramedic attended to the wounds on her face, back, and chest. Bruises and grazes lined her cheeks and chest. "Now if you later feel confused or disoriented, or experience headaches, nausea, or fatigue, I want you to go straight to the hospital. Those symptoms are usually a sign of a head injury, but it doesn't appear you hit your head that hard. And you mentioned that the attacker didn't hit you across the temple, is that right?"

"That's right."

"Also, if you have any difficulty sleeping because of any pain, check in with your doctor."

"I will do. Thank you." Her surroundings appeared surreal.

Marco returned after checking all the rooms. "Are you sure you don't want to go to the hospital?"

"No, I'm fine."

"Okay, but you're staying at Bella or Jamie's place tonight in case the perp comes back. Doubtful, but you never know. It's best to play it safe."

"Sure."

He took out a note pad. "So the officer you gave your statement to mentioned the perpetrator was tall and solid in build. Any other distinguishing features?"

"No, nothing really. But he was strong, like he might've been trained well."

He bowed his head, writing further notes. "Great. Thanks, Liz."

She touched the edge of her temple, briefly closing her eyes. "You mentioned the waiter missing at your engagement party. I think the person who replaced him might've had the same height and build as my attacker. He was tall and might've been a bit bulky, but it was hard to tell because I wasn't paying much attention to his looks."

Marco angled his head. "We'll look into that, Liz." He moved away for a moment to check on the other officers and briefly explored different sections of the living room.

After forensics did a sweep of her room and found it untouched, Liz put some clothes into an overnight bag. She followed Marco to the police station while forensics swept her entire apartment.

***

Liz was driving towards Bella's house to stay the night later that evening. She described her attacker to a sketch artist and did a mouth swab to collect DNA of her attacker. This man had a bulkier build than Domenic and looked much taller. She couldn't see his eyes due to the mask he wore.

Marco was looking at possible retail stores that sold the mask within surrounding areas of Liz's home. At least, they might get a possible lead with the man's DNA.

Her phone buzzed. She answered on her Bluetooth and stopped at a kerb. It was Matthew. "Hi, Matthew." She tried to sound normal.

"Hey, Liz I was just wondering if you'd like to come to this bar over at the Docklands for a small birthday lunch I've organised for Camilla. It's for this Saturday night. Are you free?"

Liz hesitated, unsure about whether she was ready to go out after Penny's death and the attack. It was also a matter of ethics by going to an ex-client's social event. But then again, she could use a distraction, and Matthew was a friend. Perhaps the best thing for now was to be around people she cared about. Then again, she didn't have the energy for interaction. "Can I think about it? It's still hard with Penny gone."

"Of course. But if you decide not to come, I totally understand. I can text you the details anyway."

"I'll see how I go. Thanks," said Liz. She thought about how supportive he'd been over Penny, and yearned to see him again.

"Are you okay?" He paused. "Liz, I know you're still grieving, but this sounds different. Did something happen with Domenic?"

Liz sighed, resigning herself to the situation. "I was attacked last night, but I don't think it was Domenic."

"No! Are you okay? What happened?"

Liz recounted the incident briefly. "I have to go. I'm driving."

"Can I see you tonight?"

She couldn't handle her emotions right now. "No, sorry. I need to be alone. At least for now."

"Liz, can you at least think about the party?"

"I'll think about it, Matthew. Thanks for the invite." She hung up, her shoulders deflating. If only she could get a grip on her emotions right now. Anger, sadness, physical pain all rolled into one. The bastard had to be caught, whoever it was.

CHAPTER 42
NEW DISCOVERY

Liz headed towards the fire station the next early morning. The roller door lifted up as a few firefighters checked hoses, inspected fire hydrants, and other fire equipment while taking notes on a clipboard. A man at least six feet tall swaggered towards her.

"I'm looking for Johnny. Is he around?"

"And who might you be?"

She hesitated, wondering if Johnny would want to see her. "I'm Liz. He knows me."

"He's out back. Wait here."

She looked at other firefighters peering in her direction and frowned. She turned away, looking over at the street and took a breath. Hopefully, Johnny would answer her questions about what the police wanted with him.

She faced the fire station when hearing her name called out. "Hey, Johnny. Thanks for seeing me."

"What is it, Liz?" He stared down at his feet.

Was it more interesting down there? He had no reason to look guilty, and she was the victim here and had done nothing wrong. But maybe Johnny had done something wrong.

"I wanted to know why the police were questioning you the other day. I need answers, Johnny."

"Answers to what?" He picked at his nails as if they were more interesting than her.

She calmed her breathing. "Did they question you about the death of my friend, Penny? Did you know her?"

He shrugged. "Like I said that day, I don't know a Penny. Why would you think that?"

Liz stared at his eyes, which appeared to be telling the truth. But he was hiding something, and she was determined to find out. The police must've had a reason to question him the day they'd found out about Penny, and he was getting these mysterious calls. "The day we found out about Penny, you showed up too. I'd like to know why the police had a reason to question you."

"Listen. We had great fun, even if we didn't have sex, but it's done and dusted. I know you and Matthew like each other so don't bother denying it. But it's all good. I don't need another failed relationship." He chuckled. Why was he ignoring her question? "You were just a fun time."

Liz hid her disappointment, but she deserved it. Maybe his words stung, causing her to feel rejected, yet she didn't care about him in that way. Besides, she was the one that didn't want a relationship, not him.

"I'm sorry, Johnny, but I need to know what happened to Penny, and I thought you'd be more forthcoming."

He sighed. "Routine questions, that was all."

She stared hard. "But why did they need to bring you in? For what reason?"

The tall firefighter returned and called out to Johnny. "Listen, mate. We've got that electrical appliance refresher training in about ten minutes."

"I'll be there, Rowan. Just give me a few minutes."She looked past Johnny, hoping to see Matthew, but he didn't appear to be around.

"If you're looking for Matthew, he's not here. He's doing the training tomorrow and has a shift later tonight. But I've got less than ten minutes, so make it quick."

Liz nodded, deciding to disclose her recent incident. "I was attacked a couple of days ago, and I think someone is targeting me. So I wonder if you're involved in anything or know anything."

His eyes distended. "I'm sorry about that, Liz. Are you okay?"

"I fought the guy off, but you still haven't told me why the police called you."

He looked away, shaking his head. "That's confidential, Liz. My business." His eyes gazed into hers, and he tilted his head. "You're not saying I attacked you? I was working right here if it was a couple of days ago at night." His phone vibrated in his back pocket. Pulling it out, he stared at the display. His face paled. Quickly, he picked it up. "Listen, I'll have to call you back." He stilled. "Sure, sure. I will, man. Get a grip." His hands trembled as he ended the call and put it back into his back pocket.

Liz was curious about that call. "Are you okay? That call got you a bit wired. Was it a friend?"

He peered at his watch. "Hmm." He looked around. "Yeah, sure. A friend. I have to go, Liz. Sorry."

She nodded and watched as he headed back inside the firehouse, her shoulders deflating. What more was he hiding?

186

CHAPTER 43
A NIGHT OUT

Matthew was in awe of the Docklands Bar as he turned his head to look at the suspended, glowing light-fittings, and the array of liqueurs and alcohol placed around the counter. The ambience was dark and spacious and featured rectangular-shaped red leather couches in a corner of the room, and plenty of bench space to rest drinks and food on.

He greeted his firefighter, friends, Johnny, Rowan, and Pete. A few friends of Camilla's arrived, along with her kindly neighbour and adult children. He looked towards the entrance, wondering if Liz would come. She never accepted his invitation but didn't refuse it either. His mind flashed back to the way he'd comforted her in her grief, and how right it felt to hold her in his arms. He fought back the images when a voice drew his attention.

Camilla turned to him after greeting a friend. "So is Liz coming?"

"I don't know. She wasn't sure if she could make it, but she might be coming."

Camilla held a cheeky grin. "Oh, I hope she comes. She's amazing." She gave Matthew a wink. "You like her, don't you?"

He shrugged. "Maybe, but it's not going to happen. I'm a relative of a former client, so she might see me as out of bounds."

Camilla put up her hands. "No worries, bro." She wrapped her arms around him. "Did I ever say thank you for organising a new life for me? I'm a new person because of your support and help with Mariana."

He beamed. A warmth grew inside his stomach. "No, you did it all. And you have a beautiful daughter who looks up to you. So long as you keep up with the counselling, you'll do fine."

Camilla nodded. "I know, and...Speak of the devil." She rushed towards Liz who brought Jamie along with her.

Matthew's vocal cords knotted. He took a wide stance and had a bounce in his step while heading towards her. *Wow!* He couldn't take his eyes off her as warmth radiated throughout his body and his heart raced. She wore a fitted pink blouse, with a white shawl draped over her shoulders and black jeans. As he got closer, he smelled fresh flowers and soap. Her lips looked inviting with their rosy pink shade. Her eyes shone, casting a glow in the dim bar.

"Hi Liz. I'm glad you made it." He turned to Jamie. "Good to see you again, Jamie. I'm glad you both came." His face was steaming.

"Thanks," Liz said then faced Camilla. "Happy birthday. You look stunning." She leaned in and hugged Camilla then turned to Jamie. "And this is my friend, Jamie."

She leaned forward. "Great to meet you, Camilla, and happy birthday. Nice to see you again, Matthew," said Jamie.

Camilla nodded. "Hi Jamie. And Liz. Thank you so much for coming. Much appreciated. I wasn't sure you were coming."

Liz nodded then turned to Camilla whose eyes flickered from Liz to Matthew then back to Liz. "I'm here for you, Camilla. Let's say I'm here to monitor your progress in a friendly yet professional atmosphere."

"Hmm," said Camilla. "Those ethics are crap and don't need to be taken too seriously. Besides, I'm no longer your client so you're home-free."

She ignored the comment, her cheeks blushing. She handed her a small trinket box. "This is for you."

Camilla grinned. "Oh, thank you, but you didn't have to. I'll go put this on the table." She turned to Jamie. "Let's go talk to some of my friends, Jamie. Is that okay?"

Jamie nodded then gave Liz a strange look. Whatever passed through them must've been an inside joke. "Of course. I would be delighted."

Matthew ushered her over to the counter. "What's your poison?"

Liz's hands fidgeted. "Just a champagne, thanks."

He ordered it from the bar then handed it to her. He grabbed himself a bottle of beer and took a drink. Liz leaned back against the counter, her eyes roaming as if she loved the place. "So what made you change your mind about coming here?"

Liz shrugged. "I needed the distraction. I thought that staring at the walls at home didn't hold much appeal and decided I'd much rather interact with people."

He beamed, a magnetic heat between them. Liz must've felt it too, but she was fighting it by avoiding his eyes and sipping her champagne. "So does this mean we can be friends?"

Liz nodded. "Sure, just friends."

Matthew hid his disappointment. "I understand." She waved to Johnny and turned back to him. "So how are you doing after the attack?"

Liz pushed down the dark images. "I'm fine. I've been staying at Bella's place, but I think I'm ready to go back home. I doubt the guy will be stupid enough to come back. The police were checking out hospitals for any stabbing injuries, but nothing so far."

"The guy won't go to any hospital if he's smart." A slow song came over the speaker and Matthew put out his hand. "Shall we dance?"

Liz blushed and hesitated. She looked to Jamie and Camilla who were in their own private conversation. "I don't think so, Matthew."

He frowned. "It's just a dance between friends, that's all."

One dance couldn't hurt. She smiled and took his proffered hand.

They headed over to the dance floor. He put his right hand into hers and gazed into her eyes. His lips parted, and he couldn't take his eyes off her as they swayed to the music, his hand on the small of her back. His pulse raced as Liz turned away momentarily. He got tongue-tangled and mentally fuzzy. He lost awareness of his surroundings as his eyes bored into hers, his breath slowing down. Liz pressed her lips together, and his desire led him to place a strand of hair that had strayed, behind her ear. She blushed again and looked down.

"I want to kiss you so much right now, Liz."

She drew back as if he'd slapped her. "That wouldn't be wise."

"You look beautiful, Liz. And I'm glad you came." He lifted his hand and stroked her smooth cheek. He wished he could tell her how he felt, but Liz wasn't ready.

Liz looked away. "I wonder where Jamie is."

He chuckled and turned to look behind her. "She's being introduced to Camilla's friends. I'm sure she's being entertained."

As they kept dancing, he held her tighter against him and savoured her scent. All he knew was that he was falling deeply in love with Liz.

CHAPTER 44
AN UNWELCOME GUEST

Liz walked into the bathroom and straight into a cubicle, where she put her head down and shook it. Oh God, she was falling for Matthew but didn't know what to do about it. Not only was it partly an ethical issue, but Liz didn't know if she could ever trust in a relationship again. Was she taking a huge risk by believing in Matthew when, for all she knew, he could turn out to hurt her just like Domenic had. Her gut told her otherwise, and maybe she had ignored her gut with Domenic. No more would she go there, but could she learn to trust Matthew implicitly?

A voice penetrated the cubicle door. "Liz, are you okay?" said Jamie.

She ripped a piece of toilet paper and wiped her nose with it. "I'm fine." She wandered out of the cubicle, her posture limp. When Jamie stood with open arms Liz fell easily into them.

Jamie pulled away. "Is this about Matthew?" Liz nodded. "I know the ethics are there for a reason, but you can find a way around them. You can pursue a relationship with Matthew if that is what you want. No doubt that he has feelings for you, too."

Liz half-smiled, her throat constricted and dry. "I can't help the way I feel, but what if he has another persona like Domenic?"

Jamie shook her head. "He is definitely no Domenic. He seems genuine to me. And I must say, he is a lot more handsome than that piece of rubble." A scuffle sounded outside and Liz's skin prickled with fear. What was going on outside? "Listen, wait here. I will go and see what's happening."

Liz ignored her. "No, I'd rather go and see. I'm not fragile, Jamie. Let's go." With trepidation, she ambled outside the bathroom.

"This is a fuckin' public place. How did I know you guys'd be here?" The man turned around. *Domenic!*

He shoved Johnny towards the counter. Matthew, Rowan, and Pete grabbed Domenic by the arms and pushed him towards the exit, but he wrestled with them as he tried to make his way back to the bar. Then Domenic saw Liz and smirked at her. He ignored Johnny and the others and focused on her. "Well, well, well. Who would've known my first true love was here?"

Liz took a step back. Her legs turned to jelly and her hair lifted on her nape and arms. With her hands jammed into her armpits, she fought against her bodily tension. "What are you doing here? I'm calling the police." Jamie stood by Liz, her arm around her back.

He scoffed. "For what? Being in a public place? How the hell did I know you'd be here? But now that you are, we can get reacquainted. It's been too long, Liz. You and I are a team. We'll always be a team."

"Please go, Domenic," said Liz.

Domenic glared at Matthew. "What does that guy have that I don't? I can give you the future you deserve. Prison changed me." He turned back to Liz. "I promise you I'll leave after one drink. Give me a chance to show you I've changed."

Matthew shook his head. "The lady told you to leave, so leave."

Domenic clenched his fist. "She spread her legs for me first, mate. I'm not going. anywhere."

Matthew lunged towards him and punched him in the face. Domenic fell back into Johnny's arms. "Get the hell out of here or you'll get worse than that."

A group of them pushed him out when Domenic said, "I'm going. No need to call the police, you fuckers."

Liz's teeth rattled once he left and she blinked rapidly. She stared through Matthew and her heart fell deeper. He had proven he cared for her, and she wondered why she'd doubted it.

Matthew rushed towards Liz and wrapped his arms around her, stroking the back of her head. She fought back tears and stiffened as if detaching herself from the situation. He pulled apart from her. "Do you want to call the police?"

"No, what's the point? He didn't technically do anything. Besides, he's way too smart to do anything out in the open."

"And the police will get to the truth if he's the stalker. Please don't worry."

Jamie touched her shoulder. "Do you want to leave?" Liz nodded. "Okay, but you will be staying at my place this time."

"No, Jamie. I will not let that bastard drive me out of my own home."

Matthew expressed concern in his eyes. "Then let me keep watch at your place tonight, Liz," said Matthew. "Purely as a friend that wants to keep you safe."

Liz hesitated and wondered if that was a good idea. "I'll be fine."

Jamie pursed her lips and leaned closer to her. "You either let Matthew come or you can stay at my house. It's your call."

"It's not like he's going to be stupid and come visit me tonight," said Liz.

"I'll stay in the car outside your house as a stake-out. I won't bother you at all." He smiled reassuringly.

"Alright then," Liz said as she stood cross-armed, still rattled.

CHAPTER 45
SEXUAL TENSION

Liz took a breath as she stepped inside her apartment, waving good-bye to Matthew who stayed in the car outside her building. A sense of guilt ran through her as she wondered if he'd be comfortable in his car. But she didn't think that Domenic would dig his own grave and visit her place tonight. He was too clever for that.

Biting her bottom her lip, she walked towards her bedroom. She stepped out of her dress, put on a thin camisole and pyjama shorts then entered her bathroom. Washing off her lipstick and eye make-up, she shook away all thoughts of tonight's incident.

Liz got into bed and brushed away images of Matthew sitting outside in his car tonight, possibly ending up with aches and pains. As she slowly dozed off, a chain of dreams sent her into a deep sleep that eventually roused her. She jolted in bed and stared at the digital clock on the bedside table. Two hours had passed by since she fell asleep, and now she was fully awake.

Slowly, she got out of bed and wondered about Matthew. She strolled through the living room, opened the sliding door, and entered the balcony. She looked over the railing. Matthew was still lounging in his car, resting his head back. Was he still awake? The night was chilly, and it was ludicrous for him to sleep in the car when she had a perfectly good couch in the living area. She didn't want to treat him like a complete stranger, as he wasn't. Liz was also the type of person who liked to be kind and generous towards others.

Making the decision, she called Matthew on his phone. "Come inside. I'm happy for you to stay on the couch for tonight."

"Are you sure?"

"Yes, come in." She put on a dressing gown and waited.

Matthew smiled as he entered her apartment. He walked inside and followed her to the living room. She was aware of his breath down the back of her neck and ignored the arousal at his closeness. She cleared her throat. "I'll get some blankets and a pillow. Wait here."

Matthew nodded, his eyes lingering on hers. "Sure."

Liz fumbled with the blanket and pillow as she reached above the closet. Carrying them underneath her arm, she moved into the living room and set them on the couch. "I know it's late, but would you like a drink?"

"No, I'm good."

The darkness surrounding them was a little lit up by the outside light that cast a romantic glow around Matthew's face. If she was a painter, she'd be able to draw a beautiful, sculptured outline of his jaw, lips, and tantalising eyes. The way he was looking at her made her weak at the knees. Her back tensed up.

"Okay then. Goodnight." Her feet froze, a sudden sense of paralysis coming over her. This was silly. She could manage his charms and looks, and she needed to get more sleep.

Matthew leaned forward and kissed her on the cheek, his lips lingering. Liz's breath slowed down but she came to her senses. "Goodnight."

Back in her bedroom, her breath hitched at the sound of Matthew shuffling about in the living room.

She slipped under the covers. Heat surrounded her body as she thought about Matthew in the next room.

Closing her eyes, Liz imagined the way Matthew's eyebrows turned up when he was in deep thought, or the way he carried his firefighter's uniform, looking so much in control. She remembered the way his hands felt across her cheek, and the way he had twirled her hair out of her eye.

She tossed and turned in bed, unable to take her mind off Matthew. A sound in the living room made her rise out of bed. Standing near the door, she had her hand on the doorknob but was unable to turn it. Was she checking on him or did she want something else? Footsteps! She heard him walk into the kitchen and turn on the kettle, possibly making himself a cup of tea or coffee. When she had asked him if he wanted a drink, he'd said he didn't want anything. Was that because he didn't trust himself with her?

Slipping back into bed, Liz lay on her side and closed her eyes again. Her mind turned to Domenic and the way he showed up at the party. Did that mean he was watching her and knew she'd be there? She didn't believe it was a coincidence.

As she was falling into sleep, she got roused by a light cough outside her door. Soon she fell asleep with dreams of Matthew.

***

Hot damn! She looked so beautiful at the party, and Matthew couldn't stop thinking about her in the other room. So close and yet so far. He liked the slim curves of her body underneath her flimsy dressing gown, and it had opened slightly to reveal a tanned, smooth upper chest and a slim neck. He yearned to touch her smooth skin but refrained from doing anything she wasn't ready for. He had wanted her since the first day he laid eyes on her, and his feelings had grown stronger each time he saw her.

He loved the selfless way she'd helped his sister come off the drugs. He loved the way her long, dainty fingers touched her temple as she pondered things, and the way she held her body while walking with confidence and ease. She loved people, and had a gift in helping others and would gladly deny her own pain to ease the worry of others. She was one of a kind, and he couldn't help but yearn for her in the next room.

He eased back on the couch after drinking his coffee and closed his eyes, not wanting to pressure her into anything she wasn't ready for. But sounds in the night kept him awake. The sounds of cars passing by, the sounds of planes and birds, and the creaking sounds of the apartment. He tossed and turned but couldn't sleep when his mind focused on Liz. Her mouth, her captivating hazel eyes, her dark hair, and her slim, toned body that was every man's dream. The thought of her in the next room was almost too much to bear, but he had to have control. He eventually fell asleep with thoughts of Liz in his dreams.

CHAPTER 46
TRAUMATIC PAST

The next morning, Liz yawned and stretched. She rose out of bed, pulled on a dressing gown, and wandered into the living room. Matthew sat up on the couch and watched television without the volume on.

"You're awake."

Matthew smiled. "Hmmm. Couldn't sleep much."

"Same here." She tightened the robe around her when it opened up, showing her taut

stomach and cleavage. Matthew's eyes had lingered on her chest for a moment until she covered it with the robe. "How about eggs and coffee for breakfast?"

He turned to her. "Sounds great, but you don't need to cook. We can go out if you like. Just somewhere close by."

Liz nodded. "Are you sure? I don't mind making breakfast. I love the kitchen."

He smiled. "No, it's fine. I'd rather go out if that's okay with you."

Liz nodded. "Okay. I'll go shower. And you're welcome to shower after me if you like."

"Thanks. I'll do that."

Liz grabbed clothes from her room then headed into the bathroom, an awareness that Matthew was waiting in the living room. The fact that he was in the apartment so close by made her self-conscious as she showered. She imagined him in the shower with her, but she shook away those thoughts. Crazy thoughts!

Liz turned off the tap after ten minutes. She dried off, dressed and approached Matthew. After he showered, they left the apartment twenty minutes later and headed downstairs to the local cafe.

Liz sat opposite him after they ordered from the counter, and she watched other patrons eating big breakfasts and all coupled up. Only a few couples sat in the cafe, and the day outside was glaringly bright and warm for Spring. Heat fell on the back of her neck and brows, and she wiped the heat away with a tissue.

"Listen, I know you probably don't want to talk about it, but I'd like to know the full story about Domenic. You were obviously rattled by him at the club."

Liz cringed, avoiding his eyes, but Matthew had proven his loyalty when he saved her from the accident, and when he kicked out Domenic in her defence. He was a great brother to Camilla and a great uncle to Mariana. She also knew how he'd suffered at the hands of his father. "I want to know what we're dealing with here, Liz. I'm here to help in any way I can, and if he's the one that's hurting you, I want to get that bastard back behind bars where he belongs."

"I don't know, Matthew. It's hard to go back there." She hesitated. "But I'm seeing a psychologist who has encouraged me to talk about it more with people I trust."

He put up his hands. "It's all good. You don't need to tell me now, but if you'd ever like to, I'm here to listen." He leaned forward and grabbed her hands. "I really care about you, Liz. I've never met anyone who's ever given so much of herself to others like you did with my sister and niece." She smiled and savoured the tenderness of his strokes and his fixed gaze that spoke volumes about his feelings. "I know what it's like to experience trauma at the hands of a man."

The tall waiter arrived with scrambled eggs and toast for Liz and sausages and bacon for Matthew. He set them down on the table and left with a smile.

She was ready to tell him everything. "Alright. Let's eat. We can go back to my place afterwards, and I'll tell you the whole sordid story."

His eyes softened further as he gave her a reassuring smile. "I'm glad you're talking to a psychologist as I know it helps."

Liz nodded. "Did you talk to anyone after what happened with your father?" She forked the eggs and ate.

He frowned. "How did you know about that?"

She smiled reassuringly. "Camilla mentioned it as part of her assessment, but it was very brief."

He cleared his throat after taking a bite of his sausage. "I had a great social worker as a child, but when I was about twenty, I decided to see a psychologist who helped me deal with it when I got triggered. As a firefighter, you need to have a clear head, and I didn't want my demons to affect my job. But I wanted to move forward, too. Trauma like that doesn't truly go away, but you can learn to manage it. And I think I'm okay now. I mean, I'll have my bad days but we're still human."

"I'm glad, and maybe later you can tell me more about it. I only have a very scant outline of your trauma. But if you're willing, I'm here to listen too."

He smiled. "We'll see."

***

202

Thirty minutes later, they were back in her apartment and settled in the living room. Liz sat on the couch across from Matthew who was sitting in the armchair. He clasped his hands together and rested them between his legs as he watched her. She took herself back to that time with Domenic.

Liz was standing by the sink after washing the dishes. "I can't do this anymore, Domenic. I'm leaving." She knew she was taking a risk but she'd tried to leave him countless times before. Once, she had tried to sneak away into the night, but he found her and stopped her, the beatings quite severe. This time he couldn't convince her otherwise. She was damned if she did, damned if she didn't. Either way, he would try to talk her out of it. But she needed to make him understand. Maybe she could rationalise with him. She had her friends on stand-by once she broke it off with him. They had wanted to be with her when she told him, but she had to be strong and do it on her own. She refused to be a victim any longer.

Domenic tightened his hands and clenched his teeth. "What do you mean you're leaving?" His eyes darkened and he dug his thumbnail into his palm.

She fiddled with her back pocket, the pocketknife cold in her hand as she slowly pulled it out. She kept it behind her back. "I can't live with you anymore. It's not working out. You can't keep hurting me like this."

He gave a mocking laugh, quickening his pace towards her, standing within inches of her. "Nobody leaves me. Least of all you." He leered and smirked.

Liz made her way to the living room to maintain distance, but he followed her and stood over her. She could smell his garlic and spice breath. His teeth had yellowed from too much nicotine. "I'm sorry, but I don't love you anymore."

"What the fuck's love got to do with it? We're good together and you know it."

She shook her head and swallowed. "I can't take the beatings anymore. That's not a relationship. You can find another woman who'll love you the way I can't."

He grabbed her by the chin, glaring. He shoved her and she fell back against the couch. "You're fuckin' staying and that's that."

She rubbed her back, wincing in pain, but kept her grip on the knife. If he found out she was pregnant, it would be much worse. "No, I can't stay. I'm sorry. Please let me go."

"You're not going anywhere, and if you do, I'll find you."

She rose from the couch, losing all breath and ignored her back pain. "You can't convince me this time. I have to go and live my own life. You can find someone more worthy of you. It's not like you haven't cheated on me. Instead, now you can do it freely."

He stepped closer towards her. "You're the one I want to come home to. The other women are just good fucks. But you and me, we're solid, and we'll live together forever. I control you. Damn it! I own you."

"I'm sorry, but I've already packed and I'm leaving now."He charged at Liz with full force, pushing her hard against the wall and making her hit the back of her head. He smashed her head into the wall.

He lifted up his arm and slapped her. The stinging sensation was like he was ripping open her cheek. Liz raised the knife and stabbed him in the shoulder, but it was merely a graze as he flicked the knife away and it fell to the ground. He threw her against the couch and pressed her hands tightly behind her back. He kicked her hard in the stomach. One punch after another dizzied her senses and blurred her vision.

"No, don't hurt me. Please, I'm pregnant."

He laughed. "You fuckin' bitch." His brain didn't register what she'd said in such a psychotic rage. He proceeded to pull strands of hair out of her scalp. Liz's energy waned as she wrestled with him by swinging her own punch, but he stopped the blows. "Please, no. Baby. I'm pregnant." The crunch of bones as he swung one punch into her eyes, lips, and forehead and she drooped and almost blacked out. No, she had to stay awake for the sake of the baby.

He stood up and threw her down on the floor, kicking her in the legs, bruising her and grazing skin, even breaking bones. "No, check...my...bag...doctor's letter. Nooooo..." The last thing she saw after swinging multiple blows to her entire body was Domenic's expression change to one of confusion. He stopped to search for her bag.

Liz grounded herself back to the present. "It took me about four months to

recover from the fractured ribs, internal bleeding, and other broken bones in my legs. I nearly died, and I lost my baby too."

Matthew's face had paled as he squeezed her shoulder. "I am so sorry. I want to rip that bastard's heart out." His eyes softened. "A man like that will never change." He leaned in and pulled her into his arms.

Liz would no longer be Domenic's victim.

CHAPTER 47
A NEW BEGINNING

Later that day, Liz stepped into the kitchen after a light walk with Matthew. "How about a cheese frittata and salad for lunch? I also make a mean fruit smoothie."

Matthew was checking his phone for messages. "Sure, sounds great. Let me help."

"Okay, you can grate the cheese. It's in the top part of the fridge, and the grater's in that second drawer over there."

Matthew grabbed the cheese and started grating it into a bowl while Liz cracked eggs into a separate bowl. Matthew picked up sprinkles of cheese and threw them towards Liz, the cheese landing on her face. She drew back with a light chuckle. "Hey watch it, Mister. You'll have to clean that up."

He threw another cluster of cheese in her face. "Oops, that was an accident."

Liz hit him on the shoulder playfully and he gave her a wink. Once she cooked the frittata and prepared a salad of lettuce, carrots, tomato, and salad onion, she cut up kiwi fruit, watermelon, and apple then mixed it in a blender with yoghurt and a touch of honey.

They sat down to eat with smiles on their faces, devouring the food and savouring the silence and refreshing tastes.

Matthew wiped his mouth. "That was delicious. You sure know how to cook." He paused. "Given that you've done most of the work, I'll wash up and you can put your feet up."

"I'll at least clear the table for you." Liz picked up the plates when accidentally their hands brushed as they went to pick up the salad bowl. Their eyes lingered, and Matthew gently caressed her hand, which trailed up to her upper arm. Before she knew what she was doing, her hand brushed his cheek. Their eyes remained fixed on each other until Matthew held her hand and led her to the couch.

Liz sat awkwardly on the couch when Matthew joined her. He drew a strand of hair away from her eye and rubbed her cheek with the back of his hand. Her breathing turned rapid and her dry throat made her speechless. The warmth and tenderness of his skin triggered a swarm of emotions in her.

Matthew moved his body closer, their legs touching as he slid his hand over her thigh. He looked back up at her with hunger in his eyes. "You're beautiful, Liz." Leaning forward, he brushed her chin and kissed her tenderly on the lips. Liz returned the kiss; her yearning flared and she surrendered to it. Their tongues tangled in a slow-burning heat that slowly sizzled, but Liz pulled back a moment. What was she doing? Was she even ready for this?

Matthew turned away. "I'm sorry. Maybe I should go." They sat in silence for a few minutes while Liz pondered their close connection. Her body and mind wanted him, and maybe she could listen to her gut this time. He was a decent, loving man who cared about others, and it showed in his love of his family and his work as a firefighter. In her heart, she craved his touch and his love, and knew that she could trust Matthew completely. He had shown her time and time again.

Liz shook her head. "No, it's okay. I wanted you too."

He nodded but started to rise. "I'll go."

Liz reached for his arm and set him back down. "I don't want you to go, Matthew." She knew that her eyes spoke volumes.

He frowned. "Are you sure?" Liz nodded, her desire speaking for her.

Matthew lay her on her back and he lay on top of her, his mouth reaching for hers. He kissed her tenderly until again, they became hungrier, their tongues entwined in a frenzy of emotion. Liz's pent-up energy from many months of lust drew out of her. She pressed his buttocks tighter against her while Matthew kissed her around the neck and jaw. She moaned in deep pleasure as he pulled off her t-shirt and smirked at her black lacy bra. His hands cupped one breast then another until he unclipped it and took it off. He brought a nipple into his mouth and sucked and licked, intermittently watching her get aroused as she guided his face deeper into her breast. He sucked the other breast while his hand trailed her jeans, undoing the top button and pulling down the zip. He inserted his hand into her underwear and probed in between her thighs. "I want you to come for me, Liz. I imagine you'd be even more beautiful when you're aroused."

Liz was speechless, savouring his probing fingers that brushed over her mound as he pushed his finger deep inside her. His fingers circled her clitoris in a fast motion as he brought his mouth over hers again. Liz touched his manhood, feeling the hardness as she unbuttoned his own jeans. He led her hands back to his groin and moaned in pleasure. "Come for me, Liz."

She closed her eyes and enjoyed his handy fingers until coming to a climax. "Matthew. What are you doing to me?"

He smiled then took off his jeans. Liz pushed off her own jeans and he followed her to the bedroom. "Are you sure about this?"

Liz nodded as she walked over wearing only her panties. "I'm ready."

She took off the bed sheets and he jumped in beside her. "I'm on the pill."

"That's good," said Matthew as his lips and tongue tantalised her again while his hands touched her breasts and inner thighs, teasing and circling her mound. She caressed his manhood, soon hardening as he sucked and nipped at her breasts. His mouth trailed around her neck and down to her abdomen, kissing and caressing until he guided his penis slowly and gently inside her, the rhythmic motion causing her to moan again. His own arousal soon overpowered hers as he came inside her, with Liz climaxing soon after. She was satiated and, in that moment, needed nothing else.

***

After spending an hour in each other's arms, making small talk and savouring the comfortable silence between them, Matthew rose and dressed quickly. "I have to get home and get ready for a shift. It's been a great couple of days with you, Liz. I hope you have no regrets."

Liz smiled. "No regrets. And you?" She exposed her breasts while holding the sheet down to her stomach.

He laughed, leaning forward and caressing her breast. "You keep exposing yourself like that, and I'll never leave here." His eyes turned serious. "But no regrets. Can I call you tomorrow?"

Liz nodded. "I'd like that, and take care at work. You're in a high-risk job."

"Always, but I've done this for years and I'm a pro. Nothing to worry about." He gave her a reassuring smile. "I've spoken to Marco, and he's organising temporary surveillance on your apartment. Once that stops, they'll have a car patrolling the area until they catch this guy who attacked you."

Her heart warmed. "Thanks, Matthew, but he won't come back again. I'm good."

He lay on top of her, fully dressed when his tongue delved into her mouth and kissed her hungrily again. She reciprocated until he pulled back. "I'm going before you make me stir crazy, woman." He winked. "I'll talk to you tomorrow."

"I look forward to it." He rushed out the door to avoid further temptation, she assumed, and suddenly hated the solitude in her room. Did she miss him already?

CHAPTER 48
A BUSINESS PROPOSAL

Liz walked with Gabriella towards Southgate on Monday when Gabriella answered her phone. She fished it out of her back jeans pocket and paled when looking at the display.

Liz tilted her head. "Is everything okay?"

Gabriella turned to Liz. "It's Domenic again."

Liz was tempted to tell her to not reply, but why aggravate him when Gabriella could get answers. "Reply. Put it on speaker. See what he wants. If he keeps ringing, change your number."

Gabriella nodded and put the phone on speaker, as they stopped mid-way towards the restaurants. "What do you want?"

"I heard on the grapevine that you're working with Liz?"

Gabriella frowned. "And how do you know that? Are you stalking Liz?"

He chuckled. "Come on, love. I only want what's best for you, and Liz has issues. She needs psychological help. I never hurt her the way she said I did in court. It was a huge misunderstanding."

"What the hell do you want from me?"

"I want a relationship, Gabi. Visiting me twice in prison was hardly a way for you to get to know me. I just want my girl back."

She scoffed. "After what you did to Mum, how can I ever trust you?"

"I've changed. I admit we had our damn issues, but I loved your mother at one time. But that's in the past, baby. I just want us to be father and daughter again. Give me a chance."

She shook her head. "No, just leave me alone. Stop ringing me."

"Please, Gabi. I love you, girl. And I know you still hold a grudge against me for what happened with Frances. It was an accident. I had nothing to do with her death."

Liz's stomach clenched, curious. *Who was Frances?*

Gabriella's face became ashen. "I have to go. Don't call me again. We've been over for more than ten years." She hung up before he could reply and avoided Liz's eyes. "We're going to be late meeting Nick."

They increased their pace until reaching the Italian restaurant. "Who's Frances?"

Gabriella rushed inside. "I'll tell you next time." Her eyes brightened at the sight of her boyfriend sitting at a corner table.

Liz looked around at the full restaurant, the hectic pace of waiters dodging people entering and exiting their seats, causing loud shuffles. Smells of basil, cumin, and mint permeated the surrounds and, in spite of feeling sick about Domenic, she felt hungry.

Gabriella leaned in and kissed Nick quickly on the lips. Liz shook his hand. He wore tight, ripped blue jeans and a bright gold necklace over a loose t-shirt.

"Good to see you again, Nick. Sorry, we're a bit late."

"Not a problem. I have the afternoon free, but you guys no doubt need to return to work." The waiter arrived and took their orders of two varieties of pizza to share and drinks.

After small talk, Nick smiled. "The women's refuge should be ready in the next couple of weeks. The place will have communal showers and a working kitchen for meals. And there's even space to eat that's separate from the kitchen. I think space is important, so there are lots of windows and sunlight. We need to brighten up their day. Later on, I might think about expanding into offering career counselling or general counselling. One thing at a time. I guess the priority is getting young people off the streets. But I need your help with finding volunteers to work in the shelter and getting these people you work with interested. I am marketing the service to your clients."

Liz was in awe of this venture. "This is a huge job. I mean, you need insurance, tax exemptions, the financial backing to keep it operating, a business licence. How have you financed it so far?"

Nick beamed. "Well, luckily for me I was able to get another non-profit company to fund it, and that'll keep going provided it all goes well. The website's almost done too as I'll need to market that too. I plan to speak to the local media about the shelter, and I think I should be able to get food donations from grocery stores."

Liz nodded. "I'll talk to my new manager at work. Have you got a business plan or a mission statement?"

He handed Liz a thick document in a manila folder. "Everything's in there."

Gabriella intervened. "Where were you when I was a kid? My mum and I could've used your shelter when we were trying to leave my dad."

Nick's eyes softened as he stroked Gabriella's cheek. "Darling. I'm sorry, I wish I knew you back then

214

and had this idea as a teenager." He turned to Liz. "I know your history with Domenic too, and if ever you need my help, don't hesitate to ask. You see, my poor mother had to leave my abusive dad. It's hard to do but possible. These women's shelters can help women get out of danger and hopefully reduce the amount of deaths. It's so widespread, it's scary."

Liz was speechless as she flicked through the papers in her hand, amazed by the hefty amount of work it took to open a women's refuge. He was an angel brought down to Earth.

CHAPTER 49
THE PERPETRATOR

Two nights later, Liz entered the police station and met Marco who led her to an interview room. She stared at the evidence bag. "That's the mask my attacker wore. I mean, it looked exactly like that one." She flinched at the memory of the attack. "Is he the guy who hurt me?"

Marco nodded. "It appears that way. The results of the DNA showed his identity, and with pure luck, he was arrested a number of years ago for armed robbery and assault. The mask was found in his bag. Apparently, he took over on a casual basis at the cafe near your home for the past few months to get close to you. The medication he used to drug you was also found in his bag. He stated he was ordered to drug you with your usual coffee." Marco took a deep breath.

Liz couldn't believe that this sweet-looking young man who worked at the cafe near her place had hurt her this way. "Who is he?"

"He's a low-level scumbag for hire who got himself into the prostitution business. Some of these women are aged between fourteen and sixteen years. The man's been arrested for running an unlicensed and under-aged escort service. We're looking at a possible partner in the business, but we've had witnesses mention Anne was offering sexual services on the streets. That's why we think there could be a connection here. She might've known too much, and someone was afraid she'd speak up.

Liz nodded. "She was scared and wanted to run from the business. I'm sure of it."

She succumbed to nausea, thinking about those poor girls. "Have you found the girls?" Her heart went out to those innocent girls, no doubt lost and alone in the world.

"Not yet. We have a problem."

Liz shifted her posture, frowning. "And what's that?"

Marco moved in his seat. "He won't give up who he works for in the business, so we'll have to keep working on him. Using our bad cop, good cop routine and develop a rapport so that we'll hopefully get something out of him. Or if we threaten him with fuller charges, he might give them up too."

Liz huffed, wanting this whole damn thing to be over. "So tell me about the waiter at your engagement party."

"This guy said he was working at our engagement party, but he won't say how he knew about it. He replaced the original waiter who was supposed to work at the party that night. The waiter was reported missing by his family, but we located him. Apart from being shaken up, physically he was fine." He cleared his throat. "And this man that attacked you said that the first time he slipped you the Zyprexa was the night of the party. He put it in the wine and the slice of cake you had. He was ordered to drug you over several days, for reasons unknown. Maybe to let your guard down and basically have control over you. He is not telling us about anyone else at this stage."

A chill ran down her spine as she briefly closed her eyes. She squeezed her hands tightly together, shaking her head at the thought. "Does the actual waiter know anything?"

Marco sighed. "No, he doesn't."

Liz swallowed. "Do you think this guy's a killer?"

"That's the thing," Marco said. "He denies killing anyone but admits to attacking you in your home and drugging you." He cleared his throat. "I'm inclined to believe him. He has a stab wound that corroborates the attack." He checked his watch. "I don't think he's a killer, Liz. And I don't believe he intended to kill you, but to scare you for whatever reason. We're not sure of the motive."

She rested her arms on the table and bowed her head. "So could it have been Domenic who killed Anne and Penny?"

"The Forensics team are investigating." He paused. "We're back-tracking from that night for possible witnesses." He took a breath. "Would you know of anyone else, other than Domenic, who might have a grudge against you?"

Liz peered into the distance. "No, no-one I can think of."

He gave her a reassuring smile. "If you think of something from your past, let me know."

Liz leaned forward. "Do you think that whoever killed Penny is connected to all the other murders?"

Marco avoided her eyes for a moment. "Given there's medication involved and other things that seemingly match, Tim and I believe that this is all connected. She might've got too close to something."

Liz angled her head. "What other things match?"

Marco sighed. "There's only so much I can tell you related to your case as a civilian, so just trust the system. And don't go rushing over to Domenic to demand answers, as he's very dangerous. If he was involved in the murder of these women, then he's not done with you. He might escalate, so you need to be vigilant and not go anywhere on your own. Promise me that, Liz."

"Fine, I promise." She hesitated. "Have there been any other murders similar to Penny's circumstances?"

Marco ignored her question, which meant he had something to hide. "I'll continue to have an officer patrol your street, but maybe Bella or Jamie could stay with you for a while until this is sorted out. We'll try hard to get this perpetrator to tell us who he's working with, but have your eyes and ears open."

Liz nodded. "Of course, and thanks Marco." He walked her out of the police station, when Liz turned back to him. "Please keep me informed."

Marco's eyes darkened. "Of course." He looked past her into the distance. "Stay safe. I'll be in touch, Liz."

As Liz wandered away towards her car, her legs wobbled beneath her like jelly. This man who attacked her had to be working with Domenic, but did Domenic have an alibi that night? He was the only person who had a grudge against her, but it was his fault she'd lost the baby. If she hadn't lost the baby, she'd have a ten-year-old child by now. Her grief was constant, and each time she saw a young child she imagined that child to be hers. But she trusted in Marco and he would get to the truth. Domenic's luck was running out, and she was ready to fight if he wanted to escalate things.

CHAPTER 50
A NEW INSIGHT

The following Friday night, Liz walked hand in hand through the Botanical Gardens with Matthew. The breeze was noticeably warm and dry as it blew Liz's hair in all directions, her shoulders brushing with Matthew's. She gazed out at the river with its overhanging trees, causing reflections to line the rippling water. The river evoked a sense of calm within her and of going with the flow of life in normal circumstances. It was what she needed in this moment with the man she cared about.

The scent of an array of plants, along with herbs and fresh flowers filled her senses as she took in Matthew's scent of spice and musk. He stopped in his tracks and faced her, rubbing the palms of her hands. "I'm glad I've got the next couple of days off between long shifts. It's great to relax with you, Liz."

She blushed and turned away momentarily, her heart beating at a rapid pace. "I'm glad you chose to spend part of that time with me. How are Camilla and Mariana?"

"Great. Camilla's got a job in a cafe, and she's studying youth work part-time. She'd like to work with homeless youths and give them a fighting chance, she says."

Liz chuckled. "I'm so happy for her. She's come a long way."

"And Mariana's loving preschool and fighting fit. Tomorrow, they want me to spend time with them so you don't mind, do you?"

She shook her head. "Of course not. They're your family."

"And so precious to me. I can't let Camilla suffer the way she did when we were young." He averted her eyes. His body stilled before her.

Liz knew that his father was violent and hurt her mother, but she didn't know at what level of violence. "Matthew, I know a bit of your story from what Camilla told me, but are you comfortable telling me your side of it? I know you were pretty young.?" He didn't respond. "Forget I asked anything. It's none of my business. I'm sorry." She turned away.

He pulled her chin towards him, leaning in for a chaste kiss. "No, you're part of my life now and I want to tell you."

They moved over to a bench, holding hands as they sat side by side among the billowing trees that reminded her of remaining grounded in times of pain. The trees around her kept her shaded from pain, keeping her resilient and strong, and she had the feeling she'd need to be sturdy for his story.

He caressed the tips of her fingers, his hands trailing the top of her hand. "I was ten years old when it happened. My mother was badly beaten by my father with not only his fists but a tyre iron. I heard the noise from upstairs, but never had it been that bad between them before. He'd often punch her once or twice and leave it at that, but that night was different. Something happened. He was enraged like a caged wild animal. It was as if he'd suddenly been let free with little control." He swallowed. "Anyway, I came down the stairs and my father brought the tyre iron down on her legs." He blinked a few times. "Then her stomach." His eyes were glazed. "And finally, her face. It happened so fast, and I had to protect my mother. I couldn't let her die at the hands of that bastard. I had to save her, and Camilla was in a corner of her bedroom, crying and covering her ears. She was only six and was always scared. She shouldn't have gone through that. Every night, not knowing whether he'd pick on my mother's dress, or her cooking, or the way she folded his shirts. Everything was wrong in his eyes."

Liz squeezed his hand. "I'm so sorry, Matthew." She stroked his hair.

He looked into his lap and exhaled. "Like I said, I had to protect my mother, my family, my security. I had to help Camilla from all that violence and trauma. I had no choice." Liz waited, sensing that he didn't want to go on, but had to. "I ran into the kitchen and grabbed the biggest knife I could find." His breathing accelerated. "And I stabbed him in the neck." He turned to her. "I had to stop him, Liz. I had to stop him. He would've killed my mother. He would've killed all of us."

Liz leaned in and wrapped her arms around him in silence. "It's okay, Matthew. It's okay. You had to protect your family. It was the right thing to do." His body quivered but as she caressed his back, he relaxed then pulled away.

"He died on the scene when my Mum told me to call 000 before she fell unconscious. The bastard disabled her for life. He crushed her leg, bruised her whole body, caused internal bleeding, and disfigured her face. She had to have multiple plastic surgeries, and now she still struggles to walk. The surgery she's having is for her other leg because of the pressure she's put on it." He clenched his hands together. "Not to mention damaging our souls. My poor mum rarely goes out and keeps to herself. She refuses to live here with us permanently because she's afraid of people, particularly dominant men. She even lost a lot of friends because of him. He took away her mobility and her sanity, and I'm glad that bastard's dead. No-one has the right to treat any woman that way."

Liz nodded. "My God! What you and Camilla have been through. No ten-year-old should have been through that. In fact, nobody should have." She paused. "Did Camilla and your mum get counselling back then?

Matthew looked up at her but appeared distant. "We were part of family counselling, but they didn't have much after that. I had more counselling because I needed it for my job and for my own sanity." They sat in silence for five minutes until Matthew got up. "Anyway, let's keep walking and grab some lunch. I've had enough negativity for one day out. I'm sorry."

"No, don't be. I'm the one that asked you, and I'm glad you did. I guess we've both experienced violence at the hands of a horrid man."

They rose from the bench and headed towards the cafe for lunch. "You mentioned what Marco found. Do you know why that guy would attack you?"

Liz shrugged. "I don't know. He told Marco that he was ordered to do these things, but he wouldn't give a name." She suddenly had a moment of clarity. "I have to find Gabriella's mother. Make sure she's safe. What if he goes after her, now that Gabriella's rejected him?"

"You need to tell Marco." He paused. "It's not your job to save her mother."

She sighed. "I have to at least try. I wouldn't forgive myself otherwise."

As they entered the cafe with the bustling waiters, Liz pondered the notion that things were likely to escalate. What was his next move, and would the police stop him in time?"

***

Liz set aside her bag on the table after getting home from The Botanical Gardens. "Do you mind if I take a shower. I'm feeling sweaty after the walk in the gardens."

"Sure, I'll watch some TV." He had a strange expression on his face.

She headed over to her bedroom to rummage into her drawer for fresh clothes, then stepped into the bathroom. Her mind wandered over to Matthew's story and how they were kindred spirits, both experiencing family violence. She understood him. She empathised with his past just as he did hers. Was she falling in love with him or was she just vulnerable right now?

Pushing down the thoughts, she pulled off her clothes, then turned on the shower and savoured the warm sprinkles of water soothing her skin. *Oh damn!* She forgot to lock the door. It wasn't like she was home on her own, anyway. She was safe with Matthew here.

While lathering the soap on her upper back, footsteps sounded and the shower door opened. Liz drew back at the sight of Matthew's naked body as he neared her. He pressed her against the shower tiles with her arms held above her shoulders. He leaned in and kissed her hungrily, his lips smothering hers and their tongues flicking in and out.

"Oh Matthew."

He pulled away and brushed a hair strand out of her eye. "You're so beautiful. I couldn't resist coming in with you."

She beamed as he took a nipple into his mouth and sucked while holding her other breast with his other hand, caressing it gently. His lips trailed her across to her other breast as his hands stroked her abdomen, all the while making his way down to her stomach with his lips, all hot and heavy. Her arousal made her wrap her arms around him as she threaded her fingers through his hair. He moaned in arousal and licked her around her abdomen.

Matthew held her buttocks with his hands while he continued to kneel and moved his mouth down to her inner thighs, his tongue exploring her clitoris as he squeezed her from behind.

Liz pushed his head further into her mound as he prodded and probed with his tongue until she climaxed.

He moved his body back up to her face and kissed her hard and deep, pressing his body close against her. She stroked his penis that was hard and stiff in her hands. Tenderly, she caressed it, gliding her hands around the tip. He briefly closed his eyes as if savouring her touch. His fingers then played with her breasts and he kissed her nipples with hunger. Their bodies moved in frenzied motion as he trailed kisses around her neck. Liz caressed his manhood and guided it gently inside her. Their tongues tangled as he pressed his manhood further inside of her wetness until he exploded inside her with increased arousal. "You're amazing, Liz."

CHAPTER 51
A BLAZE

Two days later, Matthew smelled smoke. It was past midnight. He lay in bed and looked around his bedroom, his sense of smell strong, but he couldn't see any smoke anywhere. Maybe they'd left something on in the kitchen or was it coming from outside?

He peered through his window but no smoke or fire spread anywhere. He walked to Mariana's room and watched her sleep, stroking her across her fringe. He smiled, then scurried to Camilla's room, but she was sleeping peacefully too. Without waking her up, he sneaked outside into the living room and was hit by a rich scent of smoke, but it seemed to be coming from the laundry, situated on the side of the living area. He touched the doorknob and flinched from the heat. "No!" he said, hearing the crackling, roaring sound of fire. If he opened the door, things would get much worse. Quickly, he took off his t-shirt, soaked it with cold water from the kitchen and folded it underneath the slight gap in the door to hold off the fire.

Matthew reached for the telephone in the kitchen, but there was no connection. Something was seriously wrong here. He quickly ran into his room for his mobile phone, but he couldn't find it in its usual place. He ran to Camilla's room and shoved her.

"Wake up! Wake up. There's a fire in the laundry."

Camilla drew back and rubbed her eyes open. She quickly jerked then rose. "Call 000."

"I tried but the phone's dead. Where's your phone?" Camilla's eyes searched beside her. "It's always on my bedside cabinet but it's not here. What the fuck's going on? And Mariana?"

He shrugged. "We have to get out of here. I'll go get Mariana and you open up that window over there and get out."

"Please, Matthew. Be safe.

He nodded, then scurried for his life. He headed to Mariana's bedroom, bent down over her and lifted up her body. "Sorry, sweetie, we have to get out of here."

She half-opened her eyes. "What? Why, Mattie?"

"Ssh, I'll explain later." He stepped over to the bedroom window, but the winding knob wouldn't budge. It appeared to have been screwed shut. What the hell! Turning back to the door, he carried Mariana, who was fully awake now, and drew back at the roaring fire seeping into the living room. "Can you walk for me?"

Mariana nodded. "Okay." Her eyes widened and her body shook at the fire that was coming from the laundry, smoke burning through the door. He grabbed her hand and picked up her jumper. He found a used towel near the wardrobe and picked it up.

"Listen, put this jumper over your face to protect you from the smoke. We'll run to the front door."

He pulled her by the hand towards the door, then wondered whether Camilla's window had been screwed shut too. Running for his life, he changed course while holding Mariana's hand and quickly rushed to Camilla's room. He breathed a sigh of relief at finding the room empty. She must've got out. But when he tried to open up the window, it wouldn't budge. He turned and looked everywhere for his sister. "Camilla, are you here? Camilla." Assuming she'd made it outside before someone had screwed it shut, he prayed that she was okay and waiting at the front. Whoever was doing this was making sure they'd closed off all exits.

She nodded. "I'm scared, Mattie." She let go of his hand and ran back to her bedroom. "But my teddy. I want my teddy."

He knew he didn't have time to get her toy, but he had to make sure Camilla got out. She might still be in the house. Maybe she tried another exit or she could be unconscious for all he knew. "Get outside and I'll go get it. Go see if Mummy's outside. If she's not there, go next door. Hurry!"

The fire had burned through the laundry door and had made its way to the living room. As they rushed past the living area, Mariana and Matthew covered their faces and he let go of her hand. He watched her exit the front door then returned to her bedroom, fits of coughing overwhelming him in spite of a towel that covered his mouth. He scurried back into Camilla's bedroom and searched the other rooms for Camilla, checking every nook and cranny. She was nowhere to be found. He prayed to God that she'd made it outside.

Matthew moved back towards the front door. A wide timber beam toppled over him. The heat of the post grazed his arm and hit his right leg as he pulled it off himself. He winced at the burn. As he was getting up, he thought about the fire extinguisher and ran into the kitchen with a slight limp to quickly grab it. He gasped, realising it had vanished. No damn fire extinguisher. Who was doing this to them?

The blaze in the living room was burning through the couch, television stand, and bookcase, and was dangerously close to the kitchen. He coughed as his body almost shut down. He walked towards the front exit, hoping in hell that Camilla and Mariana were okay. A blaze of fire got close to the front. But there was a glass side door he could exit into the backyard. A shadow flitted past the glass door. He opened the door, but the shadow returned. A large figure wearing dark glasses swung a baseball bat into his face. *What!* He fell back and everything went black.

CHAPTER 52
A FIRE RECOVERY

Liz was inches within hitting a car as she turned into Camilla's house. Flashing lights blinded her as fire engines, an ambulance, and police cars surrounded the house. Firefighters were hosing down the front part of the house while other firefighters seemed to have gone inside the front door. Was Matthew in trouble? She could barely breathe as her steps led her to Camilla who was arguing with a police officer. "Maam, you can't go in there. It's not safe. Let the firefighters do their job."

"But that's my brother in there. You have to get him out. He saved us." She rubbed at her tears and had her arm around a weepy Mariana. They turned to Liz, and instantly, Camilla wrapped her arms around her while Mariana did the same.

Camilla had called Liz in a frantic frenzy, shouting out that Matthew was in the house and that she'd better come. She wasted no time in getting to the house, her mind ruminating about all the worst possible scenarios.

"What happened, Camilla?" She explained the incident as Mariana stared quietly at the front door. Liz's heart raced a mile a minute, and she prayed that Matthew was alright. This had to be her fault. She had no doubt that this was Domenic's doing. Probably a jealous thing, thinking that Liz was his possession. "He's tough. He'll be fine."

Camilla squinted. "I went next door after Mariana rushed out, to get my neighbour to ring 000 and we waited outside for the firefighters."

"And you didn't see anyone around here? I mean, how did the fire even start?"

Camilla shrugged. "I honestly don't know, Liz. I live with a firefighter, and my house is even more fireproof now than it was before. He has to be alright."

The waiting was the worst part. If anything happened to Matthew, she'd never forgive herself. She refused to think he was hurt, or worse; dead. He was tough, so surely, he knew how to save himself, but why didn't he get out of there with his family? What made him stay back?

Ten minutes later, the firefighters carried Matthew out on a stretcher. Oh thank God, he was still alive. He had an oxygen mask over his face. She rushed over to Matthew, but he was unconscious. She slid her hands over his forehead and kissed his cheek, a slow tear burning her eye. Camilla and Mariana touched his face with tears lining their faces. Turning around, she spotted Johnny and Rowan who nodded to her with serious gazes as they pushed the stretcher into the waiting ambulance. Camilla and Mariana rushed inside the ambulance after saying goodbye to Liz.

"I'll meet you at the hospital," said Liz. The ambulance put on its lights and drove away.

Johnny headed towards her with dark eyes and a sombre posture. "Hi Liz."

"How is he?"

"He's in bad shape. Inhaled a damn lot of smoke. He's got an injury to his leg and face. I'm praying he'll be okay. But it's hard to tell with the amount of smoke. Do you need a ride?"

232

She shook her head. "No, I've got my car. I'll head on over to the hospital. Thanks, Johnny. You guys saved him."

He nodded. "No worries."

Liz cleared her throat. "Do you know how the fire started or if it looked suspicious?"

He shook his head. "Hard to tell without a proper investigation, but it seemed to have come from the laundry and spread from there. We'll know more once it's properly searched." He paused. "Anyway, if there's anything you need, let me know." He walked off and helped the other firefighters pack up. They controlled the blaze, but the house had a fair bit of damage and no longer looked liveable. It would need extensive repair and a good clean-out.

Liz walked to her car with a slumped posture and entered. She started it up, her mind on Matthew. Once inside the safety of her vehicle, she drove along the road with an uneasy sense of being watched. She looked in the rearview mirror and in front of her, but nobody was in sight.

***

Liz headed to the waiting area where Camilla and Mariana sat with serious faces. "What's happening?"

Camilla gave her a reassuring smile. "He's still being treated so I haven't heard anything yet."

Liz nodded. "He's a fighter. He'll get through this. I know he will."

Camilla lay a hand over hers and bowed her head. They sat in silence for a few moments until Marco arrived. "Detective? What are you doing here?"

"Have you spoken to the doctor?" Marco asked Camilla.

"No, nothing yet. Still waiting," said Camilla who was holding her daughter's hand.

Liz stared at him. "What's going on? You didn't answer Camilla's question."

He prodded them over into an empty tearoom of the hospital. Toys lay in a corner of the room and Mariana headed over to a tea set, playing while he spoke to both women. "Listen, did either of you see anyone in the vicinity of the fire?"

Camilla shook her head. "No, I was with my neighbour and then we came out, but I didn't see anyone."

He turned to Liz. "And you?"

"No, no-one. Is there any reason to think the fire was suspicious or deliberate?"

"Hmm," said Marco. Liz waited for more. "We found a firefighter's uniform in the backyard. It's being checked for prints and DNA."

Liz gasped. "That's bizarre."

"I don't want to speculate at this stage." He swallowed. "The arson team will be doing a thorough investigation of the incident, and I'm sure they'll let you know whether it was accidental or deliberate." He turned to Camilla. "I would suggest you not stay with Liz for reasons I can't divulge. Is there anywhere else you can stay until you can return home?"

Camilla nodded. "A close friend of mine. I'll give her a call later." She looked strangely at Liz but said nothing.

"Anyway, I'll go chase up the doctor or a nurse and find out what's going on," said Marco. He ambled down the corridor.

"Something's wrong, Liz. What is it?"

"I just can't tell you. It's best you don't know for your own protection. Otherwise, I'd let you stay at my apartment. Sorry."

Camilla didn't press her. "All good. I'll respect your privacy. I'm just happy for your support. I mean you could be sleeping right now."

"Sleeping's overrated. I'll stay until we know what's happening."

They both sat on chairs, watching Mariana move away from the tea set to assemble blocks into a tall tower. Camilla broke the silence. "He's crazy about you, Liz. He talks about you all the time. And I'm happy for both of you. He has to be alright."

Liz smiled but said nothing. She was fighting the urge to cry because if he didn't pull through, she didn't know how she could live without him. She was all in now.

CHAPTER 53
A BLACK CAR

Liz roused herself from sleep at the sound of a voice a week later. She opened her eyes, disoriented, her neck aching from the hospital armchair. She looked up and smiled at the droopy eyes of Matthew lying in a hospital bed. He wore bandages over his arm and leg and had bruising around his face. He winced as he attempted to shift his body upwards. "Stop! I'll help you." She leaned forward and gently hefted his heavy muscular weight into an upright position. He jiggled his body upward. She stared into his blood-shot eyes. "How are you feeling?"

"Like I've been put through a furnace and beaten with a bat." His eyes darkened. "I saw a firefighter coming in, thinking he was about to get me out of there, but boy was I wrong."

Liz angled her head, wondering. Was Domenic working with another firefighter? Or did he pose as one? "Marco mentioned finding a firefighter's uniform. Did you recognise who it was?"

Matthew shrugged. "No. He was in a disguise. I thought he was going to help. I couldn't see his face, but then he hit me with a baseball bat. Did they find that anywhere?"

"No, nothing mentioned about a bat. Just the uniform." She pondered. "It wouldn't be Johnny, would it? Out of a jealous rage?" Liz said. No, that was crazy. He wasn't a suspect.

"I couldn't tell and I don't know anymore. My head feels like it's going to explode. I thought I was going to

236

die in there. I thought Camilla was still in the house but she made it out. I was still in the house when the fire got out of control."

She took hold of his hand. "I'm sorry, Matthew. This is all my fault. I shouldn't have got involved with you, and now your life's in danger too. So stupid. I am so stupid."

Matthew hid the disappointment in his eyes. "What are you talking about? If it was Domenic, then he's responsible for his actions." He winced in pain but kept a smile. "Do you really think that Domenic would pose as a firefighter?"

"That's what I'm thinking. They're checking the uniform for any evidence."

"I think he had gloves on so it won't show anything. He's probably too clever for that. And I guess they'll question all the firefighters too."

She turned at the sound of a screech. It was Mariana jumping up and down, yelling, "Mattie. Mattie. You okay?"

His smile was memorable as she ran and wrapped her arms around him. Matthew appeared to be fighting his pain but beamed at her anyway.

Camilla shook her head and grabbed Mariana off her uncle. "Enough, darling. Your uncle's in pain. Take it easy there."

She sat at the edge of the bed. "Sorry, Mattie."

He stroked her face, looking into her eyes. "It's okay, sweetie. I'm going to be fine. Nothing to worry about."

Mariana nodded. "The house's all burned."

Matthew looked at Camilla then at Liz with an air of concern. "It will all work out. We can get some parts of it built again, and it'll be brand new. Just think how much nicer we can make the house."

Camilla approached him, leaned forward and kissed her brother on the cheek. She put down a large overnight bag. "I managed to get into the house today to get some clothes. The bedrooms were thankfully mostly intact, but the living room, kitchen and laundry were completely wiped out. At least it's partly salvageable."

"And thank God for the insurance," Matthew said.

Liz stepped closer to Matthew on the other side. "Matthew if you guys could stay with me, I would let you stay in a heartbeat, but it's best you stay away."

Camilla gave Liz a questioning look. "You still won't tell me?"

Matthew stared at Mariana. "Liz, I think she needs to know. At least so she can be on her guard for anything suspicious. You have to tell her."

Liz wanted to protect them all, but maybe he was right. If she knew what was going on, she could better protect herself and keep her family safe. She eventually nodded. "Okay. I'll take Mariana for a walk while you tell her and be back soon."

"Thanks, Liz."

She grabbed Mariana off the bed and held her hand as they walked outside the ward and down the corridor. The tearoom was close by, so she'd take a walk with this gorgeous girl by her side. "And how are you doing, Mariana? After the fire?"

She shrugged. "Happy that Mattie, me, and Mummy are okay."

Liz nodded. "You must've been scared, but Matthew saved you."

Mariana's hands flailed. "He's my favourite uncle. And I got to see all those men helping Mattie."

Liz smiled. "I'm glad you didn't get hurt, but Matthew's a firefighter and he knows how to fight fires."

She frowned. "And I saw this man running across the road, but Mummy didn't see him. He helped Mattie later."

Liz suddenly cringed. "What man?"

"He was one of those men with the fire."

She stopped walking and headed into the tearoom. Luckily no-one was inside as they sat on a low couch with tea and coffee facilities lining the bench. "You mean a firefighter?"

"Yeah, one of those."

She swallowed hard, wondering if this was the break they needed to catch the bastard. "Did you see his face?" It couldn't possibly be Johnny, could it? Or was it Domenic?

Mariana shook her head. "No, I just saw him wearing those clothes and getting into a big, black car."

Liz rummaged for her phone out of her bag and dialled Marco's number. "Hi Marco, we might have a lead and I need you to chase it up."

After hanging up, she wondered if Domenic's arrogance caused him to think he wouldn't be spotted. He blended in as a firefighter. They might finally get evidence of the type of car Domenic drove.

CHAPTER 54
FADED MEMORIES

The alley was dark and narrow. A young woman looked up at the two visitors, tightening the strap around her wrist to give herself a shot. An older woman on the other side of the alley pulled down her panties while the man ogled her legs. Syringes and bongs lined against the edge of the dirty building.

"It fuckin' smells like a dirty rat 'round here."

The other visitor turned. "I don't care about that, you bastard. You better hope that kid didn't see your face." The woman pulled up her panties, licked her lips and approached.

They smirked. "She didn't, but if she did, I can fix it."

The other person smiled. "And how do you plan to do that?" The woman pleasured the visitor who moaned in arousal.

"You'll see."

***

Liz, Bella, and Jamie toasted a glass of wine in honour of Penny. They returned to Liz's apartment after attending her funeral wake at Penny's aunt's house. The turn-out had been huge, and her aunt had kept her memories alive through old photos and videos. Even her poor mother had come with a nurse, but she'd been confused about who Penny was. Thank God for small mercies.

Liz's heart almost got caught in her throat at her memories of Penny. "It was a beautiful service, don't you think?"

Bella smiled, deep in thought. "It was. A great tribute to Penny and her accomplishments."

Jamie nodded. "A woman who will continue to be cherished forever."

They clinked their glasses and sat in silence on the couch, listening to the gentle voice and rhythms of Celine Dion in the background.

Not long after, Liz buzzed in Marco who swung inside her apartment and grabbed Bella's hand. She kissed the back of his hand and followed him to the couch. Jamie and Liz sat opposite them.

"I have a small lead on the case," Marco said.

Liz leaned forward. "What lead?"

Marco lifted his shoulders and looked at Bella meaningfully. She ambled over with Jamie towards the balcony outside so that Liz and Marco could have privacy. "Domenic didn't appear to be at the scene of the fire. We checked partially visible footprints in the paved backyard and found they didn't match his shoe size. It was someone else who hit Matthew with the baseball bat."

Liz tilted her head. *Interesting!* "Could it be someone working with him? Another firefighter perhaps?" She remembered Johnny's mystery call at the fire station.

He cleared his throat and shuffled his feet. "We've questioned everyone but Johnny. He's taken time off work and we can't seem to locate him as yet."

Marco intervened. "What can you tell us about Johnny?"

241

Liz recounted her encounters with Johnny and how he got a strange phone call while meeting him at the fire station.

Marco squinted. "Matthew mentioned that Johnny was spooked over these secret phone calls at work. We need to establish probable cause to request Johnny's phone records, but at this stage there's nothing more concrete we can go on. But the fact that he's not returning my calls is questionable."

Liz hugged her body tight. "I feel like it's never-ending, Marco. When will it stop?"

Marco shrugged. "We're looking further into Johnny's background, but we are getting close, Liz. Very close." He ushered Bella back inside and Jamie followed.

"We're leaving, Liz," Bella said as she kissed her on the cheek. "I'll ring you later but call me if you need anything."

Liz nodded. "I will, and thanks again for your support." She turned to Jamie. "You too, Jamie."

Jamie approached Liz and wrapped her arms around her friend. "Stay safe."

He turned to Liz. "Okay, we're going. Take care." He moved towards Bella, and together with Jamie, they made their way back to their respective homes.

Was Johnny involved in this or was it someone else entirely? Liz started to wonder if she had it all wrong. Maybe it wasn't Domenic who was doing this to her, but what other enemies did she have? If she stopped ruminating about it, a fresh mind might give her answers.

CHAPTER 55
POLICE WHISPER

Liz walked into the police station a week later, searching for Marco as she approached the counter. A smiling policeman nodded in her direction.

"Can I help you?"

"I have an appointment to see Marco. It's Liz Randiza."

He gestured his palm towards the waiting area. "Take a seat. He shouldn't be too long, Liz."

"I've been here before, and it seems pretty quiet. Where is everyone?"

"An incident maam, but we have other detectives and police out on the road. Only a few left back here." He fiddled with papers then grabbed the phone to alert Marco.

Her head pressed down into her neck as she pondered whether Marco had a lead on the investigation. Maybe he'd managed to find Johnny or discovered who the guy was who had hit Matthew.

She approached the policeman again. "Actually, can I use the ladies' room?"

The policeman hesitated. "It's straight through that corridor, on your left."

"Thank you." She headed to the toilet with her back straight. The cubicles were all empty. The staff must've had an important case.

Once she finished, she headed outside and nodded to two policemen immersed in their own conversation. She remembered that Marco's office wasn't too far from here, so instead of waiting, she decided to meet him there. Walking towards it, she squared her shoulders when muffled voices arose. She stood outside, her ear turning in the direction of the voices. It was Marco and Tim in conversation.

"Dammit Tim, I can't tell her anything. She's a civilian, so why scare her any more than she already is?"

"But she deserves to know. I mean, she might have insight into that old case. These are women coming off the streets, taking drugs, prostituting themselves, and making money for these guys. But when they seemingly try to get out of the business and know too much, they're killed. Maybe Liz knows more than she thinks. We could try hypnosis."

"I don't think so. We'll have to dig deeper into who had access to that drug two years ago, perhaps look at other states. It might not even be linked to Liz, given that Domenic was in prison at the time."

"Maybe he's had a lot more help on the outside."

"Hmm, that's what I'm thinking, too," said Marco.

Tim sighed. "And I'm not talking about Liz's attacker. It's someone else."

"Back track on those drugs and move forward. We'll get him." He hesitated. "Anyway, I better go get Liz. She's been waiting a while now."

Liz quickly made her way down the corridor to avoid detection, but it was too late. "Hey, Marco. I was coming to meet you at the office. I needed the ladies' room."

Marco shook his head, his eyes dark. "And how much of our conversation did you hear?"

She shrugged. "Enough to know that someone's using drugs to kill women. Possibly

244

making it look like suicide."

He ushered her inside the office while Tim smiled briefly. "Take a seat." Marco and Tim sat across from her. "Listen, Liz. I don't appreciate you eavesdropping. Police business is not your business. We don't want this case tainted by any means, and when civilians find out too much, it can affect the trial of a case. And sometimes civilians think they're good enough to investigate on their own but end up getting killed." He stared hard.

"I'm sorry. I just wanted to meet with you in your office after going to the bathroom. It won't happen again."

He pursed his lips. "Damn right it won't." She waited with her hands clasped. "Anyway, we had no witnesses spotting Domenic or anyone else in the vicinity of the fire, apart from Mariana. Domenic had an alibi too, and it checked out. Also, we're wondering if you could look at a few cases from a couple of years back. Some of these women could've come across your service. And we'll need to possibly request case files if any of these are relevant."

"I'll do anything I can to help."

Marco gave her a reassuring smile. "Great." He grabbed three case files and one by one, flicked them open and discussed the cases, but Liz didn't know any of these women. These files were based on two previous women who had died of a suspicious drug overdose.

He gave her a deeper rundown of the third woman who had a connection with Domenic. "A woman had been writing letters to Domenic for several years in prison before she died of an overdose. Domenic even got special privileges with her."

Liz's stomach wanted to heave. "You mean sex? A room to themselves?"

Tim nodded. "Exactly that, so the question is, why would Domenic have her killed whilst he was getting his fun in prison? As far as we know, she wasn't a threat to him in any way. She didn't have any strong connections to anyone and was pretty harmless, actually. And she had help in a women's shelter, getting away from a violent ex-husband."

Liz dug her nails hard into her palms, wondering what had happened to these women. "And this woman died two years ago?" She peered into the distance. "The name doesn't sound familiar, so she might've not come through our service. Was she living on the streets?"

Marco nodded. "Here's what I'm thinking, Liz. The case with Penny and the last case is too similar to be coincidental."

Liz's spine chilled as she shifted in her seat. "So whoever killed Penny also killed this other woman, but for what motivation?"

Marco's eyes darkened. "I know we asked you this before, but I think we might've missed something then. We want you to trace back to a few days before Penny died. Try to get a handle on what she might've done that could make someone pay attention. Did she ever mention any enemies or disgruntled family members of your clients?"

Liz shook her head. "No, nothing. Penny was the sweetest person you could get."

"Can we try a brief relaxation exercise and see if anything new pops up?" Tim asked.

"Of course. I want to find Penny's killer." She settled more comfortably into her seat and soaked in Marco's voice as she brought herself back to the past.

CHAPTER 56
RESEARCH

Later that evening, Liz used her security card to access the building where she worked. The office was empty and deserted. Chills prickled her spine and her heart rate accelerated.

She mentioned to her new boss that she needed to complete case files on one of her clients and would also be researching the family's background. In actuality, Liz wanted to check the company database regarding the case of a woman overdosing on a drug a number of years ago. Once she got her facts straight, she would let Marco know and he could investigate it further.

The relaxation exercise didn't give Marco any leads into why Penny was the target of a killer. She knew that Domenic had to have someone working with him on the outside, but that man who attacked her kept quiet about others involved.

Liz rested in her chair and booted up her work laptop. She punched in items on the database, the clicking of the keys loud in the dark silence.

Keying into the database, she did a search history of the last five years but couldn't find anything. She filtered her search by typing in family violence, sole parent, and deaths by drug overdoses. Her heart pounded against her chest as she skimmed through a case note about a woman who had almost died from a morphine overdose. There was speculation that it had been an accident and not intentional. Her eyes searched the date of the incident. Approximately two years ago. She found an address.

Gabriella's address. It had to be her mother, Jean, who was affected at the time. What was going on?

It couldn't have been Domenic as he was in prison, but he had a connection with the other woman who had died of an overdose. It couldn't be a coincidence. He had to be involved somehow.

She turned off her laptop, grabbed her bag and headed towards the exit after entering the security code. It was eight o'clock, so it was still early enough to visit Gabriella's mother. The area was still deserted, but the dark of the night made her uneasy

A black station wagon sat parked near her vehicle. *Domenic.* Her mind was running away with itself. The vehicle was likely empty. But what if... Was he going to jump her from behind at any moment? Her instincts told her to move fast. She ran towards her own car across the other side of the road. The station wagon moved very slowly in her direction. Her heart hammered and her teeth rattled. Picking up her pace, she gasped and shivered and made a run for it, but her legs weren't long enough and her feet weren't fast enough. *Oh hell!* The car stopped and she turned. As soon as she clicked on her car's fob, footsteps sounded behind her.

A gentle touch on her shoulder caused her to gasp. She turned and took a few steps back, rummaging into her bag for a bottle of perfume and pointing it at Domenic. "Stay away."

Domenic chuckled. "Come on, Liz. I just want to talk. That's all. I won't hurt you. I've changed. In fact, we've both changed and been through some heavy shit. I understand what I did now was wrong, but that doesn't mean you have to turn me against the cops. Give me a fuckin' break."

"Did you hurt Matthew in that fire?"

He drew back, staring with hard eyes that showed no signs of recognition, but, then again, he was a great actor. "Don't know who you're talking about."

"Did you kill Penny?"

He knit his brows. "Who the fuck's Penny?"

"My friend who worked with me. Well, did you?"

He shook his head. "No, I didn't." He edged closer towards her while Liz backed to her car, fumbling with the fob as it fell out of her hands. It fell to the ground, and with her heart speeding a mile a minute, she quickly picked it up. It almost slipped out of her hands again. She looked back at him as he smiled and winked. "I'd like us to be friends. I promise I'm not here to hurt you. I've learnt a lot in prison, and you and me are carved from the same stone. We both like thrills, excitement, and rough sex. We'll always have that in common, you and I." He winked. "I miss you, Liz."

"Please leave me alone, Domenic. I won't mention you coming near me to the police as you know you're not allowed to be this close."

"I know you're not snobbish, Liz." He stood with his arms crossed against his bulky frame. "I know I'm a bit of a low-life who's been in prison, but I'm the man you fell in love with." He punched his chest. "Sure, there have been other women, but you're the one meant for me."

She ignored his comment. "I'm leaving, but if you hurt me, I'll go straight to the police." He peered at his watch. "It looks like you've got a pressing appointment. Why don't you get to it?"

He turned his head. "What are you doing at your place of work so late anyway?"

He was fishing. Her gut told her never to trust this piece of garbage who had always put on a mask. "And what makes you think I work here?"

"My daughter, Gabi, told me. Why she was so keen to work with you in the first place, I'll never know. But she feels a sense of responsibility towards you."

She shook her head, a chill permeating her entire body. "You've been spying on me."

He scoffed. "Of course not. Why so paranoid? I've spoken to Gabi and she mentioned it, like I said." He was about to leave then turned back. "You can never be too careful, so I understand your paranoia."

She opened up her car door and slid inside without a response, chilled. He angled his head and stared, then turned and walked away. What the hell was he doing here? Was he there to distract her for some reason? Or was it to show he still had control over her?

She sped off into the night as her hands quaked before her, wondering when the hell he'd be out of her life for good.

CHAPTER 57
A WORTHY VISIT

Liz's eyes flicked back and forth into the rear-view mirror, her hands grasping the steering wheel tightly while her chest felt like it was squeezing the life out of her. She had to make sure Domenic wasn't following her.

Gabriella and her mother lived in Coburg, and she knew that Gabriella would understand the reason for her visit. As soon as she turned into the street, her heart thudded loudly. She might have a lead here, one to divulge to Marco. Not that he'd be happy that she did her own investigating, but she had to do something. She was going nuts. It was her fault Matthew was in the hospital. She couldn't sit back and wait for Domenic to destroy her life. Whoever else was helping him, she would find that out too.

Stopping by the kerb, she looked out over the large block featuring a white weatherboard house with worn-out black roof tiles. The front garden was bare, and the low-concrete fence in front of the house needed paint. Towards the back of the house was a rusty steel shed that had seen better days.

As she ambled down the concrete path with its cracked, uneven ground, she took a few steps along the side of the house then made her way to the dented, timber front door. Ringing the doorbell, she waited and picked at her nails.

When the door swung open, Liz cringed at the sad woman before her. She had glossy, blonde hair, sad, dark eyes, a full mouth, and was petite in build. She appeared to be in her late forties and wore a faded t-shirt over black leggings. Her face and neck appeared to have old scars. The woman was attractive, but her eyes were deep pools of gloom and morbidity. Her good looks enhanced with those expressive eyes. She was holding a cordless phone.

Liz cleared her throat. "Are you Jean?"

"Who's asking?" She lay the phone on the ground behind her then toyed with her knuckles. The door remained half-open.

"My name's Liz. I'm a social worker and I work with your daughter, Gabriella. Is she home?"

Her eyes lit up at the mention of Gabriella. "She's out with her boyfriend, Nick. Did you need to speak to her about work tomorrow?"

Liz shook her head. "No, I came to see you actually."

The woman's hands clenched as she pulled back momentarily. "Oh no. You're Liz. Domenic's Liz? I remember you in Domenic's trial, but you didn't hear me speak though, did you?"

She looked behind her, making sure that Domenic hadn't followed. "Yes. Has he been in touch?"

Her teeth rattled and she had a distant look, placing her hand over her heart. "He came over once, but I quickly called the police then he left. He mentioned he was a changed man."

"And did you believe him?"

The woman shrugged. "I don't know what to believe anymore." She sighed, picked up the phone, and opened the door wider. "Why don't you come in?"

Liz's eyes roamed the narrow foyer as she made her way into the living room. A tall bookshelf stood opposite the television, and the carpeted flooring was frayed and stained. Her body sank into the green chequered couch while Jean sat across from her on an armchair, clasping her shaky hands into her lap.

"I read about your case two years ago, when you were hospitalised due to a drug overdose." The woman's eyes widened. "A friend of mine died from the same drug, so I had a few questions."

"How do you know that?"

"I have access to relevant cases with the company I work for." She explained her stalking incidences. "I've been looking at similar cases to yours. Do you know who tried to hurt you from the overdose two years ago?"

She shook her head. "No, I don't. It was like some kind of home invasion, but I can't remember a thing, and Gabriella was out at the time. Thank God. But she got home just in time to get me help." The woman's eyes drooped. "My daughter visited her father several years ago as he'd summoned her, and she wanted closure. I told her to visit, but that he'd probably never change. I didn't want to aggravate him either. If she turned him down, then it came from her and not me. I don't think he'd hurt his own daughter. He genuinely loved her and still does. But when she asked how he was doing and if he was lonely, he told her how he'd made a new best friend in prison, but she didn't see the guy."

Liz tapped her foot gently against the carpet, gripping her bag strap tightly over her shoulder. That had to be his helper. "Has Domenic been harassing you since that time?"

Jean pressed her lips together. "No, only that one time. The fact that he left me and not the other way around means he might not have a grudge against me. I've already spoken to the police and told them all this."

Liz frowned. "At the time I didn't know Domenic was married."

Jean smiled. "I ought to thank you for taking him away from me as I struggled to leave him. But I'm sorry for what happened to you. You were just a child. But now you think he's stalking you? Do you think he hates you for leaving him?"

Liz nodded. "I'm sure of it, but the police have my back." She rose. "I'd better go, and please don't tell Gabriella I was here. I don't want to worry her. Thank you for your time."

Jean rose. "You take care."

***

Liz sat in her car, parked a few houses away from Jean's house. She wanted to see whether Domenic had followed her.

After an hour, she got tired of waiting and was about to leave when a black SUV pulled into her driveway.

She flinched as Domenic exited the car and stormed into the house, banging hard on the door. He obviously didn't see Liz, but she could make out his tall frame as the lights turned on. Jean answered the door and he barged in ahead of her. Why was he driving a different car?

Liz grabbed her phone and called Marco. She obviously knew Domenic but was he going to hurt her?

"Marco, listen. You need to get to this address quickly. Domenic's pulled up in a black SUV and is meeting up with Gabriella's mother, Jean. Get here quickly."

Liz moved the phone further from her ear while Marco shouted. "What the hell are you doing, Liz? I could charge you for obstruction of justice. You cannot get in the middle of this investigation and taint things. Now you've probably gone and made things worse. I want you to go home and I'll deal with it."

A flicker of guilt filled her senses as she calmed her fast breathing. *Oh damn*! Did she make things worse for Jean?

CHAPTER 58
A CHILDHOOD NIGHTMARE

Liz greeted the policeman who was parked by the kerb in front of her apartment the next afternoon, keeping watch as she stepped into her building. Surveillance had been on for a while, then off, and now it was back on, as per Marco's instructions.

Not long after she entered her home, a policeman rang her mobile phone, asking about a visitor. It was Gabriella, so she explained that it was fine to let her into the apartment and met her outside.

Gabriella wore dark glasses and a scarf around her neck, in spite of the warm air. "Hi Liz. Sorry to bother you at home, but I have to speak to you about something."

"Is everything okay? And why are you wearing glasses? I can't see your eyes."

She hesitated. "I'll explain everything once we get inside."

Liz led the way into the elevator until it got to the first floor. She unlocked her door to the apartment. Something didn't look right with Gabriella, and she wondered if she'd been having issues with Domenic. Maybe he wouldn't stop ringing her. "Take a seat on the couch. Make yourself comfortable."

"Thanks." Gabriella sat with her knees hunched up and her head bowed. With shaky hands, she took off her glasses then scarf and winced.

Liz moved back, drawing back at the red marks around Gabrielle. "What happened to your neck?"

Gabriella averted her eyes. "It's not what you think. And it's not why I'm here, but my mum mentioned your visit last night. And it's okay. I'm not mad."

"I had questions about her overdose but she said she couldn't remember anything."

Gabriella nodded with tears streaming down her puffed-up cheeks. She lifted up her calves underneath her thighs and rested back against the couch. "That was a horrible time, Liz. If I'd been home a few minutes later, she would've been dead. But I didn't see anyone and the police never found the guy." She bit her bottom lip. "Anyway, I've spoken to the police about this, but I thought you should know too."

"What are you talking about, Gabriella? You're scaring me."

She seemed to be holding her breath and scratched her knee. "The reason I pressured Penny to make me work with you was because I had to protect you from my dad. I have no doubt he killed my babysitter, Frances, when I was about five years old. Fifteen years ago, she reported him to the police about her witnessing his abuse towards my Mum as she was too scared to report him. After that, Frances wanted us to leave with her, to some hotel as she knew she wouldn't be safe at home. Her brother and mother told her to leave so she stayed in the hotel, even though she wanted to stay home. I never met her family, but Frances's brother—I think his name was Bryce—he had gang-type friends. He said he'd make sure that their mum was safe, should Domenic turn up at her house."

"And did he?"

Gabriella nodded. "But he didn't seem interested in hurting them, even if Bryce's gang friends were there.

He was determined to find Frances, and I believe that he eventually found her."

Liz's hands turned numb and a tension in the back of her head made her wince. "And what makes you think he got to her?"

Gabriella fought back tears. She bowed her head. Both her hands rested on either side of her head. She shook it as if trying to clear her head. "It was all my fault. When he couldn't find her at home, he forced me to tell him where she was. He said he wanted to make sure she was okay, as he didn't think she'd be safe in a hotel on her own. She stayed in the hotel for a couple of days, thinking my mum might change her mind. I gave him the name of the hotel and a few days later, she was found beaten to death. Her tongue was cut out after she died like someone wanted to silence her for good." The tears streamed out and her eyes looked hazy and tired. "It was all my fault she died. If I didn't give him the name, she might still be alive."

Liz shifted her body on the couch and pulled Gabriella into her arms. "This is not your fault. You were only a child. If it was your dad, he would've found her eventually. He was always too smart for his own good. You were only five, so put that idea out of your head."

Gabriella pulled apart from her. "I know you're right, but it still hurts, you know? It hurts that he's out of prison now and getting away with her murder. It was bad enough to hurt you and mum, but I have no doubt he killed Frances. God knows how many other women he's killed too."

Liz squirmed. "It will all work out in the end, Gabriella." She sighed. "But your mum thinks that your dad loves you and wouldn't hurt you. Do you believe that?"

She shrugged. "I honestly don't know." She fought back tears. "All I do know is that he's angry that I don't want to see him. And he's called a few times, but I've now blocked his number."

"Did you tell him where you work, and that you work with me now?"

Gabriella shook her head. "No, I didn't tell him anything about my life." She got up. "Anyway, I promised my mum I'd take her out to dinner tonight. I have to go."

Liz followed her. "Wait up, Gabriella. How did you get those red marks around your neck?" Gabriella peered into the ground, shifting her feet. "Please tell me. It's okay."

"It was my father. I got home, probably not long after you left, according to my mum. And I was so angry by the way he was talking to her. So demeaning. I called him every name under the sun and he lost it. But only for a minute. The police eventually arrived, but they missed him by a few minutes."

Liz stroked her on the shoulder. "He hit you?" Gabriella nodded and fell into Liz's arms, crying incessantly.

Liz's body quaked as goosebumps penetrated her skin. He hit his own daughter, and if he was capable of that, he was capable of anything.

Domenic had always been a manipulator and liar. If he had murdered that poor woman, then Liz was in a lot more danger than she thought.

CHAPTER 59
DEVASTATING NEWS

Matthew was at the firehouse on a Tuesday afternoon. He returned from a factory fire with no casualties. All safe. He turned to Johnny who was sipping coffee in the kitchen. "So are we okay? With Liz, I mean?"

Johnny hit him playfully across the shoulder. "Listen, mate. Water under the bridge. She was a bit of fun, nothing serious. We only kissed a couple of times. That was it." He changed the subject. "Anyway, you've recovered well."

He flashed back to the fire. "Yeah, I had some good time off, I guess."

Johnny nodded. "So what did the arson investigators find out? What was the source of the fire?"

Matthew swallowed, wondering if Camilla accidentally caused the fire. "It was one of Camilla's candles sitting on a cabinet in the laundry. But she claimed to have never lit the candle. She would never have left a candle on a wooden cabinet. My guess is that whoever hit me with the bat was the one that started the fire." A sense of guilt permeated his bones, as he'd wondered if Johnny was the culprit who had hurt him. How well did he even know Johnny?

"Sorry about that. Any idea who it might be?"

Matthew shrugged. "Possibly Liz's ex-boyfriend but we can't be sure."

Rowan and other firefighters piled in and helped themselves to freshly made bread that had been baked by Pete who loved to cook. Matthew grabbed one and bit into the steaming bread, savouring the softness and moisture as it melted in his mouth. It was like eating a cloud.

His mind was on Liz. He hadn't seen her much lately, and she mentioned how she was busy at work. He wondered if she was lying. She was up to something, and whenever he called her on it, she mentioned being busy. He missed her like crazy, and he wanted to make sweet love to her again. He couldn't get her gorgeous face out of his head. He dreamed about her every night, and she distracted his mind from other things. Maybe tonight he'd surprise her.

But this ex-boyfriend of hers was a big problem, and he wondered if he was the one who orchestrated the fire.

His phone buzzed in his pocket. Retrieving it, he hoped it was Liz. It was Camilla. "Hey Camilla. What's up?"

She shouted out. "Mariana's missing. I've called the police and they're looking, but I'm scared."

He barely breathed, the men around him staring. "What happened?"

"I went to pick her up from school but she wasn't there. The teacher told me that she smiled at the person picking her up, but they couldn't remember what she looked like. Even her name."

"A woman picked her up?"

"Yeah, and I called all my friends and her friends' mothers, but nobody had picked her up. Apparently, instead of picking her up in front of the building, this woman was in the car pick up line, so they didn't even get a good look at this person."

"Have you called the neighbours or her old foster mother?"

"Yes, goddammit. I've called everyone I know." Her breathing sounded loudly over the phone. He worried she was having another panic attack.

"Listen. I'm on my way. Are you home?"

"No, I'm at the police station, being interviewed by this detective, Tim. Please hurry. We have to find her."

Matthew ended the call and quickly rose from his seat. "My niece is missing. I have to go."

Johnny's eyes widened. "Oh my God! Is there anything we can do?" Other men slapped him on the back offering reassuring looks of support.

He cleared his throat, darkest thoughts rising. "No, I have to go."

He stormed towards his locker and got his things ready then rushed out like a headless chicken.

While driving in his car, a black SUV behind him was right up close, revving the engine. Matthew looked in the rearview mirror and floored the accelerator, careful to avoid slow drivers in front of him. He managed to see part of the registration number. A flailing arm poked outside the driver's window with a prominent tattoo that he remembered from the night of Camilla's birthday. But Liz mentioned that Domenic drove a station wagon. He changed lanes to get the car behind to pass him, but the driver followed him. Again, the SUV was right up his tail when Matthew picked up speed to lose this person. He couldn't make out the driver as the windows were all tinted. It had to be Domenic chasing him, but was he driving a different car? He decided to change tactics and slowed down for a few seconds. He had to stay one step ahead of this person who was obviously trying to intimidate him. When the car behind him, slowed down too, he changed tack by accelerating as fast as he could and turned into a side street rather than stay on the main road. He quickened his pace and turned into a number of side streets to lose him. He looked in the rearview mirror then entered someone's driveway to possibly avoid detection by being off the road. He waited to be sure he wasn't being followed.

He regained his breath and dialled the police. He asked for Marco, but he wasn't in. "Yes, someone in a black SUV was following me, and I want you guys to be on the lookout. I got a partial plate. I believe it's a man by the name of Domenic so check his alibi for today. When you speak to Marco, he'll know who I'm talking about."

Matthew started up the motor again then made his way to Camilla, hoping to God that Domenic was off the road.

If Domenic had anything to do with Mariana going missing, he'd have his head on a platter. He wouldn't be lying down, taking it all.

CHAPTER 60
INVESTIGATING TEAM

Matthew demanded. "Tell me you found the damn car." He sat in an interview room at the police station, his arms resting against the tabletop.

Marco shook his head. "Sorry, mate. Not yet, but the team's still working on it. Tell us exactly what happened."

Matthew recounted the incident with confidence in his voice. "I know it was Domenic because of his tattoo. Why isn't he down here?"

"Listen, Domenic's missing right now. But in the meantime, keep yourself safe. Don't go doing anything. Let us handle it."

He scoffed. "Oh, what, like you handled Liz getting attacked and her car getting damaged? Like you're damn well handling the fact that my niece is now missing, and that I know it's that dirty bastard doing this? He's trying to send me a message, trying to gain the upper hand. Do something, dammit."

Marco nodded. "Look, this guy's very smart, but right now we're following a couple of leads. We've placed one of his old friends at the scene of that fire, and that makes Domenic a definite person of interest. That's all I'll say at this stage. But you need to hang tight."

He received a text message. "Camilla's finished with Tim, so I'll go wait for her in the waiting room."

Marco sighed. "Fine, but I want you both to stay here, purely for your safety. We don't know what this guy has planned if it is him."

Matthew shook his head. "Camilla called everyone she knew so this can't be a coincidence. It has to be someone working with him."

He headed out of the interview room and met up with Camilla in the waiting area. His arms held her tightly while the side of his neck dampened from her tears. "I am so sorry."

They pulled apart and sat down side by side. "This isn't your fault." She looked at him with a curious expression. "Do you think it's that guy that's been stalking Liz? Her ex-boyfriend? Is it, Matthew?"

"We think so, but right now they can't find the bastard, and I'm worried. They have no solid evidence against him, but we'll find Mariana. You have to believe that."

Camilla's eyes were black and her face looked paler than usual. Her hands were shaking, but she tightened her grip to stop the tremor. "Why the hell would he take Mariana? Oh my God. He's a madman and he has my daughter." She bowed her head and cried into her hands, moving her head in all directions. Matthew let her vent and stroked her gently on the shoulder. He suddenly realised something.

What if this was Domenic's plan to get Liz to go to him? What if he wanted her and planned to get Liz in exchange for giving Mariana back to them? But he hadn't made any contact, and a psychopath like that would have ways to find his number. He couldn't leave Camilla in her distraught state like this.

"I'll call Liz." Matthew dialled her number but it went straight to voicemail. He called again, but her voicemail came back on the line. Why wasn't she answering? It was Tuesday evening and she would've finished work by now. She should be home.

Camilla stared straight ahead after venting and took Matthew's hand. "So Liz isn't answering?"

He stiffened. "No, but I'll try again in ten minutes."

"You should go to her. She might be in trouble. What if he's using Mariana to get to Liz? It's possible, Matthew." He shrugged, but his mind was churning about all the worst-case scenarios. He refused to think that Liz was hurt. She might be in the shower or out shopping and hadn't heard her phone. There could be any number of reasons she wasn't answering her phone. "I want you to go find Liz. I'll be fine here, Matthew. I can't be any safer than in a police station. You need to leave."

His heart yearned to find Liz, but he wanted to support his sister too. "Let me try again." He retrieved his phone from his back pocket and rang her number again. It went to voicemail, and this time he left a message. Now he was starting to worry even more. "I can't leave you, Camilla. It's fine. I'll keep trying."

She shoved him. "Get out of here. Liz has done so much for me and Mariana, and I know you love her. Go help her. What if she is in danger?"

Matthew angled his head. "Are you sure, Camilla? I mean, I can ask Marco to check on her."

"No, Mariana has to be his priority, and right now, you need to be there for Liz. There's nothing you can do about Mariana, but if Liz is hurt, you'll live to regret it. No more regrets, remember?"

He rose from his seat. "Okay, fine. Just tell the detectives I had to run an errand and will be coming back. I don't want to send the police on a wild goose chase if we're wrong about this."

Camilla nodded. "Be safe, brother."

He gave her a reassuring smile and wandered to the exit, his heart tightening with each second he hadn't heard from Liz.

The only way he could get answers would be in her apartment. She gave him the code and key to enter so he could see for himself whether she was home or not. Maybe she was having a long shower. Surely, she was okay?

CHAPTER 61
IN HOT WATER

Liz's hands sweated against the steering wheel, manoeuvring from lane to lane to beat the slow drivers on the main road. She was heading towards an abandoned warehouse on the outskirts of Melbourne. Someone had called and explained that Mariana had been kidnapped. She didn't recognise the voice. He'd given her an address and she jotted it down quickly before he hung up on her.

This mystery caller mentioned how he'd kidnapped Mariana for the sole purpose of making an exchange, but she couldn't stomach what they planned to do with Mariana. All he said was, "Fuckin' get to this warehouse or she dies. And no fuckin' cops or she dies."

Her mind turned to Matthew. She realised that Matthew was the right man for her. If she was to die today, at least she would die with a smile on her face, knowing that she had found love and happiness with Matthew. Even if it was short-lived.

If she did survive this, she would tell him she loved him and would gladly risk a relationship, and her heart. But right now, she had Mariana to think of, and if she could save that poor, sweet girl, her death would be so worth it.

Before leaving home, she had inserted a small pocket knife inside her bra. She hoped they wouldn't notice it. But she needed protection. At least she'd die trying as she refused to go down easily.

She stopped at a traffic light that took forever and a day to change to green, huffing and puffing with the long wait. Rubbing her forearm, she realised her nails had dug deeply into her skin, anxiety overtaking her. With a quick breath, the light changed and she sped forward towards her destination.

The truck in front of her was driving at only forty kilometres. She beeped. "Hurry up, dammit. You're killing me here."

The driver wouldn't budge and refused to change into the left lane. As soon as she got a little space, she drove into the left lane, steering back into the right lane in front of the driver who beeped back at her. She snorted and ignored the sound, pressing her foot hard on the accelerator, wondering how long it would take to get to the warehouse.

Spotting a sign for the turn-off, she drove off the main road and slowed down along a side street to locate the large building that housed Mariana. She hoped that whoever held her, had fed and hydrated Mariana, or she'd definitely hurt them.

***

Matthew unlocked Liz's apartment and called out. "Liz, are you here? Liz?"

He ran into her bedroom and peered underneath the bed, in the bedroom closet, the laundry, then the other rooms. She was nowhere to be found. He walked out on to the balcony, but it was empty. His stomach clenched as he tried her number again, but it went to voicemail. Where the hell was she?

He took a breath and wondered what to do next. Maybe he could ring Marco and let him know she was not around. If Liz planned to go out, she would've told him. Her being missing had to be connected to Mariana going missing. It couldn't be a coincidence.

Looking around the kitchen, he spotted a pen resting on top of a notepad. He ripped out a page underneath the top page then placed it on top of the page with an imprint of the pen. He scribbled over it, and managed to see an address. Maybe this was where she was headed. Quickly, he ripped off the page, put it in his pocket and raced out of the apartment. She had to be there. It had to mean something, but in his experience, getting the police involved could only make things worse. He'd check out the place first as it might not mean anything. Once he was there, he'd call the police if this was where he'd find Mariana or Liz.

CHAPTER 62
A DANGEROUS TURN

Liz took a breath as she stepped out of the car, chills
spreading down her shoulders and into her lower back.
The building was a murky grey with several smashed
windows on the second floor. It seemed to stretch for
miles alongside a river. The red-brown roller doors and
timber doors aligned beneath the windows had graffiti
etched into them. The mystery caller mentioned an
entrance at the first door, and that she had to knock
once she arrived. Scurrying on uneven ground almost
made her trip. Chills continued to run up and down her
spine, and she struggled to block out images of
Domenic's fist in her gut and face.

Liz knocked hard on one of the locked doors. She
waited. She recalled one time how Domenic had pushed
her out of his warm car in the stormy rain purely
because she'd spotted and spoken to an ex-boyfriend at
a restaurant. She walked in the rain, almost passing out
from the cold and waited an hour before he returned.
Another time, he had played a dangerous game of
choking her then letting go a few times. His arousal by
her pain was clear in his eyes, but she had to succumb
to his sick games of torture purely to save herself.
Leaving him was the last straw. She couldn't take
anymore of his beatings, sexual weirdness, or calling
her stupid and a moron on a daily basis. No, he was one
damn sick puppy. Was he here with the mystery caller?

She lost all breath when the door opened. She
fought against numbness that penetrated her body and
shifted uncomfortably. Someone swung open the heavy

door, but it wasn't Domenic. Her body flinched and her heart raced a mile a minute. *Nick!* He stared her down. She stayed in her spot. "Oh my God! You?"

He glared. "Don't be so surprised, Liz. We're master manipulators. Don't take it personal."

"But...but you're supposed to be helping women in shelters, and here you are kidnapping a child."

He shoved her inside. "It's just a front for the escort and drug trade. Now, get in and shut your damn mouth."

Liz put her head down, stepping inside the coldness of the building. When he said 'we,' was he talking about Gabriella? Was Gabriella involved in this with Nick, trying to evoke sympathy by claiming that her father had hit her the other night? What if she planned to get close to Liz purely to take vengeance against her? She might be close to Domenic and hated Liz for testifying against him and now wanted revenge. What a clever plan to gain Liz's trust all for the joy of plotting her demise.

"Where is she?" Liz asked.

"I said, shut up." Nick's eyes turned to the door as if waiting for someone. Was it Gabriella?

The inside of the warehouse was huge with subtle light shining in from the windows, dirty concrete flooring, and a few cardboard boxes strewn in all directions. The stench was stifling, as if it hadn't been aired for many months and she pushed down her terror.

Nick pushed her from behind and she fell down on her knees. Picking herself back up, Liz froze. No, this couldn't be happening. Poor Mariana was tied to a chair with her hands behind her back and a blindfold over her eyes. Even her mouth was covered with a dirty cloth.

Her hair was dishevelled and her arms looked slightly bruised. Why would Nick resort to kidnapping? She was only five years old. Five, and he couldn't care less. Completely soulless, with a poor innocent girl getting in the middle of her mess. Liz had to make it right, even if it cost her life.

"It's okay, Mariana. Everything will be okay," said Liz. "You'll be going home soon." Liz's heart broke, a tear streaming down her cheek. "You'll see your mum soon, sweetie." The poor girl's body shook, and Liz wanted to cry.

Nick pushed her further into the warehouse when footsteps sounded behind her. She turned then slowed down her steps. A prickle of fear caused her to stay still. Someone else was in the warehouse, but who?

She looked at Nick. He had a stupid smirk on his face. The footsteps drew closer. Before she could turn around, a hand closed around her shoulder and another held a gun to her head. The new arrival looked her up and down in an all too familiar manner. "Oh, you're still as sexy as ever, Liz. I'll enjoy our love games again. Can't wait!"

"Please let Mariana go. Please, Domenic."

Domenic moved inches from her face. "Oh, keep quiet, Liz, or she'll never get home. Now, move."

Liz glanced over her shoulder. Nick followed behind with a stiff posture. He looked robotic.

They walked down a number of metres, far from Mariana, but at least she wouldn't hear their conversation. At least she wouldn't be witness to this psycho's degradation of her.

Her body shook, but she braced herself and spoke up again. "I knew the other night was a facade, a trick to let my guard down. You never changed in prison, did you?"

Domenic pushed her onto a dirty mattress without bedding. "I said shut the fuck up, bitch. Always wanting the upper hand, but I'm in control now. Not you." He grabbed a thick rope, shoved her arms behind her waist and tied her hands against a steel post. "Now, I reckon I'm gonna have my fun with you before..."

She shook her head, her eyes widening and her hands clammy. "Before what? Are you planning to kill me?"

Domenic pressed his lips together and shrugged. "You don't get to ask the questions. I do. Now, what does that stupid detective know about me?"

She took a calming breath. "I don't know. It's not like he's going to tell a civilian anything."

"Bullshit. You're friends with his girlfriend so don't lie to me." Domenic retrieved a blindfold from his pocket, placed it over her eyes, and tied it behind her head. "Okay Nick. Drop the kid off at her house then make an anonymous call from this phone. Dump it later." Nick was releasing Mariana. Thank God! Footsteps gave her the proof he was letting her go.

Liz's body turned cold all over as her lack of sight gave her less control and made her more unsettled. It was like her head could no longer support itself due to the heaviness of it all. "Why is Nick working with you, Domenic? He's supposed to be helping women not hurting them."

He chuckled. "I've trained my friend, Nick, to take over in my footsteps. His speaker persona makes him trustworthy. But he's someone who's been managing our escort business. My friend handled a couple of the bitches that knew too much about selling drugs on the side. About the escort business. So what if they were fifteen? If they were old enough to run away from home, they were old enough to have sex." He laughed again. "I'm thinking of expanding though, and you're a liability, Liz. Like Penny and another girlfriend bitch of mine. They were all liabilities."

"But why Penny? She was innocent in all this."

Domenic shook his head. "I ordered Nick to kill Penny. She was caught doing a search on those women who died of drug overdoses. She would've eventually connected them to me or my friends in the business." He paused. "These bitches were a part of my escort business and wanted to get out. Wanted to rat me out. No-one leaves a lucrative business. And no-one leaves me until I say so. Ever!"

Liz thought the worst. "They were just kids, Domenic. How could you do that?"

"Hardly. They were sixteen when they started, and two years ago, they would've been eighteen, but who gives a rat's ass? They were old enough to damn well spread their legs."Liz scoffed. "You beat those poor women to death, Domenic. Don't you have an ounce of sympathy or remorse?"

He grabbed her hard by the shoulder. "Those women deserved it. No-one challenges me or leaves me, and if they do, they pay the price. I make the decision to leave, not them. I have control. Always."

Liz's body shook, the rope against her wrists cutting into her skin. Her shoulders ached like hell and her vertigo grew stronger. "Why would you get Mariana involved? A child, for God's sake."

Domenic kicked her. "Don't worry. She's gone now. She's sweet, and I'd never harm a five-year-old child. I love children, but you women are all bitches."

Liz was doomed. She wondered if there was any way out of here. If only she could reach the knife stuck inside her bra, but her hands were out of reach. If she'd put them in her back pocket, Domenic would see it and take it off her.

Liz turned to Domenic. "What do you want with me?"

He sat over her mid-section, took off her blindfold, straddling her. "I want you to suffer the way I suffered for ten damn years. You couldn't leave well enough alone. You had the fuckin' nerve to leave me when you were pregnant with my baby. No fuckin' right to keep my baby from me. Maybe I would've let you leave, but no way were you leaving with my baby. If you'd have told me sooner about the kid, we could've had a life together. I would've loved that child just like I love Gabriella."

"Please, Domenic. If this is your idea of love, then you really are sick. You need help." Goosebumps permeated her skin. "And if you love Gabriella so much, why did you hit her the other night? That's not love."

He hesitated. "She caught me at a bad time, but I would never intentionally hurt her."

Maybe Liz could appeal to his humanity. "I'm sorry I wanted to leave, but you were hitting me over and over. There was only so much pain I could take. I wanted you to get help for the anger, but you never listened. I loved you. At times, you were a good person. And I can see how much you love Gabriella, so I know there's a good person in there." He said nothing. "Please let me go, and I won't say anything to the police. You can still be free."

"You'll fuckin' say anything just to get out of here, but I'm not a fool. You deserve to die just like your friend."

"You didn't have to kill Penny. She might not have found anything."

"She got what she deserved. I don't know any woman worthy of my respect anymore, and that includes you."

Poor Penny! Her heart was empty over the loss, and all because of her. She had to fix this. She had to come up with a plan.

CHAPTER 63
INTERVENTION

Matthew accelerated all the way to the location but stopped by a kerb when his phone buzzed beside him. He grabbed it and shuddered at the sound of Marco's voice.

"Where the hell are you? I told you to stay put."

"I have an address, and I'm pretty sure Liz and Mariana are there."

"Well, wherever you're going, you need to turn back and come to the station. We have a lead."

"What lead?" Matthew asked.

"We cut a deal with this man in custody who's been working with Domenic. He told us he occasionally uses this abandoned warehouse on the outskirts of Melbourne. Where are you going?" Matthew cited the address to Marco. "Christ, Matthew. You need to turn back. Do not approach. If Domenic's there, it's not safe. I am ordering you to stay away or I'll arrest your arse."

"Fine. I'll turn back," he lied.

"Good. An officer will greet you at the station and will keep you in a secure facility with Camilla."

Matthew pulled back out on the road and headed to the warehouse. He had a head-start on the police, and in no way was he putting his niece or Liz at further risk. He had to save them. Who knew how much time they had?

He wondered what Domenic's plans were for the exchange. Would he want Liz back or was he planning to kill her? He didn't want to think the worst as he pushed hard on the accelerator, cursing at slow drivers. "Move, move," he said to the slow driver in front of him. His breathing turned rapid and the back of his neck broke out in a sweat. Even his hands were slipping on the steering wheel, but he had to get it together. He had to be mentally strong and fight like he'd never fought before.

Matthew might've kept his distance from women. He might've played the field for years because of the lack of trust, and fear of turning into his father. But he wasn't his father, and never would be. He'd never once been tempted to drink alcohol to the point of blacking out. He would never ever contemplate hitting a woman. Hell, he wouldn't even hit a man unless it was in self-defence.

When Matthew arrived half an hour later, he parked at a kerb in an isolated area and exited his car. He walked along and wondered how he would even get into the place when all the doors appeared to be locked. Looking around, he found a small rock and pushed it into the door that slightly opened. With a bit of a nudge, it finally opened. He peeked inside but couldn't see anything. Sneaking inside, he cringed at the sight of a decrepit chair with a rope placed over it. He gasped. Was that where Mariana had been sitting, or was it Liz? Where were they now?

Moving further along, in the corner of the warehouse and a few metres away, he slowed. A bulky man that looked like Domenic lay over Liz. Muffled voices sounded and they became clearer with each step. He held the rock in his hand but kept it behind his back in case it was spotted. Creeping closer, his heart tore in two at watching Liz trying to turn her face away as

Domenic, forced his tongue into her mouth. She kept fighting him off her, but he didn't stop. A blindfold lay on the ground.

"Please, don't Domenic. Please, no. No," Liz cried.

The urgency in her voice urged him further along as he rushed like an earthquake in her direction. Matthew lifted up his right arm that held the rock, but it was too late. Domenic had seen him.

Domenic grabbed his arm and yanked it hard behind him. The pain was gut-wrenching and he dropped the rock. Domenic punched him hard in the nose. He fell back and hit his head against a steel post. He almost blacked out and stumbled as he forced himself upright. Domenic kicked him hard in the ribs, a searing pain tearing through his chest.

"Domenic, no. Leave him alone. Come after me instead," said Liz. "Please, don't. I'll do exactly as you say."

Matthew summoned the courage to lift up his right foot and kicked Domenic firmly in the face. Domenic fell back but, before he could hit him again, he rose and charged at Matthew. Where was that damn rock? He slid away from Domenic, his eyes roaming for the rock. He found it! Matthew ran for the rock. Domenic pushed Matthew forward, his face hitting the cold ground and he moaned. He kicked back with his leg, but Domenic avoided it.

Domenic grabbed him hard by the neck and had him in a choke hold. He was low on air, his eyes closing at the stabbing pain. No, he wouldn't die because of this bastard. He refused to die. Liz needed him. He pushed his head back, hitting Domenic hard in the nose, giving him an opening to rush for that piece of rock. He leaned forward and grabbed the rock when a stabbing pain knocked him out.

***

Liz was shaking, her heart breaking in two at watching Matthew's courage and bravery. Luckily, he was still alive, but how long before Domenic would kill him?

Domenic grabbed the rope resting on the chair then tied him up against another steel post opposite Liz. He walked back to her, licking his lips and holding his crotch. "Now, where were we?"

She put her plan in motion, and the only thing she could do to save Matthew and herself was to pretend she wanted Domenic all over again. Liz knew what turned him on. She could use that. It would make her sick to have his hands all over her, but what choice did she have? All she needed to do was get him to free her hands then she could grab the knife inside her bra before he could undress her. It had to work. Otherwise, both she and Matthew were dead.

CHAPTER 64
FIGHT FOR FREEDOM

Liz's body chilled at the grimace on Domenic's face. He rubbed his hands together. The stomping sounds he made as he approached were unnerving. He put his hands around her neck. Liz's eyes fluttered at the loss of breath, but he chuckled then let go.

"Don't worry. I won't kill you till I've had my fun." His grasp trailed from her neck down to her breasts, squeezing tightly enough for Liz to wince in pain. *He cannot discover my knife or he'll punish me even more.*

"Don't you think I need a free hand if you want me to excite you?" He ignored her as his hands moved down to her belly button while hovering over her face and planting a wet kiss over her lips. She wanted to vomit. She might've once loved this psychopath, but she had since grown and developed actual taste in men. He stared down her body from head to toe with desire in his eyes when his lips circled around her throat.

He stopped for a moment and watched her frozen state, then slapped her hard across the face. The pain stung, but she steeled herself. She had to if she wanted to survive. "You were always beautiful with a hell of a body, and these past ten years I only lusted for you more. But you're still a fuckin' bitch who doesn't know when to shut her mouth." He avoided her eyes for a moment and turned back to Matthew who had come to. She watched him with pain in his eyes. *Please don't hurt Matthew. Please don't hurt him.* "Turn back to me and forget about him. For old time's sakes. Maybe you can arouse me again." She put on the bravest act of her life, ignoring the nausea. Domenic watched her closely, processing her. If Matthew died on her watch, she'd never forgive herself.

Her prayers were answered when he smirked at Matthew. He faced her again with lust in his soulless eyes. He unbuckled his belt, his eyes never leaving hers.

"I guess the boyfriend can watch while you pleasure me. It'll be my joy to see him lust for you too before he dies."

Liz suppressed sickness and pressed on. "Happy to, but I need my hands to give you pleasure. That's exactly what you liked in the past." He stepped out of his pants down to the board shorts that he wore. She had to get one of her hands free. "Come on, Domenic. If you plan to kill me, grant me this one last wish."

He moved over to the steel post and grabbed his gun then turned back to her. "Fine. I'm only untying one hand, but I've got the gun. If you try anything, you're dead."

She peered over at Matthew. He shook his head and pushed against his restraints; he was trapped. His chair was moving, but he stopped fighting when Domenic turned to watch him.

"Now, watch closely and see how this bitch can get me off. Enjoy the show!" He hovered over her, holding his gun in his right hand while taking off the rope with his left hand. Then he took off his shorts and lay over Liz, trailing his lips from her neck down to her breasts, kissing over her bra. Liz pictured Matthew in her mind as she shifted her body and took Domenic's manhood in his hand, stroking it. A sick sensation in her stomach made her turn away. She had to get him excited to the point of distraction, so he wouldn't be thinking about the gun. He couldn't get to the knife either, so she continued to stroke him hard as he moaned. His eyes partially closed as he held the gun with a slightly shaky hand. She was taking a risk here. He could easily shoot her as she grabbed hold of her knife, but she had to try. He was going to kill her anyway, so she might as well die trying than die without trying at all.

Domenic probed inside her mouth again then pulled away and stroked her breasts. "Harder. Stroke me harder, bitch!"

She complied.

"Why don't I take my bra off? You always liked my breasts."

He smirked. "I always loved your tits. Take your fuckin' bra off then."

She took her hand off his penis and shifted her right hand towards the inside of her bra as he kissed her hard again. Her fingers strained to find the pocket knife, manipulating her hand at the right angle. She had to get to it before he realised what she'd done, not wanting to experience his wrath.

Her fingers grasped the hardness of the handle. Quickly she pulled it out, flicked open the knife from the stud when Domenic shifted and stopped kissing her. "What was that?" Without wasting time, she stabbed him hard in the leg and the gun went off.

***

Matthew looked away, disgusted by the view in front of him. Poor Liz had to endure giving her ex-boyfriend pleasure. It must've been humiliating for her. He couldn't watch any longer. Out of the corner of his eye he realised she was reaching for something inside her top. What the hell was she doing? Why risk her damn life when the gun was on her?

He watched as she stabbed him in the right leg with a pocket knife. The gun went off. Liz cried out. My God! She was hit. The bullet grazed her left leg while Domenic fell back against the ground, screaming in pain. Liz winced in pain as she forced herself towards Matthew, but Domenic grabbed her by the hair and threw her back on the ground. She kicked him in the groin. "You fuckin' bitch!" He pulled the pocket knife out of his leg and held his hand over the seeping blood. His eyes were cold, raging, and black. He gave her several blows to the face and knocked her into a submissive state. He slowly made his way towards Matthew, but she yelled, "No! Kill me, not...Not Matthew. Please."

He chuckled, seeming to enjoy her pain as he limped over to Matthew, pressing hard against his wound with the butt of the gun while holding the knife in his other hand. "You can suffer, watching this dirt bag get shot first. Then I'm coming for you, Liz."

Matthew realised he'd lived a good life, knowing Liz and getting to know his niece and sister again after all these years. He would at least die, knowing he had loved the most amazing woman in the world. It was out of his hands now. He knew that Liz would fight and win. Marco should be here soon to rescue her. She would be okay. She had to be okay.

Domenic lifted up his hand and pointed the gun towards Matthew.

Matthew stared up the barrel of the gun, awaiting his death.

CHAPTER 65
A SHOOTING

"Police! Stop or I'll shoot," said Marco.

"Domenic stared down the detectives, Marco and Tim with several police officers behind them, all pointing their guns towards him. He threw his head back and laughed but lowered the gun. As Marco and Tim rushed towards him, Domenic raised the gun again. Marco shot him straight into the shoulder blade, and Domenic fell back with a large thud.

Liz breathed a sigh of relief. "Oh, thank you!" She was wrapping the blindfold around her blood-soaked leg.

"Where's Mariana?" Marco asked.

He moaned, his eyes drooping. "In....a safe....place, det....ective." Domenic closed his eyes, passing out. Paramedics came up behind her and tended to his wounds, shoving an oxygen mask over his face.Liz drew her hand roughly through her hair. "I heard him tell his friend, Nick, to drop Mariana off at her house. This guy should've called the station. Check...there." A woozy sensation overcame her.

Marco untied Matthew. Once he was free, he hobbled over to Liz. He wrapped his arms around her and squeezed tight. She had almost lost him, but now she had a second chance. They pulled apart, and Matthew kissed her hungrily on the lips, trying to kiss away the horror she had faced. A person clearing their throat caused them to stop and face the person. It was Marco.

"Sorry to interrupt, but how are you guys doing?"

"Good now, thank you so much, Marco. If it wasn't for you..." Liz's voice broke and tears welled in her eyes.

Marco nodded, holding her up. "Your wound's just a graze, so you shouldn't have long-lasting effects, but stay off it until the paramedics treat it."

Matthew intervened. "I'd surely be dead. Thank you." He shook Marco's hand.

"Any time. Now, listen, you both need to go to the hospital. I'll come by later and get your statements." He ushered over paramedics and they put both Liz and Matthew on to stretchers. They tended to Liz's leg and Matthew's wounds. "We'll go get Mariana, don't worry."

Matthew's eyes darkened. "Please find her."

"Hold up," said Marco to one of the paramedics. He gestured for the other paramedic to take Matthew. "Liz, did Gabriella mention a guy by the name of Bryce?"

Liz's spine chilled. "Yes. He was the brother of Gabriella's babysitter. Why?"

Marco swallowed and peered at his watch. "Any idea where Gabriella might be?"

Her spine chilled. "No, why do you ask?"

"We were told that a young woman picked Mariana up from school. It might've been Gabriella as no other friends or family have seen her. Gabriella would be someone Mariana knows through your work."

Liz wanted to sleep for a hundred years, as hearing that bit of news made her tired and sick. She trusted Gabriella. Gabriella and Nick must've been in on it all along. Gabriella played Liz, pretending to be sweet and innocent when all she did was get her revenge for Liz testifying against her father. Was Gabriella's mother in danger because she had testified against Domenic, too?

Liz remembered the black SUV in front of Jean's house, but Domenic didn't have that car the other times she'd seen him. So maybe someone else owned it. An uneasy sense overcame her as she turned to Marco. "Go to Jean's place. You have the address. I have a feeling that Domenic's friend might be there. He might've got his friend to hurt Jean. His ultimate act of control because Jean testified against him. Gabriella might be a part of it too."

Marco frowned. "And how do you know about that story, Liz?"

She cleared her throat. "Gabriella gave me the shortened version." She was fighting drowsiness.

Marco gestured to the paramedics to take her away. "I'll talk to you later, Liz." He stormed off like a speeding train, with Tim following behind.

Liz thought about her ordeal with Domenic while being wheeled to the ambulance. What a pity the bastard wasn't dead. He was evil personified. Her mind was in a daze, and she felt nothing for a man who had done nothing but terrorise her for so long.

***

Liz, Matthew, and Camilla sat huddled in the hospital, waiting for Mariana by Liz's bedside. She hadn't heard from Marco in a while and wondered what was taking so long. But Domenic had instructed Nick to take her home so surely Mariana would be there? But if Bryce had come back, what was his story?She turned to

290

Matthew who squeezed her hand. "Are you okay?" he whispered.

Liz nodded. "A little worried, but I know they'll find Mariana."

Camilla looked into the distance, talking to herself. Liz guessed she was praying.

When Liz heard footsteps, she jolted in her bed. But it wasn't Mariana. It was Bella and Jamie running towards her.

Bella ran into her arms as Liz shifted herself in bed, fighting against the pain. "Oh, thank God you're okay."

She pulled away from Bella and Jamie hugged her too. "Liz. He didn't do anything, did he?" Jamie asked.

Liz unwrapped herself from Jamie's arms. "No, I'm all good."

Bella grabbed her by the hand. "We'll talk more about this another time. Right now, I'm sure that little girl will be back safe."

Bella and Jamie approached Camilla who came out of her daze and smiled. She remained silent, her body shaking. The poor woman was looking fragile, and understandably so.

Time pressed on until she heard new footsteps in the ward. Gabriella held Mariana's hand for a moment until the little girl broke away and ran inside the ward.

"Mariana," said Liz.

Camilla got up so quickly she almost tripped and ran into Mariana's arms while Gabriella was handcuffed by waiting policemen. They took her away, her eyes drooping as she ignored everyone. She avoided Liz's eyes and stared straight ahead as the police officer pulled her in the opposite direction.

Mariana and her mother hugged tightly. "Mummy, Mummy. I love you, Mummy."

"I love you too, darling. Never forget that," said Camilla.

It was a beautiful thing to watch, but Liz's mind kept turning to Gabriella. She had obviously trusted the wrong person again.

CHAPTER 66
TWIST OF FATE

The tall man waited until the security guard fell asleep in his chair, the night after Domenic had been shot. The story of the infamous lady killer was all over the newspapers. It made him want to puke. He snuck into the ward, looking over his shoulder and gently closed the door behind him. He flicked on the lock. It was almost midnight and the hospital was dead-quiet.

Domenic was half-asleep when the man's footsteps roused him. "Hey, bud. Good to see ya. Where have you been?"

The man held the gun behind his back. "Good things come to those who wait, my friend. Great things, in fact."

Domenic squinted and scratched his temple. "What the fuck are you talking about?"

The man glared, nearing the bed. "Did you kill her?"

Domenic swallowed and tilted his head. "I've killed plenty of women, but don't forget you were the one who drugged them to death."

He chuckled and moved a few steps, standing on the side of his bed. He raised his gun. "But the difference is that I had remorse and was acting on your orders. You're the sick son of a bitch. Not me!"

"But I thought we were mates. From prison. What's going on?"

"Did you kill Frances?"

Domenic's face turned ashen as if he'd seen a ghost. "You can't be! No way."

"I was a young fat gang-banger kid with pimples and long hair back then, but I grew up. Over the years, my anger festered and festered. I made sure I met you in prison because I made a promise to myself and to my dear sister that I would avenge her death. And now the time has come."

"But how did I not recognise you? I met you back then."

He pressed his lips together. "Like I said, I grew up and you only met me once. I'm no longer Bryce, but Nick. And I'm sure your mind was full of the ways you would beat and kill my sister. I became your friend and your enemy, and I honoured your wish to watch over Gabriella. Not that I expected to fall in love with her, but I did. And now I hope she'll forgive me for all the horrible things I've done and the people I've killed. I don't want this life anymore and now you have to pay." A banging on the door made Domenic jolt.

He yelled out. "Help me! He's got a gun. Help!" The security guard tried to kick open the door, but he failed miserably.

Bryce shook his head. "By the time someone comes, you'll already be dead. I must say, I never really liked you." He turned towards the door then faced Domenic again.

"Come on, Nick. I'll disappear and leave you, but don't kill me. Please, mate."

"I'll give you one last chance, or I'll make you suffer worse than the gun. Did you kill Frances?"

He shifted his body. "She reported me to the police. I couldn't go to jail when I had my little girl. I couldn't. She had no right to report me."

Nick clenched his hands and in one swift movement, punched him in the face. Domenic's head swung back, hitting the bed head. He shivered.

He looked towards the door and several officers shouted out. "Drop the gun." Once they eventually unlocked the door, it was too late.

Nick shot Domenic straight into the eye, a sense of relief washing over him.

EPILOGUE
TWO MONTHS LATER

Liz sat on the balcony of her home as Marco stood overlooking the view of the city. Matthew sat beside her, holding her hand.

Matthew had changed her. No more would she be opening herself to strange men in nightclubs or searching for a fun time. No more distractions from her pain. She was over all that and wanted to settle with Matthew. She wanted children with him. If he would have her in the way she wanted him. If he proposed, she'd say yes right away. No hesitation. No regrets.

Marco breathed in the fresh air. "For the breaking news, guys; Bryce, or should I say, Nick, will be on trial for the murder of Domenic, Penny, and two eighteen-year-old girls who were also ex-girlfriends of Domenic. He liked them young. Bryce killed the real Nick and took on his identity. Bryce had a long-standing criminal history. He learned to be a speaker and was pretty popular, too."

Liz nodded. She could sleep well at night knowing he could no longer hurt her. "And I take it Domenic killed Anne, and God-knows how many other women, overdosing them on drugs and beating them to death?"

Marco shifted and drew a hand through his glossy hair. "Yes. He got away with a lot of murders and almost killed you, Liz. He had Bryce as his partner in crime, but Bryce had more of a conscience."

Matthew nodded. "So was there anyone else involved in these murders of young prostitutes or just the gang of three men?"

"No, that's it. But, at least now, we've located all the women in the escort business who can make a new life for themselves. A lot of them fell to the streets after their families abused them. I guess that's where social workers can help out." He winked at Liz.

"And what happened to Jean when she almost died of a drug overdose? Was that Domenic?"

He shrugged. "I suspect it might've been but there's no evidence for that. So many unknowns now that Domenic's dead. But then Bryce might fess up about things. We'll see."

Marco stretched out. "And Gabriella's in shock. She loved the man." He sighed. "But to find out he was a murderer and a fraud. She was forced by Bryce to kidnap Mariana just so Bryce could keep up his charade of working with Domenic."

"And what's Johnny's story? At one stage, I thought he was involved with Domenic, but something was going on with him," asked Liz.

Marco nodded. "Those mystery calls he was getting were about a gambling debt. He's in over his head but we're helping him out. The condition is he needs to get treatment for his addiction, and he's willing to stop."

Matthew turned to Liz. "I was meant to tell you Liz, but Johnny's taking time off to get help for his gambling. The chief's willing to support him through this."

Liz's heart warmed. Johnny wasn't involved. Now that Johnny was getting help, he'd be fine. "That's good. He's not a bad guy."

"Anyway, I'm out. Bella's cooking me my favourite dinner tonight. We'll see you both over at the house soon."

Matthew shook Marco's hand. "Thanks for everything, Marco. You saved me and you saved Liz."

"Anytime." He turned to Liz. "Now you rest easily tonight. You've earned it."

"Thanks, Marco. Say hi to Bella, and we'll catch up soon."

***

Matthew wrapped his arms around Liz later that evening. "I love you, Liz, and I want to express my love to the world." He stroked her cheek, gazing adoringly into her eyes.

Her heart warmed, and she touched his hand. "I love you too, Matthew, and I'm sorry about everything I've put you through."

He huffed. "Come on, Liz. It's crazy to think that way. None of this was your fault. You had a psychopath as an ex-boyfriend and he wanted vengeance. But now he can no longer hurt you."

She nodded, a warm glow rising from within. "I am finally free, Matthew."

He chuckled and moved his head back, resting his arms around her waist. "I'm yours forever, Liz, and I hope you'll be mine forever."

They sealed their love with a kiss when Liz's phone interrupted them.

"Jamie, hi. What's up?" Silence. "Jamie?"

"Can I come over?"

Her voice didn't sound right. "Of course you can. Is everything okay?"

"I have bad news, Liz."

Reviews are gold to authors and allow Lucy to keep writing. If you enjoyed this story, please consider rating and reviewing it on Amazon here:
http://mybook.to/TwistedObsession

Check out Jamie's Story, *Web Of Lies* in Book 3 of the Friends In Crisis Series here:
http://mybook.to/EbookWebOfLies

ABOUT THE AUTHOR

Lucy Appadoo is an author of fiction and nonfiction books. She writes in the genres of romantic suspense/thrillers with significant life themes, contemporary romance, and 20th-century Italian-themed historical romance/coming of age.

Lucy is a qualified counsellor and works as a rehabilitation counsellor for the Australian government. She draws on her life experiences to write inspirational stories about authentic, driven women who manage adversity with strength and heart.

Her favourite authors include Toni Anderson, Kendra Elliot, Blake Pierce, Cheryl Bradshaw, Erica Spindler, Nicholas Sparks, Adriana Trigiani, and James Patterson (to name a few).

Lucy enjoys reading romantic suspense, romance, thrillers, crime novels, family/historical drama, and sagas. She has enjoyed travelling to exotic places such as Madrid, Mauritius, and Italy, and uses her travel experiences to strengthen her creative writing.

Her interests include travel, exercising, journal writing, reading for entertainment or knowledge, meditation, spending time with her husband and two daughters, and socialising with friends and family.

To sign up for a monthly newsletter and download a FREE Romantic Suspense novel, go to: http://www.lucyappadooauthor.com.au

ALSO BY LUCY APPADOO

FICTION

The Friends In Crisis Series - Romantic Suspense/Thriller
Haunted By The Past (Book 1)
http://mybook.to/HauntedbythePast

<u>Web Of Lies (Book 3)</u>
http://mybook.to/EbookWebOfLies

The Hearts Series - Romantic Suspense
Rising Hearts (Book1)
http://mybook.to/RisingHearts

Forbidden Hearts (Book2)
http://mybook.to/ForbiddenHearts

Kindred Hearts (Book 3)
http://mybook.to/kindredhearts

Broken Hearts (prequel to Forbidden Hearts)
http://mybook.to/Bhearts

Short Story Thrillers
Evening Interrupted -
http://mybook.to/Eveninginterrupted

The Dreamcatcher -
http://viewbook.at/Thedreamcatcher

Red Flags - http://mybook.to/Redflags

Collection of Short Story Thrillers - http://mybook.to/collectionofthrillers

The Italian Family Series - Coming of Age Family Drama/Romance
A New Life - http://mybook.to/ANewLife

The Beauty of Tears - http://mybook.to/TheBeautyofTears

Dancing in the Rain - http://mybook.to/dancingintheRain

A Life By Design - http://mybook.to/Alifebydesign

NON-FICTION

Grief & Loss
Moving Beyond Grief - How To Shift From Grief &
Loss to Joy & Peace
http://mybook.to/MovingBeyondGrief

Stress Management & Anxiety
Holistic Spiritual and Mental Health - Building
Resilience and Creativity by Conquering Anxiety
and Managing Stress -
http://mybook.to/Holistichealth

Career Guidance
Your Holistic Career Path - Create Career Change,
Satisfaction, and Work/Life Balance
http://mybook.to/YourHolisticCareerPath

**Journal and Record Of Books You've Read (with
Quotes)**
Readers' Journal
http://mybook.to/ReadersJournal